S0-BCK-004

A passionate surrender . . .

Alex's emotions had shifted so often in the last hour that she hardly knew what she was doing. Guilt. Pain. Shock. Excitement. Euphoria. When his mouth crushed into hers, it set off an explosion that drove every rational thought from her mind.

His body was as hard as she'd remembered, and far hotter. He radiated heat, excitement, passion. . . .

She clung, amazed to feel almost fragile in his arms. Her hands roamed freely over his back, around his shoulders, into his hair. She opened her mouth to him, the exchange of breath raising a desire that weakened her knees.

SIGNET
REGENCY ROMANCE

On Sale November 15, 1999

A Fine Gentleman by Laura Matthews

Lady Caroline Carruthers was enjoying her visit to the Hartville home. But one thing made life at the estate complicated—Lady Hartville was intent on convincing her son that Caroline would be the perfect wife for him. Who could think of marrying such an obstinate, infuriating man as Richard? But an unexpected surprise arriving on the doorstep turns a far-fetched plan of wedding meddling into startling possibility....

0-451-19872-7/$4.99

The Irish Rogue by Emma Jensen

Ailís O'Neill is not the average Dublin debutante. She spends time teaching English to Gaelic peasants—and painting the local wildlife. But with her brother running for British Parliament on behalf of Ireland, Ailís is expected to socialize with the political set. Her disdain for the English partisans is evident, but no more so than for Lord Clane. And she knows nothing of Lord Clane's notorious past—or that his future includes plans to steal her heart....

0-451-19873-5/$4.99

My Lady Nightingale by Evelyn Richardson

Mademoiselle Isobel de Montargis had a passionate soul, a strong will, and a proud determination to become more than music tutor to the dashing Lord Hatherleigh's niece and nephew. Her dream was to become an *actrice de l'opera*. But how could a lady, respectful of her reputation and social standing, be able to ever fulfill such a daring dream? Leave it to Lord Hatherleigh....

0-451-19858-1/$4.99

To order call: 1-800-788-6262

Double Deceit

Allison Lane

A SIGNET BOOK

SIGNET
Published by New American Library, a division of
Penguin Putnam Inc., 375 Hudson Street,
New York, New York 10014, U.S.A.
Penguin Books Ltd, 27 Wrights Lane,
London W8 5TZ, England
Penguin Books Australia Ltd, Ringwood,
Victoria, Australia
Penguin Books Canada Ltd, 10 Alcorn Avenue,
Toronto, Ontario, Canada M4V 3B2
Penguin Books (N.Z.) Ltd, 182–190 Wairau Road,
Auckland 10, New Zealand

Penguin Books Ltd, Registered Offices:
Harmondsworth, Middlesex, England

First published by Signet, an imprint of New American Library,
a division of Penguin Putnam Inc.

First Printing, October 1999
10 9 8 7 6 5 4 3 2 1

Copyright © Susan Ann Pace, 1999

All rights reserved

 REGISTERED TRADEMARK—MARCA REGISTRADA

Printed in the United States of America

Without limiting the rights under copyright reserved above, no part of this
publication may be reproduced, stored in or introduced into a retrieval system, or
transmitted, in any form, or by any means (electronic, mechanical, photocopying,
recording, or otherwise), without the prior written permission of both the copyright
owner and the above publisher of this book.

BOOKS ARE AVAILABLE AT QUANTITY DISCOUNTS WHEN USED TO PROMOTE PRODUCTS OR
SERVICES. FOR INFORMATION PLEASE WRITE TO PREMIUM MARKETING DIVISION, PENGUIN
PUTNAM INC., 375 HUDSON STREET, NEW YORK, NEW YORK 10014.

If you purchased this book without a cover you should be aware that this book is
stolen property. It was reported as "unsold and destroyed" to the publisher and
neither the author nor the publisher has received any payment for this "stripped
book."

Chapter One

"Is he gone?" Alexandra Merideth Vale poured tea for her cousin, who served as her companion.

Sarah Vale nodded, limping to her usual chair near the fireplace. "But you should have seen him off, Alex. He was annoyed that you chose to sulk in your rooms."

"Hah!" Her snort lodged a crumb in her throat, triggering a coughing fit that increased her irritation.

Her father's pique had been feigned, as usual. He never stopped manipulating people. She had given up hope that he would change, though she saw no reason to join his games. Dutiful-daughter-saying-painful-farewell-to-beloved-father was not a role she enjoyed at any time, but after a week of argument and recrimination, she refused to even try.

"Why should I regret his departure?" she demanded once she caught her breath. "You know how unpleasant life is when he is here."

"Manners." It was the closest Sarah ever came to criticism.

Tea soothed Alex's throat. "All right. I am unmannerly. But I could not tolerate another lecture. He has done nothing but scold since he returned last Tuesday. *Sit down, Alexandra. Don't display your indecent height.*" Her voice matched Sir Winton Vale's growl to perfection. "*Put that book away, Alexandra; you must cease flaunting these ridiculous pretensions. How dare you contradict Mr. Bowles; can't you act like a lady for even one hour? Such vulgar enthusiasm; people will think you escaped from Bedlam. Oh, why was I cursed with an abnormal freak instead of a son?*"

"He doesn't mean to be disagreeable," said Sarah soothingly.

"Of course he does. He was born disagreeable."

"Alex!"

"Sweet Sarah, who can find a kind word for the most debauched reprobate in the realm." She forced the sarcasm from her voice when Sarah flinched. "You know little about gentlemen, Sarah. Even the best are condescending fools, lacking either wit or substance. Father is worse. He despises any female capable of seeing his faults—like Mother, God rest her soul. He never forgave her for exposing his questionable logic, even when she saved him money and embarrassment. Nor did he pardon her for producing only me in twenty years of marriage."

"She also produced Richard."

"That was in year twenty-one. You were fortunate not to have been here, Sarah. He celebrated her pregnancy, positive that it was a son at last." Her voice betrayed remembered pain. He had made no effort to hide his satisfaction that he would finally have a child he could point to with pride. His daughter was merely a misbegotten female.

"He was right. That one was a boy."

"Yes." She clamped a firmer control over her tone. "Once Mother performed her wifely duty by conceiving an heir, he publicly excused her twenty years of stubborn intransigence— even the doctor choked on that one. Of course, she betrayed him by dying of a fever two weeks later. So no spare. He's never forgiven her."

Nor did he care a whit for Richard. The heir's existence was all that mattered. He'd rarely been home in the ten years since, leaving her to raise her young brother. Richard's departure for school last month had ripped a hole in her heart that she had not yet filled. "Did you notice that he did not mention Richard even once this trip?"

Sarah sighed. "His guilt is growing. He cared for Aunt Sophy and knew she was too old to bear another child. That is why he ignores Richard. Seeing him is a reminder of the selfish way he killed her."

"Men care nothing for their wives when it comes to begetting an heir. All that matters is the perpetuation of their precious names." She snorted. "He has heaped so much dishonor on the name of Vale, I wonder how Richard will bear it."

Sarah refrained from comment, picking up her needlework.

But Alex was still seething with frustration from a week of arguments. "Now that Richard is gone, I am useless to him. His revulsion shows whenever he looks at me. He hates me."

"You could try to be conciliatory." Sarah's needle flashed, fashioning a perky bird perched on a pine branch.

"How? By pretending to be something I am not? I despise deceit. And overcoming his objections is impossible." Unable to sit quietly while turbulence churned in her stomach, she rose to pace the room, striding faster with each word. "He hates me for understanding more than one word in ten that I read. He hates me for caring more for his dependents than he does. Half of our recent arguments arose because he is stripping the estate of capital to finance his gaming. How can we manage repairs? Milton's barn is ready to collapse. The Howitches need a new roof. Doris Timmons will starve before spring without help. Summer was so cold that the harvest is the smallest in years. Some crops failed entirely."

"Don't work yourself into a megrim over things you cannot control," advised Sarah.

"I never have megrims. But I hate injustice. Would you have me ignore it? Yes, I lack the authority to effect permanent change, but thinking only about things I can influence requires closing my eyes to everything around me, for you know I have no control over any aspect of my life." Her hand stopped Sarah from interrupting. "Father may be the author of my current frustration, but I know better than to expect change from him. He will never approve of me. The last straw was growing a handspan taller than him. He despises looking up to anyone, especially his own daughter."

Sarah nodded.

"What really galls me is that others treat me no better— ladies, gentlemen, it doesn't matter. Even perfect strangers look at me with suspicion just because I refuse to squander my days on needlework and gossip. Why wasn't I born a man?"

It was a question she had asked since childhood. Her mother had understood, for she had also resented the restrictions women endured. Thus she'd used her pin money to buy Alex lessons with the vicar. Sir Winton never knew, for he had rarely visited the estate even then. One pregnancy in ten years of marriage had erased his hope for a son.

But education had merely increased Alex's unhappiness. Fate had played her a dastardly trick, first trapping her in an ungainly body, then filling her with curiosity about subjects ladies usually ignored, and finally thrusting her into a society where men made all the rules.

Education had taught her how much she was missing and had raised unanswerable questions. Why must ladies remain quietly in the drawing room while men attended universities and ran the country? Who had decreed that only men could explore the world or think great thoughts? How could men justify ignoring her when her logic was sounder than theirs? And when had women agreed to live their entire lives under the thumb of a father or husband? If only she could escape long enough to do something for herself.

Not that it would do any good. Who would know? Men did not listen to women. Nor did they recognize any female accomplishment beyond music, drawing, needlework, and entertaining.

She tried to relax her jaw, lest it snap under the pressure of grinding teeth. Gathering her control, she returned to her chair.

The butler rapped on the open door.

"What is it, Murch?"

"A letter, Miss Alex."

Her heart pounded, for she recognized Lord Mitchell's frank. The vicar must have delivered it the moment her father's carriage passed through the village.

Lord Mitchell was a well-known antiquarian. Six months ago, she had taken the enormous risk of writing to him, in the vicar's name.

A clearing in the woods had long served as her refuge, a place where she could read or study, free from eyes that might report her activities to her father. A year ago, unusually heavy rain had pounded the clearing, exposing the corner of a foundation. Curious, she had dug down to its base, but had hesitated to excavate further until she knew what it might be. Study convinced her that there were actually two buildings—a Roman temple atop an earlier Druid shrine.

But confirmation was tricky. Interest in Roman sites had grown in recent years, yet most of the searchers sought only gold or other treasure that would lead to fame and fortune. Her own fascination lay with the buildings themselves—what they had looked like and how they had been used. Since her small collection of books contained no authoritative works on the subject, she'd had to devise her own theories. Yet without confirmation from a reputable antiquarian, her ideas were little better than idle speculation.

Seeking help had been a frightening, but necessary, step. No man would take a female's questions seriously, so she'd borrowed the vicar's identity. Revealing the site's location was also dangerous. If her father discovered it, he would loot anything of value, destroying the rest in the process.

She had deliberately chosen Lord Mitchell because of his age and health. He rarely left home, having contracted a painful gout condition some years before. Since he lived in a remote corner of Yorkshire, he was unlikely to visit her or request that she call on him. And he was one of the few who showed as much interest in the ancient Romans themselves as he did in their treasure.

Despite his initial caution, he'd soon warmed, and had actually sent her copies of papers that had been presented to the Antiquarian Society. Even though she knew his secretary had done the actual transcription, it was an enormous kindness. For the first time in her life, a man was treating her as an intellectual equal.

But each new contact increased her wariness. She made light of the find, describing only the foundation stones and omitting any mention of roof tiles, Latin inscriptions, or her growing collection of artifacts. If she raised too much curiosity, he might send an assistant to investigate.

She hated the deception—all her deceptions—but she had no choice. More than the site was at risk. Her father owned it, so if he chose to desecrate it, she could do nothing to stop him. But the staff would also suffer if word of her work reached his ears. They knew she was digging, but said nothing. If he discovered their secrecy, he would turn them off for disloyalty, then lock her away. Her interests had always embarrassed him. Learning that his freakish daughter enjoyed mucking about in Roman ruins would be the last straw.

Pushing her father from her mind, she read the letter through, then did so again, hardly believing her eyes.

> *I congratulate you, sir. Your thesis on the siting of early Roman temples would account for the rapid decline of Druidism . . .*
>
> *Organize your thoughts into a treatise for the Antiquarian Society, to be presented at the winter meeting . . .*
>
> *I will sponsor your membership.*

She was breathing too fast.

This opportunity might never come again. But how could she present a paper without appearing? Dressing as a man would never work. Her bosom was too full—another bane; she was tired of fending off men's advances.

But she would think of something. Could she plead illness at the last minute, sending the vicar to read her paper? He would have to use a false name, of course, for she was already using his.

More deceit. Her head spun.

Another thought tempered her excitement. A formal treatise would reveal the temple's location. Even deliberate vagueness could not disguise the general area.

She couldn't do it. The risk of discovery was too great. Recent test holes had convinced her that other, larger buildings had once stood nearby—a definite attraction.

But could she insult Lord Mitchell by refusing to share her ideas? Turning down this opportunity might prompt an investigation. At the very least, it would prevent him from ever helping her again.

"Not again!"

Crumpling the summons, Anthony Torwell Linden hurled it at the door. Who was carrying tales this time?

Fisting his hands controlled their shaking, but several minutes passed before he overcame his fury.

Not that the tale-bearer's identity mattered. His father had many correspondents, any one of whom might assume he was neck-deep in the River Tick because he'd lost ten pounds at White's last week. Or perhaps a meddler had seen him driving in the park and mistaken Ralph's sister for a light-skirt. Or Mr. Tolliver could have . . .

It didn't matter, he reminded himself firmly. Nothing mattered. Knowing who was exaggerating would make no difference. He ought to be used to the charges by now. Seventeen years of condemnation had cast his reputation in bronze. But protest was useless. No one cared that the rumors were false.

"Fool," he muttered, retrieving the letter. Many times a fool. He could blame no one but himself.

Taking a deep breath to steady his temper, he read the missive again.

Nothing had changed.

> *A matter of grave import requires immediate consultation. You will call at Linden Park no later than Thursday.*
>
> *Linden*

The wording was as stilted and condescending as ever.

"Idiot," he grumbled, again directing the epithet at himself.

Why the devil had he started this? Granted, he had been young, but even a frustrated fifteen-year-old should have realized where it must lead. Chucking his reputation away was the most stupid thing he had done in a life full of stupid behavior.

He shook his head, for the question itself was stupid. His reasons may have been childish, but he could still recall every moment of that infamous day.

His father, Lord Linden, was the most rigid, disapproving man he had ever known. Nothing satisfied him. Every word he uttered was either a complaint, criticism, or accusation—or assigned another penalty.

Punishment had been part of life for as long as he could remember, even when his behavior was no worse than any other boy's. He had endured it as long as possible, but his temper had finally snapped.

Sighing, he dropped his head into his hands.

That day was not one he was proud of. Seventeen years later he was still living with the consequences. But what else could he have done?

He'd arrived home for long break, happier than he had been in years. He had enjoyed the term, discovering a serious interest in the classics that had brought praise from all his tutors. Even the harsh school discipline had softened, for no one had indulged in pranks for more than a month.

But he'd hardly reached his mother's sitting room when his father summoned him to the study.

The confrontation was no different from a hundred others. Linden cared nothing for his son's school performance or his plans for the future. All that mattered was behavior. His correspondents had reported a host of infractions, proving that Tony was an incorrigible hellion hovering on the brink of ruin.

He was a disgrace. His language alone would guarantee an eternity in hell—someone must have reported the oath he had flung at his horse for scraping him against the stable wall last month. Or maybe his friendship with Haskell's heir was enough to condemn him; Mark could put a sailor to the blush.

Linden then launched his favorite rant against the evils of gaming, decrying his son's penchant for impulsive wagers and canceling a quarter's allowance to prevent even greater losses.

It had taken a while to work out that charge. Though playing at cards and dice were common at school—indeed, eschewing such activities would draw ridicule from the other students—he rarely lost more than a few shillings, usually breaking even over time. The past quarter he'd actually come out ten pounds ahead, though there had been one game several weeks earlier that had cost him twenty pounds.

But his father refused to listen, listing other indiscretions in a tirade that lasted a full hour. His punishments were more severe than ever before. Besides forfeiture of his allowance, he was to spend four hours a day in the chapel, contemplating his crimes. "And you must remain inside the Park. You are weak-willed, Anthony. Duggat hired a new maid for the Striped Cat, but the girl is naught but a harlot, leading lads straight to the devil. I'll not have you disgracing your name. Since you've proven yourself incapable of control, I must keep you away from temptation."

The tirade had finally snapped Tony's temper. Living up to Linden's standards was impossible. If he was going to pay anyway, why should he not enjoy himself? Thus had begun a bitter clash of wills. He found a hundred ways to slip in and out of the Park without being caught. He sampled the Striped Cat's ale, its maid, and two of her friends. He indulged in card games whenever possible, wagering on anything and everything. And he laughed at each new punishment. By the end of that summer, he'd acquired a reputation for debauchery and excess that surpassed hellions ten years his senior.

Linden believed he was worse than ever, though the excesses of that summer were long behind him. Even in the early years he had not been as wild as rumor claimed. While it was true that he had hovered on the brink of expulsion a dozen times in the terms that followed, he had always stopped short of actually being kicked out. He'd made a great show of gaming, but had never lost more than a few pounds. In fact, his investments had grown until he could almost live on the proceeds. In like manner, his debauchery had been mostly show, as was his legendary drinking.

But none of that mattered.

His sigh filled the room. That childish rebellion had once been satisfying, but it had been years since he had done anything to maintain the fiction. Yet his reputation worsened every Season. No one knew the real Tony Linden. No one wanted to know. Young bucks actually admired the imaginary rakehell. Others envied his supposed disdain for society's rules. And while parents tried to keep their daughters out of reach, the girls themselves often sought him out, thrilled to flirt with the danger he represented.

You are such a fool.

"True." Though he was still admitted to most drawing rooms—unlike Devereaux, who truly *was* despicable—his reputation made it impossible to relax. He had to constantly think ahead, examining every word lest it be misconstrued, behaving more formally than anyone else so nervous hostesses would not bar their doors, and hiding his identity whenever he needed people to listen seriously to his ideas.

It was time to redeem himself. He was tired of living two lives. His alter ego could only skulk in isolated places, cutting him off from society. He had hesitated to reveal the truth for fear he would lose everything he'd accomplished, but until he did, both lives would suffer. And the need that had led to his alias no longer existed.

He smoothed the summons.

Ten years ago, his lurid reputation had made it impossible to find funding for his excavations. No one had believed Tony Linden was serious about anything but debauchery, so he'd invented Anthony Torwell. The antiquarian was now a renowned authority on Roman England, though establishing that expertise had been difficult. Too many people knew Tony Linden, so Torwell could only work in remote areas. He had to avoid sites owned by lords, for they might recognize him, even if they had not previously met—Lindens shared a strong family resemblance. And Torwell had to cultivate an image as a recluse. Even correspondence from other antiquarians went to an anonymous address. England had enough eccentrics that no one questioned his habits, but the stress of keeping his two lives separate made relaxation impossible.

It was time to live in the open. And the first step was to convince his father to cease persecuting him. Since Tony Linden could not disappear completely without raising speculation, he had to spend time in London and other gathering places. But his father encouraged his correspondents to report every hint of vice, keeping his reputation alive. Even impeccable behavior could not counter Linden's constant reminders.

So he must answer this summons. Never mind that he needed to organize his summer notes and had promised *The Edinburgh Review* an article. He would go to Linden Park and try to make peace with his father.

But reading the summons one last time raised a frown. The tone was off. Something was wrong—very wrong.

Please don't let it be Mother, he prayed before issuing a spate of orders to Simms, who doubled as his secretary and valet. His mother had kept him sane through his childhood. She was one of only two people he could count on for support.

Never had his isolation seemed so stark.

Chapter Two

A wave of excitement caught Tony by surprise when his carriage turned through the Linden Park gates for the first time in nearly a year. Shadows swallowed the hill beneath the manor, the sun's last rays turning the house into a fiery castle that seemed suspended in the air. Magical. Otherworldly. He had long imagined that Avalon resembled Linden at sunset.

Its core was nearly ancient enough to qualify as Avalon. After centuries of alterations and additions, it now sprawled across several acres, but none had erased its brooding gothic look. Crenelated walls and an ornately arched entrance remained, though enlarged windows now allowed light into the ancient rooms.

The family occupied a wing constructed during Queen Anne's reign. Tony planned to add a new master suite when he came into the title himself. Recent innovations made it possible to set up permanent bathing rooms with facilities for heating piped-in water. Years of digging up ruins in all sorts of weather had made frequent hot baths his most coveted luxury.

But that was for the future.

The house faded to sullen gray as the sun slipped below the horizon. The Park's herd of red deer gathered near the stream. A stag nervously studied the coach clattering across the bridge.

Tony smiled. Linden was his favorite place in the world, despite his father's antagonism. It was good to be home.

But contentment died the moment Pollard opened the door. The butler's demeanor could not hide a gray face. "Thank God you came quickly," he said, the lapse in formality raising new fears.

"Is Mother—"

"Lady Linden is quite well." Pollard's face twisted into apology.

Tony exhaled in sharp relief, though this second slip proved that something was seriously amiss. But he would deal with it. And doing so might even lead to peace with his father.

The house had been a battleground long before his own rebellion. Though never religious, Linden had adopted very puritanical notions. He refused to let his wife visit London or consort with those who did. He railed against most entertainments, prohibited wine, and even ale, from being served at his table, and complained bitterly when servants left for more congenial households.

Tony had rarely discussed Linden's oddities with his mother, but to spare her, he often deflected the man's wrath onto himself. She did the same for him, sharing a wordless understanding that they did not deserve such treatment. He never minded assuming her guilt. Taking the blame for her mistakes was easier than enduring lectures and punishment for his own.

Pollard's words had eased his greatest dread. From the moment he'd realized that this was not the usual summons, he'd feared that Linden's irritation had moved beyond tirades into the sort of brutality that could inflict physical damage on his wife.

"Is Father in his study?"

Pollard nodded. "But you would do well to change and take a bite of dinner before meeting him. Shall I send a tray to your room?"

Is it that bad? He suppressed a frown. This couldn't be about his behavior. None of the crimes he had imagined during two days on the road necessitated fortifying himself before facing his father.

"I ate in Costerton. Tell Father I will join him shortly."

Dread seeped into his bones. He had barely returned to London after a summer away from society, so there should be no new rumors. The two people who knew he was Torwell would never mention it. He was due for another lecture on securing the succession, but that would hardly account for Pollard's gray face or the footman's tension as he delivered warm water to his room.

Was his father ill?

He had not considered that possibility earlier. Linden had always been larger than life. But even the most stubborn man could fall prey to disease . . .

Twisting a clean cravat into an imperfect knot, he headed for the study. *Please let this be another misunderstanding . . .*

The door stood open. The usual footman was absent. Pollard must have sent him elsewhere. He shivered, forcing suddenly reluctant feet into the room.

Linden sat behind his desk, as usual. It was his favorite position for handing down punishments.

"Thank you for coming so quickly." His voice was somber, but bore no hint of censure.

Startled by the unprecedented greeting, Tony mentally revised his own opening. He leaned casually against the mantel, ignoring the miscreant chair facing the desk. "Is Mother well?"

"Quite."

"And you?"

"As usual."

He could think of nothing further to say. Conversation was alien to their relationship.

Linden rose, pacing as if he were also at a loss for words. "A problem has arisen," he said at last, swallowing hard as he resumed his seat.

Tony thrust down the familiar mixture of helplessness and fury, noting the man's appearance for the first time.

White face.

Sunken eyes.

Disheveled hair.

Grease spots on coat and waistcoat.

Shaking hands.

Linden looked old—or mad. The realization severed the last

link to past confrontations. Something was seriously wrong. Stepping closer to the desk, he rested his hands on the back of the chair.

Again Linden swallowed, finally forcing out words. "We must leave the Park."

"Leave the Park?" Tony repeated slowly. "Why?"

"I—" His voice broke. Licking his lips, he tried again. "I lost it."

This cannot be happening.

Tony ran shaking fingers through his hair, his eyes never leaving his father's ghastly face. "Start at the beginning."

"What is there to say?" demanded Linden harshly. "The Park was mine. It was unentailed. Now it is gone."

No!

Inhaling deeply, he fought to awaken from this nightmare. "How?"

"A wag—"

"You wagered the estate?" He nearly shouted the question. "You? Mr. Holier-than-thou Puritan?"

"How dare you question me?" roared Linden, rage turning his face red. "Your betting is notorious."

Tony lunged, leaning across the desk to glare into his father's eyes. "I have never wagered anything I could not afford to lose." The words hissed through gritted teeth. "What devil possessed you?"

Linden recoiled.

"Can't you buy it back? You've enough in Consols—"

"No."

His breath froze, dropping his voice to a whisper. "You lost everything?" Only his hands atop the desk kept him from collapsing.

"I wouldn't have if you weren't such a debauched fool!" snapped Linden, rising so his face nearly touched Tony's. "The man needed a fortune to dower his deformed daughter. I tried to talk him into taking you instead of the estate—it would have amounted to the same thing—but he wouldn't hear of it. Your reputation has ruined us."

"Your gaming has ruined us!" Fury shattered Tony's fragile control. Linden had actually offered his son's hand to save himself from his own stupidity. For the first time in his life, he blessed his reputation. "How dare you preach about the evils of gaming, then throw away the family fortune on the turn of a card?"

"It was dice."

"You bet the roof over your family's head on an idiot's game like hazard? You've been impersonating God's deputy for so long you think you are God himself. What possessed you?"

"I was drunk!"

Tony's knees gave out, dropping him into the punishment chair. "Did you decide to commit every one of your infamous sins at once? How stupid can you get? Don't you know enough to cut your losses while you still have a shirt on your back?"

"Lady Luck always returns," swore Linden. "In the end, she is always there."

The gamester's creed. Shock doused Tony's fury as the ramifications of those words registered. "Do you mean you have wagered the estate before?" His hands shook.

The whisper sliced through Linden's shout like a sword. He paled, collapsing into his own chair.

"How many times have you risked it?" Tony asked.

"Only once—"

"Did you learn nothing from the experience?"

No response.

Tony paced the room as he tried to come to grips with the catastrophe. The how and why made little difference. What mattered was recovering as much as possible. The money was gone, but perhaps Torwell could buy back the estate. It would require a bank loan, but Torwell had sufficient assets to impress a banker. His cousin Jon could act as go-between for the reclusive antiquarian.

"Who won it?" he asked, hoping it was someone who might be reasonable.

"Sir Winton Vale."

"Dear God!" Temper engulfed him. "How could you be so

stupid? Sir Winton is a dedicated gamester! Even *you* must have heard of him. He wins and loses at least a fortune a month." Running his hands through his hair, Tony stalked to the window, no longer able to look his father in the eye. "He has probably already lost the Park to someone else."

"No. I transferred ownership to his daughter's dowry trust. It will go to her husband." He slammed his fist onto the desk. "You are the fool. If you hadn't turned yourself into a pariah, we would not be in this fix. His daughter is a deformed freak who has reached the advanced age of six-and-twenty without a single offer. But he would rather she wed a gazetted fortune hunter than you. I've warned you for years about your vices."

"You are in no position to cast stones." He fisted his hands against the window casing to keep from smashing the glass. "If anything, your sins exceed my reputation. I've never lost an estate at the tables. I've not even lost enough to postpone paying my tailor. Haven't you noticed that not once have I asked for an advance on my allowance? And not once have you received duns on my behalf. You sit in that chair with a sanctimonious sneer on your face, casting aspersions at anyone who refuses to kiss your feet. Yet you never question whether your charges are valid. You would rather cling to your prejudices than admit you might be wrong."

Don't bother, Tony. He's not listening.

It was true. When he turned back to the room, Linden's head was in his hands. And sniping at each other was pointless. Sir Winton never gave up an advantage, so redeeming the estate was impossible. "How long do we have?"

"Wh-what?"

"When—must—we—leave?" He spoke each word with deliberation. Why was Linden moping? At least four days had passed since that fatal meeting. Shock should have given way to planning by now, yet the man had obviously done nothing but brood on his woes and twist the blame elsewhere.

Linden's mouth worked soundlessly.

"When must we leave?" he repeated.

"A month. Less. Where will we go?"

The plaintive voice was the last straw. "You should have thought of that before risking the roof over your head."

Unwilling to remain, Tony stormed out. Most of his possessions were already in London. The rest would easily fit into his coach. He would survive. He might even prosper. There was a small estate in Somerset he had his eye on. The grounds contained a mound that might hold an ancient tomb. He would look into buying it—but he'd be damned if he would offer a roof to the hypocritical fool seated in the study.

How many times had Linden ranted about the evils of gaming, accusing him of throwing his money away through reckless wagers? Yet all the time, he was hiding his own weakness. What could have prompted him to drown himself in wine, then offer his entire fortune to a known gamester?

And why had none of their ancestors entailed the estate? It had been in the family long enough.

The questions circled uselessly through his head. But the biggest one of all stabbed new pain into his heart.

What would happen to his mother?

Linden's punitive orders had hurt her enough already. She had ceased corresponding with school friends years ago, ashamed to admit that she was a virtual prisoner at Linden Park, yet unwilling to lie. Her local friends were wives of other rigid moralists, who would repudiate the connection once Linden's gaming binge was known. Not that Linden would remain in the area. He would move to a place where no one knew of his stupidity. How would she cope with a dour husband and no friends? Could she manage without servants, possibly without even a home?

She was waiting in his room. "He told you?"

He nodded. "How could he—" He bit off the words when he spotted her glittering eyes. Drawing her close, he let her cry against his shoulder. Several minutes passed before she pulled herself together.

"I thought I was past that," she said, sniffing into a handkerchief.

"Did he mention that this is not the first time he has wagered the estate?"

She swayed, making it to a chair only with his help. "So that explains it."

"Explains what?"

"He was not always like this, Tony." The barest hint of a smile lifted one corner of her mouth. "During my Season, he was the gayest of my suitors, always laughing, or flirting, or reciting extravagant poems to my beauty. His wit made him welcome everywhere, and there wasn't a gentleman in society who did not envy his flair for dress. Half the girls were in love with him, but I was the one he stole kisses from in the garden."

"Father?"

She blushed. "My parents thought him a trifle brash, but he was considered a good catch. I had no regrets until you were two years old." Pausing, she dabbed once more at her eyes. He handed her a dry handkerchief. "He loved society as much as I did. Our balls were always squeezes, and we received invitations to everything. You wouldn't believe the prince's gala when he moved into Carlton House back in '84. And the month we spent in Paris—salons, balls, the court at Versailles . . ."

He choked, failing to picture Linden at the French court.

"I don't know what happened in the end," she admitted, her momentary excitement gone. "We'd been in London only a fortnight when my maid woke me at dawn. Linden announced that we were leaving. We never returned. I learned a month later that he'd sold the town house. And from that day, he changed, growing dour and disapproving, forbidding all the activities he used to love, locking himself away until he no longer recalled those days."

Tony said nothing as she again dissolved in tears. Her memories bore no resemblance to the man he had known all his life.

"Forgive me," she begged. "I cannot quite believe we must leave."

"Where will you go?"

"I don't think he knows. We have not spoken since he informed me that he no longer owns the estate. You must help him, Tony. At least make him decide something. For four days he has done nothing but brood—and drink."

"Drink?" So the departure from abstinence had not been a one-time event.

She nodded. "I was hoping that he would tell you something."

His laugh contained no trace of humor. "He blames the loss on me."

"What?"

"If I were less notorious, Sir Winton would have agreed to shackle me to his deformed ape-leader of a daughter instead of demanding the estate. Apparently Sir Winton wanted a dowry for the girl."

"Linden would have done that to you?"

"My refusal would have given him a new complaint. He must be mad." He paced the room, trying to find words of comfort in a situation they both knew was hopeless. He couldn't invite her to live with him without also inviting Linden—another impossibility. Even doubling the amount of time he spent on excavations would leave months when he must be home. They had no relatives who might take them in—he discounted his cousin Jon, for the vicarage was only a mile from the Park. Linden's pride would never consider it.

Absently bidding his mother good night, he continued pacing. Fireplace to window. Window to washstand. Washstand to fireplace. His thoughts followed the same path, around and around. Reliving the confrontation in the study. Naming every friend and relative they had, with all the reasons why each could not help. Balking at any suggestion he share his roof with his father. He needed a drink.

But he froze with his hand on the bell-pull. This was Linden's solution—hide the pain beneath a haze of wine.

Is wedding Sir Winton's chit really so mad?

He jumped. Where had that idea come from?

Refusing Linden's suggestions was an automatic reaction, he realized. Since childhood, the man had demanded blind obedience. That contest of wills intruded into every other disagreement, building even minor skirmishes into major battles.

He had long considered Linden a religious fanatic, but in truth, his obsession bore little trace of church dogma. He wasn't opposed to sin. He merely railed against enjoying life, condemning everything pleasurable: dressing in the current mode, visiting the clubs, a glass of port, a willing maid, an innocuous hand of cards, an invigorating set of country dances. But his most fervent lectures were always reserved for gaming.

He paced faster.

He might wish his father in Hades, but anger did not extend to his mother. She had always supported him against Linden's tirades, easing his punishments, concealing incidents she knew would trigger a new round of disapproval, giving him her unqualified love and support. How could he blithely pick up the threads of his own life, knowing that she faced poverty with no guarantee she would even have a roof over her head? Linden had nothing left. Even spending his remaining years in an endless round of house parties would not work. Few would welcome a guest who could not pay vails to the servants when he left.

He must explore every possible solution before condemning his mother to such a life. And one solution was recovering the Park. His parents could remain there while he lived elsewhere.

Marriages of convenience had been the custom for centuries. Most worked well enough. Excavating would keep him occupied, offering an excuse to avoid his wife if she proved too annoying. The idea of forming an alliance with Sir Winton set his teeth on edge, but he would deal with it.

Somehow.

A night of thought convinced him that it was the only honorable path. Yet his reputation stood in the way. Though he rarely lacked willing bed partners—many considered him handsome, and his aura attracted the adventurous—this situation was different. The courtesan class might enjoy the thrill of dallying with the notorious Tony Linden, but no respectable lady considered him eligible, not even those who flirted outrageously with the danger he supposedly represented.

Sir Winton had already refused a match, so he must approach Miss Vale directly. But she would only consider him if she judged him on his merits, which meant hiding his identity. Even deformed maidens incarcerated in the country would have heard the rumors.

Could he manage such a deception? Wedding under a false name—or even an incomplete name—could lead to an annulment for fraud, so he must disclose the truth before marriage. Only love might prompt a woman to overlook his deceit. And only revealing his real self would convince her that his reputation was false. He must also hide the fact that he was a fortune hunter.

He cringed, for he despised that term and all it stood for. But he could not deny that he was, in fact, a fortune hunter. He was willing to wed a stranger, described by her own father as a deformed freak, because he needed her dowry.

He paced the length of the gallery and back, scanning his ancestors as he wrestled with the problem. He must court Miss Vale, hide his identity and purpose, convince her he cared, and win her heart so thoroughly that she would forgive his imposture and wed him anyway. And he must do it under Sir Winton's nose.

Damnation! It wasn't possible.

He stared at his mother's portrait. It had been painted shortly after her marriage and revealed a carefree happiness he'd never recognized. Her smile was wide, her eyes sparkling. He could see her twirling around a ballroom, charming every gentleman into slavish adoration. But that girl was gone, replaced by a timid woman struggling to survive in a harsh world. Could he release her from her long imprisonment? She had often sacrificed her own pleasure to protect him from Linden's wrath, so he owed her his best effort. Even restoring the security of Linden Park would not balance all she had done for him.

He resumed pacing, this time looking for ways around each obstacle. Approaching Miss Vale as Tony Linden was impossible. Even a recluse would associate the name with vice. So he must conceal his identity and accept the consequences of such a deceit.

But concealing his identity posed serious problems. He had never spoken to Sir Winton, but he knew the man by sight. Thus, he had to assume that Sir Winton would recognize him. The conundrum beat against his temples. How could he hide in a house headed by a man who knew him, a man who had already refused to consider him as a suitor. . . .

His great-grandfather stared down from the wall, brown eyes twinkling with humor.

Brown eyes.

The Linden looks.

Jon.

Every detail fell neatly into place as he rode toward the village. From a distance, he and Jon were nearly identical—same height, same build, same dark brown hair. At close quarters, the resemblance ended, but Sir Winton had never been close.

In light of the family looks, hiding his connection to Linden Park was impossible, but if he and Jon exchanged identities, he could appear as an innocent bystander. Jon could be the rake-hell fortune hunter that everyone avoided. It should not be difficult. Jon knew him better than anyone and could copy the flamboyant bow and exaggerated formality that made Tony Linden stand out in any crowd. The contrast allowed Anthony Torwell to fade into the background.

Ten-year-old Jon had moved to Linden Park after the death of his parents. Tony had welcomed him, delighted to have a playmate only a year his senior. Despite their differences—Jon was quiet, conformable, and avoided trouble—they had become closer than brothers. Tony had been the leader, his insistence drawing Jon into numerous pranks. But Jon had never complained, just as Tony had never begrudged Linden's preference for Jon's quiet obedience or the way he held Jon up as a pattern card during every lecture. Only the boys knew how often Jon covered up Tony's escapades.

The closeness remained. Jon continued to protect him by

keeping his secrets. He was the only one besides Torwell's single servant who knew the antiquarian. That was a secret even Lady Linden did not share.

"Tony!" exclaimed Jon when he arrived on the vicarage doorstep. "I did not expect you here until Christmas."

"You don't know?"

"Know what?" Jon sent his housekeeper for refreshments, then ushered him into the library.

"Father lost the estate in a dice game."

Jon choked. Tony had to pound him on the back before he could breathe again. "D-dice?"

"He also lost everything else." He explained. Jon's shock matched his own.

"What will Aunt Mary do?"

"I will have to provide for her." Tony shrugged.

"Living with Uncle Thomas will land you in Bedlam in a week."

"Exactly, which is why I must recover the estate. But Sir Winton will never allow me near his daughter—which is why I need your help."

"You want me to court the girl?" Jon blanched.

Tony grimaced. Jon's adherence to Linden's puritanical demands had left him unusually innocent. How was he to find a wife when he had no experience of the fair sex? But that was a problem for later.

"No. I won't put you through that. But you must assume my identity at Vale House. She cannot find out who I am until I have won her heart."

Jon again choked.

"You have to help me," said Tony firmly. "And not just for Mother's sake. What will happen to the tenants, the villagers, even the staff if a fortune hunter gains control of the Park?"

"Dear Lord above." His face was now stark white. "They would be ruined."

Tony nodded. "A fortune hunter would not care that they have served the Lindens for centuries. He would strip the estate of every penny, raise rents to exorbitant levels, and dismiss anyone who objected. He might even remove you—the bishop would never keep a vicar over the objections of the principal landowner."

"But why must I impersonate you? Can't you approach her in secret?" Jon's voice squeaked.

"Father claims she is deformed—quoting Sir Winton, I've no doubt, since he can't know the wench—so she is probably secluded."

Jon nodded. Locking up the imperfect was common among the great families.

"When Father offered my hand, Sir Winton turned it down, citing my reputation. So he would hardly allow me to court her."

"That damnable reputation!" Jon snorted. "How many times have I begged you to redeem yourself?"

"Society does not easily admit fault." He shrugged. "There is little I can do about it at the moment, and time is of the essence. Sir Winton demands that we leave within the month." He paused while the housekeeper delivered cakes and a pot of tea. "The plan is simple. You will be the depraved Tony Linden. To protect her virtue, Miss Vale will naturally stay close to the soft-spoken vicar. Sir Winton probably knows me by sight, but only from a distance, so you should pass easily enough. Once she is firmly caught, I will reveal the truth, but by then it will not matter."

"This cannot possibly work," protested Jon. "How can you court a woman under false pretenses?"

"I'm not. I must lie about my name, but everything else will be the exact truth. My reputation is false, as you well know. Why should I allow rumor to condemn me without a hearing?"

"It sounds too easy. You can't have thought this through. Remember what happened with Squire Perkins?"

"I was only twelve. Of course I overlooked a few details." But he grinned, remembering the red-faced squire's indignation. The man was nearly as disapproving as Linden.

"Take time to think, Tony."

"I have. It will be easy. We will stage an accident near the gates. Sir Winton can hardly refuse us refuge—reputation aside, Tony Linden outranks him. And he will be accompanied by a vicar, who can keep his baser instincts under control. Miss Vale must be starving for company. She is already six-and-twenty, but I'd never heard of her, so Sir Winton must keep her incarcerated. Attention from an infatuated gentleman will warm her heart. A day or two should see the matter finished."

"Very well. Aunt Mary has always treated me as her son. I have to help her. But I cannot believe this will work. No matter what face you put on the matter, you plan to deceive the girl. I despise dishonesty."

"But it is occasionally necessary." He thrust his conscience aside. "I will use the name Torwell to prevent confusion. I am accustomed to wearing it and doubt anyone at Vale House knows it. Two Lindens might raise questions."

Mounting his horse an hour later, he headed home, details circling his mind. This was the only way he could protect his mother, he reminded himself as regrets pricked at his resolve. They surged into a stab of pain as he passed a copse of trees where a young couple swayed in a passionate embrace.

The intensity of those regrets took him by surprise, spawning a wave of yearning. He would never know love now, thanks to his father. But he had no choice. His course was set. Turning back would make it impossible to live with himself.

He stiffened his spine, setting heels to his horse. The copse was soon far behind. But though regret dutifully followed conscience into oblivion, he couldn't quite banish his loneliness.

"Sir Winton has returned," announced Murch when Alex reached the house. "He wishes to speak with you in the library."

"I thought he went back to London," she muttered, frowning. She was covered in mud from working on the temple. Digging so soon after a deluge had not been her brightest idea, but she'd wanted to make up for the time she'd lost during his last visit. Winter was fast approaching, which would put a halt to further excavations until spring.

"His coachman claims he went to Lincolnshire."

"There and back in a week? What was he doing?" Even with ideal traveling conditions, he couldn't have spent more than a few hours at his destination. And why return to Gloucestershire instead of London?

"The hip bath is in your room, Miss Alex. As is hot water."

She heard the warning in his voice. Murch had been more of a father than Sir Winton. It had been Murch who'd summoned a doctor when she broke her arm; Murch who'd protected her the time Sir Winton tried to blame her for the horse he'd lamed in a drunken rage; Murch who kept her excavations secret and persuaded the staff to do likewise. He had offered comfort, support, and even advice when she was unsure how to deal with Richard, and he'd detected the vicious nature Richard's first tutor had successfully hidden from her, allowing her to replace the man before serious damage was done.

But he never forgot his place, so the warning note in his voice was a shock. Whatever awaited her in the library would not be good.

Half an hour later, Alex approached her father.

"Congratulations, my dear." Sir Winton actually smiled. "You will make your bows to London next spring."

"What absurdity is this?" she demanded, narrowing her eyes. He'd cursed for years because she was unmarriageable. A come-out was thus a waste of money. He'd even forbidden a visit to Bath, claiming she would only embarrass herself by flaunting her failings before the world. How could he drag her to town when they both knew that advanced age added a new fault to the list? She'd been on the shelf for years, as he frequently reminded her. Did he mean to make her into a laughingstock?

For once he read her face. "You need not fear failure, for your dowry is large enough to guarantee success. Gentlemen will beg for your hand. And about time, too. I thought I'd never find a way to get rid of you."

"Dowry?" she asked suspiciously, even as pain from this new proof of his disdain stabbed her heart.

"Forty thousand pounds and a productive estate."

Her eyes widened until she feared they would bounce onto the floor. "And how did you acquire so much?"

"Dice." He shifted to avoid her accusing stare. "Is it my fault the man is a poor player who demanded throw after throw when he began to lose?"

"What man?"

"Lord Linden." He shrugged.

"You will return every shilling, for I do not want a Season." She glared at him. Did he actually expect gratitude for forcing her to fend off every fortune hunter in the country? The man was a bigger fool than even she had believed.

The usual frown snapped onto his face. His eyes glittered. "The fortune is already in your name, in trust for your husband. You will participate in the next Season, and you will do nothing to discourage suitors. I will bar you from Vale House if you try to return unwed. I've had enough of your appalling manners and vicious spite. And I've had enough of your scheming. Don't think belligerence and swearing will ever drive gentlemen away again. No one will care. Unless you marry, I'll see you stripped, tossed into a taproom, and wed to whoever has a strong enough stomach to ravish you."

The subject was closed. Alex stumbled to her room, furious to find tears streaming down her cheeks. She never cried. Doing so over a man who wished she'd never been born was absurd.

She should have expected something like this. Now that Richard was in school, he need no longer put up with her reminders of his duty as a landowner. So he'd concocted this scheme.

She shivered. Tossing her to a pack of desperate men was beyond her worse nightmares. She had to find an escape.

Could she return the dowry? Something must have been wrong with the game. He won and lost enormous sums so often that fortunes meant nothing to him. So why had he refused to meet her eyes when he mentioned this one?

"Damnation!" She slammed a fist onto her bed. He must have fleeced Linden. "How could even he stoop so low?"

But the idea gave her hope. All she had to do was prove his dishonor.

"You have known Father most of your life, haven't you?" she asked Murch when he brought her dinner tray. She refused to eat in the dining room.

He nodded.

"Does he know how to cheat at dice?"

Murch froze, but finally nodded. "He once owned a fine pair of uphills, though he swore he never bet with them—gentleman's honor, you know. I thought little of it, for his usual game has always been cards. But he could make them do just about anything."

"That is what I feared, though how can I prove it to Linden's satisfaction?"

"Linden?" His gaze sharpened.

"What do you know of Linden?"

Murch sighed. "Not much, but Sir Winton knew a Linden at school—he used to brag about winning his allowance every quarter. The lad was a terrible card player who could be goaded into betting wildly. Apparently he viewed gaming, drinking, and wenching as proof of his manhood."

"Any idea where those dice are now?"

He shook his head. "I've not seen them in twenty years or more, Miss Alex."

Alex nodded, having expected that answer. Retrieving them might explain her father's first unexpected visit—he usually passed autumn at a series of hunting parties. Perhaps his week-long stay had given him a chance to recover his skill.

It was a nice theory, but worthless. Conjecture proved nothing. No one had seen the dice in years. If the game had been crooked, she could guarantee that there were no witnesses. Without evidence of cheating, Linden could not demand restitution. The trust would prevent her from returning the winnings outright.

A sleepless night brought no solutions. Women had no rights even without the complication of a trust, though she had to try. The moment he left for London, she summoned her carriage.

But her solicitor dashed any hope. Sir Winton had tied up the trust so she could touch nothing. The moment she wed, everything transferred to her husband. In the meantime, it was administered by a London banker, whose instructions could be modified only by Sir Winton—and even Sir Winton could not withdraw a shilling.

She was powerless, lacking even the authority to permit Lord Linden to remain in residence. They were both victims of a cunning she had never suspected.

She cursed all the way home.

Chapter Three

Alex vigorously brushed a twisted piece of bronze. Two weeks of daily scrubbings alternating with vinegar soaks had finally removed the centuries of grime, but she was far from satisfied.

Wrapping her hand around the ridged handle, she stared. What the devil was it? A rod protruded from each end, terminating in a flattened finger. Both rods and fingers were oddly bent. Were they supposed to be that shape, or had something deformed them?

She turned her fist, scrutinizing the piece from every angle. The handle fit too comfortably to be meant for anything but gripping. The silver inlays spoke of wealth. If it was a tool, its owner must have been high-ranking. But what could a tool like this do? The fingers were too blunt for piercing, too sharp for crushing, and too flat to use as spoons. Besides, why would anyone attach two, at opposite ends of the handle? Surely that would be awkward to use.

Perhaps it was a door pull—yet she could detect no way to attach it.

"Damn all men to perdition," she muttered, pacing her workroom.

Identifying this was impossible. None of her meager references described anything like it. Sending a sketch to Lord Mitchell was too risky, for if it were truly unique, he would send someone to investigate—or at least demand further details. Admitting that she had an artifact of silver-inlaid bronze confirmed that this was a rich site that might contain other treasures. Most excavations unearthed little beyond stone, bits of pottery, and an occasional coin. Metal objects were usually corroded or smashed beyond recognition. Only gold survived unscathed, but it was rare.

Excitement churned with frustration. If only she could share her finds with someone. Sarah had no interest in antiquity. Even approaching the vicar was out of the question. While he cared little about the stone foundations of the pagan temple, he was as susceptible to the lust for treasure as any other man.

Sighing, she sketched the object, then completed her notes on its condition—not that anyone would see them. Finding this piece underscored the gulf separating her from the antiquarian community. No one would read her careful records or consider her theories.

Lord Mitchell's letter taunted her from its pigeonhole in her desk. She had not yet replied. How could she explain turning down an offer that any normal antiquarian would grab?

Freak! Her father's voice echoed through her ears.

Stifling it, she shook off the blue-devils. Her work might not be accepted in her lifetime, but someone knowledgeable would eventually visit the ruins. They would find a complete, professional account of her excavation.

She unlocked the trunk where she stored valuable and unusual artifacts. Keeping them out of sight was another precaution. The staff would never steal anything, but she was less certain of their tongues. Remaining silent about odd bits of stone and broken tile was easy. Secrecy would be much harder if they knew she'd found anything exciting.

Depositing the unidentified bronze, she turned her attention to the letter from her father that had arrived that morning. She was still groping for a way to prove he'd cheated. It was her only hope for avoiding a Season.

She could no longer postpone reading his demands. Unfolding it, she frowned. His scrawl was nearly illegible at the best of times, but this was the worst she'd ever seen. He must have been drunk.

Phrases stood out from more muddled scratchings. *Kestler's idea . . . easiest way to find a husband . . . sacred oath . . . only using your money to settle your future. . . .*

If she interpreted his excuse-laden maunderings correctly, his friend Kestler had conceived the idea of winning her dowry from Lord Linden—he didn't admit to cheating, though. To improve his chances of success, her father had sworn an oath on his immortal soul that he would put all the proceeds in trust. Yet he had retained enough to pay for her Season—hardly a surprise; the way he had set up the trust precluded spending even a shilling of it before marriage. But he had lost that sum in a gaming hell barely an hour after reaching London. While staggering back to his rooms, he'd fallen, breaking his leg. He would be confined to bed for several weeks and might limp for years.

I accept this inconvenience as Divine retribution for reneging on my sworn word, he continued on a second sheet—his excuses had crossed and recrossed the first—*and am most grateful that He did not exact a harsher penalty. I vow to repay every shilling, with interest, the moment I rise from this bed,* he added piously.

She laughed. The man belonged in Bedlam. But at least this would keep him out of trouble for a few weeks. His latest vow meant nothing. She had long ago accepted that gamesters were as helpless as drunkards when faced with temptation. Word of a game drove every other thought from his mind—which was why setting up the trust was so astounding.

Perhaps Armageddon was at hand.

Murch rapped on the workroom door.

"Is dinner ready?" she asked. She often lost track of time.

"Two hours yet, Miss Alex. But a carriage met with an accident near the gates, laming one of the horses. No one was hurt, but the passengers request beds for the night."

"Passengers?"

"Two gentlemen."

"Do they have names?" Murch had never been so close-mouthed.

He extended a small tray. Two cards lay in its center, corners turned up to indicate a personal call.

"The Honorable Tony Linden," she read from the uppermost, stifling an oath. "Who is Mr. Torwell?" she asked, holding out the second.

"Mr. Linden's cousin. He serves as vicar to the village near Linden Park."

"Ah." She met Murch's eyes. Both knew there had been no accident. Cursing her father for putting her in this position, she sighed. "Put them in the west wing. I will see them in the drawing room before dinner. Is Sarah back?" One of the tenants was ill.

"An hour ago."

"I will warn her."

Once Murch left, she stared at the cards, pacing her workroom as she pondered this new complication. She should have expected Linden's heir to track her down. How else could he recover his inheritance? She ought to bar the door, but she couldn't.

"The Honorable Tony Linden," she repeated, staring at a London address not far from her father's. Everyone knew that the very dishonorable Tony Linden cared little about rules, taking what he wanted, without regret.

Was this her father's real goal? If Linden dragged her off to the altar, Sir Winton would be spared participation in the Season—and he could keep the cost of one for himself. Did he not care that she would be tied to a monster?

She snorted. Of course he didn't care. Ridding himself of an unwanted daughter was his only goal.

Banishing images of her father, she considered Linden. Unsavory stories had abounded for years, even in this remote valley. He was a rakehell who had ruined more than one innocent, though his legendary charm still made him welcome in all but the strictest drawing rooms.

After so many years of dealing with her father's debauched friends, his rakish adventures did not bother her, but his reputation as a drunken gamester did. The only reason he was not in debtor's prison was the generous allowance he received from his wealthy father.

Forty thousand pounds and a lucrative estate.

The allowance was now gone. Not only his inheritance, but his very livelihood was locked into a trust that could be recovered only by wedding her.

So he had come to seduce her. And he had gone about it quite cleverly. The staged accident. The vicar in attendance. Did he have a special license tucked away in his luggage?

Her feet picked up speed.

Damn the man! And damn her father for putting her in this position. Even if Linden gave up and left her alone, others would be close behind. Sir Winton would already be spreading the word that she was an heiress. Why would a desperate man wait until she arrived in London, where he must vie with others for her attention?

Linden was beyond desperate. He would also be furious that he must abandon more interesting diversions to recover what should never have been lost. To conclude this distasteful business as quickly as possible, he might break into her room, his vicar cousin in tow, and wed her that very night.

She shivered, but guilt was stronger than fear. She knew, deep in her bones, that her father had cheated. Even his shattered leg could not atone for so despicable an act. He had deliberately destroyed an entire family for his own convenience. Reparation was possible only by wedding Linden's son.

So she must consider his offer.

Yet his reputation was terrifying. Accepting marriage was bad enough with any man. Could she condone it with one she could never respect? The answer might well be no.

She pondered her dilemma as she headed upstairs, searching for a way out.

Perhaps she was being too harsh on her father. Her only evidence that he'd cheated was her own instinct and Murch's hints. What if Tony Linden had learned his vices at his father's knee? If the viscount was also a gamester, she owed him nothing.

Yet she had even less evidence for that scenario, she admitted wearily. Could a confirmed gamester keep his family fortune intact for decades? Her father couldn't. And what about Linden's wife, mother, daughters, younger sons? Were other family members being hurt through no fault of their own? Gamesters cared nothing for others, but that did not mean their families were culpable.

In the absence of facts, her own beliefs were all that mattered. It was unconscionable to strip a man of everything he owned, so she must do whatever she could to rectify this crime. But until she determined whether marriage was possible—his reputation made her shiver every time she thought of it—she must protect herself from a compromising attack.

There was only one solution, she decided, rapping on the door to Sarah's bedchamber. She hated deceit, but this situation was too dangerous.

"Tony Linden is here," she announced when Sarah answered.

"*The* Tony Linden?"

She nodded.

"Dear Lord! Why did you let him in? He is in league with the devil. Whenever parishioners strayed from righteousness, Papa would remind them that they risked the same damnation as Linden."

Alex bit back a sarcastic retort, for her uncle had been far from saintly. "I am well aware of his reputation, but I could hardly turn him away after Father stripped his family of every penny." She explained her fears.

"Do you honestly believe you can live with so debauched a man?" Her needlework fell unnoticed to the floor.

"I don't know. That's why you must help me. I cannot risk a compromise, so you must pretend to be me. Even a hardened libertine would balk at attacking so obvious an innocent."

It was the closest she could come to mentioning Sarah's clubfoot. A man accustomed to escorting beautiful women would be even less tolerant of imperfection than her father, whose pointed disgust forced Sarah to hide whenever his friends visited. Those friends were just as free with insults. As were the neighbors, who rarely called and never included Sarah on invitations. Linden would hesitate to attach a cripple until he was sure he could live with the consequences.

"You must be mad," countered Sarah, her eyes wide with shock. "Deceit never works. And how will you explain employing it if you do decide to accept him?"

"He will not care. All he wants is his inheritance." Her conscience cringed at the choice she faced, but it had to be done.

"What about the staff?"

"Murch will see that they behave."

"And what about callers? I grant that we receive few, but Mrs. Nobles has not been here in more than a fortnight. And news that we have two gentlemen in residence is bound to excite interest."

"Mrs. Nobles was called away to her sister's sickbed last week."

"I had forgotten," Sarah admitted.

"And Murch will keep news of this from spreading. The masquerade cannot last more than a day or two. Linden's excuse for seeking shelter will stretch no longer, and I will know by then if I can accept him."

"You should decide tonight. With your luck, one of Uncle's friends will appear at dawn. You know they never warn us that they are coming."

Her irritation grew at each new objection. "Those who visit London in autumn are already there. The others are unlikely to travel again until spring."

"You cannot have thought this through," Sarah protested. "No matter what his motives, a man of Linden's reputation will be slow to forgive trickery."

"I have no choice!" Alex barely controlled her temper. "If I followed my heart, I would refuse him admittance. You know I have no interest in marriage. Placing myself under the thumb of a husband would be far worse than having to deal with Father. But Linden would not accept so summary a dismissal, and I cannot ignore the probability that Father cheated. I must consider accepting this offer, but I must also protect myself from coercion. A man of his reputation would think nothing of forcing himself on an antidote, but I believe he retains enough decency to respect you."

They argued for half an hour, but in the end Sarah agreed. The only change she suggested was with names. To avoid confusion, Alex would become Miss Merideth, companion to the crippled Miss Vale.

Sarah had known quite well why Alex considered her safe from Linden's advances, for her own father had made it clear from birth that well-born ladies and gentlemen would never tolerate her. She decided to exaggerate the infirmity, even pulling out her hated crutch.

Alex returned to her room to look over her wardrobe, then realized that anything would do. None of her gowns were stylish, and all showed signs of wear. So the only change she would make was with her hair. Instead of bundling it haphazardly atop her head, she would pull it into a knot on her neck. A companion could not afford new clothing, but she would at least make the effort to be neat—unlike Miss Alex Vale, who had long ago abandoned any attempt to make a good impression on the world.

The admission raised nervous trepidation for the first time. Her usual attitude around men was belligerence. Could she behave like a normal lady tonight? And a subservient one, at that . . .

Tony tied his cravat into an undistinguished knot, then donned Jon's worn evening jacket. Already the imposture was causing problems. Though Torwell's work clothes would suit the role he was playing, his evening wear was clearly a product of Weston's genius. So he had traded with Jon. The fit wasn't perfect for either of them, but a country recluse would hardly notice.

And it was too late to change tactics.

He cursed. If he had known that Sir Winton was in London, he would have introduced Jon as the vicar and Torwell as an antiquarian, removing his reputation from consideration. But he'd found out too late. Asking about Vale House in the village would have put his supposed accident to the lie. And he'd already produced his own two calling cards before requesting an audience with Sir Winton. Changing stories now would turn Miss Vale against him. The play was in progress. He could only pray that she was tolerable.

Deformed . . .

The description had plagued him for days. It must be truly serious for her own father to describe her so. Even confirmed gamesters usually guarded their families.

"It doesn't matter," he said aloud, trying to convince himself. He must protect his mother.

He opened the connecting door to Jon's room—the two had once formed a suite—then choked. "Good Lord! You can't go down looking like that!"

"What's wrong?"

"That cravat would shame a tradesman." Ripping off the offending cloth, he dug out a freshly starched square of linen and fashioned an impeccable Oriental, drawing Jon's squeaking protest when he pulled the knot tight. "Why did Simms not tie this?"

"I sent him for a posset. My stomach is roiling so badly I fear it will rebel at dinner."

"Nonsense." He slapped Jon's hand aside, preventing him from loosening the cravat. "Why should you be nervous? You are not trying to make a good impression. Quite the opposite."

"B-but—"

"You are not mimicking *me*, but the dishonorable Tony Linden, product of imagination. Not only is his reputation a sham, but his mannerisms have always been an act. If I can manage them, you can." His arm swept dramatically through the air as he executed a theatrical bow.

Jon stiffened, but gamely tried to reproduce the motion.

"Relax. You look like a puppet."

Jon clutched his stomach.

Tony grimaced. "Try it again. Think of a swallow sweeping across the sky, or a swan gliding along the Thames." He should not have offered criticism when they must soon meet their hostess. Jon was unaccustomed to attracting attention and sometimes panicked when faced with unfamiliar situations.

The next attempt was worse. Brick would be more flexible. A drunkard showed more grace.

"Much better," he lied.

Simms returned with a glass.

Jon gulped the greenish liquid. An enormous belch filled the room. "Please reconsider, Tony," he said, setting the glass on the washstand. "This idea is insane. Nothing good ever comes of lying."

"Which is why we are in this pickle to begin with!" He strode to the window, running his hands through his hair. "My reputation is the lie, Jon. But I haven't time to convince Miss Vale of the truth—you know our poor, lame horse will have to recover in a day or two. We must conclude this project by then."

"But—"

"Don't lose sight of why we are here. Does Mother deserve to lose her home?"

Jon flushed. "No, but—"

"Jon—"

He flung up his hands. "Very well. But I am no actor. And I'll never be able to cut a dash the way you do." Grimacing, he flung open the door and strode into the hall. Within ten feet he stumbled, knocking over a ginger jar and nearly falling down the stairs.

I am no actor . . .

What had he wrought? But it was too late to change course. Tony descended to meet his fate.

"Mr. Linden and Mr. Torwell," the butler intoned, preceding them into the drawing room.

Tony followed his gaze. The lady nearest the fire was a petite blonde. A very pretty blonde, with sparkling blue eyes and a sweet smile.

"Miss Vale," announced the butler.

Deformed? The girl was enchanting. But even as the thought surfaced, he spotted a crutch. She shifted, revealing a grotesquely twisted foot.

Relief weakened his knees. He could live with a clubfooted wife. As could society, though they usually shunned anyone less than perfect. But people had become accustomed to Byron.

Locking eyes with his quarry, he hardly noticed the second introduction.

"Your generosity will surely be rewarded." He smiled into those blue eyes, careful to overlay impeccable manners with the merest hint of sudden infatuation. "Offering shelter to strangers in need reveals the goodness of your heart. You have our eternal gratitude, Miss Vale."

"Thank you, sir." Her responding smile produced twin dimples. "I trust Mr. Linden's horse was not seriously injured."

"A strain; no more. With luck, we can continue our journey in the morning and count meeting a charming lady as an unexpected blessing. Life is full of rewards."

Jon jumped in front of him, executing a bow that resembled a stooping hawk more closely than a graceful swan. Grabbing Miss Vale's hand, he raised it so briskly to his lips that he smacked it into his nose. "A goddess, forsooth! Why has such remarkable beauty remained secluded where no one can enjoy it?" But the demand lacked force. Already his nose was swelling, combining with his tight cravat to turn his voice to a nasal squeak.

Grimacing, she rescued her hand. "This is my home."

"Are the neighbors dullards that they've allowed so tasty a morsel to remain unclaimed? Gloucestershire must be peopled by fools."

Battling an urge to laugh, Tony frowned at his cousin.

"Will you please be seated?" Miss Vale cringed. "I do not enjoy people looming over me."

Jon nodded, vehemently. "Of course, my dear lady. I would not dream of discommoding my delectable hostess. You must forgive me." He jerked an armchair closer, ramming it into her shin. Sweeping his tails aside, he sat, but the gesture flung his arm out, jostling a tea table. A decanter of sherry crashed to the floor.

Miss Vale gasped.

"Damme! What a clumsy oaf I am tonight," he exclaimed, jumping to his feet and treading on her good foot. His face flushed crimson. As he bent to apologize, his hip knocked the table onto its side even as his head cracked against her shoulder.

Satisfied that Jon was making an ass of himself, though irritated that he was adding new vices to a reputation that already had too many, Tony turned to the companion—and nearly tripped over his own feet.

She was an Amazon. And not just in size. She was glaring at Jon as if she'd like nothing better than to drive a spear through his heart.

His body stirred. He'd always had a weakness for combative women. This one could offer a real challenge. Those flashing eyes alone had his blood moving. When added to blazing hair, a generous bosom, a—

You are a vicar, he reminded himself. Though many a vicar was more sinful than the flock he led, he was determined to play the role of a saint. He could not afford any connection to Tony Linden's reputation, no matter what temptations he faced.

"Dinner, Miss Vale," announced the butler, rescuing Jon from further apologies.

Tony extended his arm. "I fear I did not catch your name."

She answered his deprecating smile with a knowing look. "Miss Merideth, companion and cousin to Miss Vale."

Her eyes tunneled into the deepest recesses of his mind, raising considerable discomfort. What did she see?

But the question vanished when she stood. Amazon, indeed. Taller than many men, the top of her head reached his eyes, though he stood over six feet tall. Her complexion spoke of hours in the garden without benefit of a bonnet. She had pulled her hair into a severe knot, emphasizing the masculine planes of her face, but already strands were escaping, adding to her vibrancy . . .

His mind went blank when his eyes dropped to that glorious bosom. Lust coiled in his gut, sending tremors through his arm as he escorted her from the room.

Not now.

He repeated the admonition, stifling his instincts. Recovering the Park was too important to allow diversions, no matter how pleasant.

Dinner was served in an intimate family dining room, which would allow easy conversation, relieving one of his concerns. He had feared a formal setting and larger household, for a vicar would hardly have a claim to his hostess's side.

Jon practically threw Miss Vale into her chair.

Tony hid a grimace. They would have to discuss behavior tonight. Jon would do better to move slowly. No one would believe this act. Tony Linden might be considered a rakehell, but he was also noted for grace and charm.

But this was not the place. Jon collapsed into his own chair and gulped a glass of wine, signaling the footman for more even before the butler finished serving the soup. Wishing he'd taken more time to soothe Jon's nerves, Tony turned to Miss Vale.

"Please forgive my cousin, Miss Vale. He has always been a poor traveler. I fear he is not quite himself this evening." He flinched when Jon dropped a fork on the floor, the clatter drawing all eyes.

"Travel can be quite wearying." But her gaze stayed on Jon.

As the meal progressed, he made a determined effort to soothe her, asking quiet questions about life at Vale House, sticking to topics he could reasonably expect a recluse to understand. She gradually relaxed, though she rarely accorded him her complete attention, watching Jon as if he were an adder.

By the time they started the dessert course, Tony knew enough to be thankful that he was in disguise. The charade was necessary, for Miss Vale was even shyer than he had expected. Her answers were brief to the point of curtness. She cringed at every reference to Tony Linden, flinching when Jon's braying laughter interrupted conversation.

His reputation had obviously preceded him, and it was equally obvious that she knew his purpose and had done what she could to protect herself. Every time Jon tried to flirt, Miss

Merideth distracted him, snapping out questions about his life like an angry major general. Jon stumbled more than once before giving up and turning to food.

But she was sharp. And determined. Abandoning the personal questions her employer wanted answered, she switched to others that revealed her own burning desire to escape her lot. She was too spirited to enjoy incarceration in the country or entrapment in a menial position. He had to sympathize with her, for he would have hated such a life.

"Tell me about London, Mr. Linden," she asked when he stopped eating long enough to signal for more wine.

Jon responded with a mishmash of half-truths about places no lady should know. But Miss Merideth either cared nothing for propriety or was so desperate for entertainment that she would discuss anything. When Jon turned back to Miss Vale with a leer and an impertinent comment, she interrupted him with a question about last week's Newmarket race meet.

Tony wrenched his own attention back to Miss Vale. Jon's distortions did not matter. Even if the ladies caught him in a lie, it would merely add to their aversion. And he needed to concentrate on his own plan.

"What does Gloucestershire offer its visitors?" he asked.

"Very little this time of year," she said absently, her attention pinned on Jon. Was she shocked by his antics or merely protective of her companion? "Most estates are embroiled in the harvest, and—"

Miss Merideth's voice overrode the rest of her response. "Are the rumors about Byron true?"

Tony jumped. "It depends on which rumors you mean," he said, his eyes keeping Jon quiet. Jon loathed Byron, becoming incoherent whenever his name arose—like last night. Another traveler had mentioned the latest rumors, igniting a tirade that ended with Jon wondering why God had not struck the man dead for his sins.

"The affair with his sister, of course." Her voice had an edge he had not expected. Had finding Tony Linden at her employer's table triggered such belligerence, or was it something else?

You are supposed to be a vicar. Act like it. "I hardly think that is a proper subject for gently bred ladies, Miss Merideth." Miss Vale relaxed at the words. Clearly, she did not wish to pursue the subject, so he terminated it. "He has left the country, so further speculation is pointless."

Miss Merideth's eyes flashed, stirring his body. Tossing an irritated scowl in his direction, she returned to Jon. "Have you seen the Elgin marbles, sir?"

Jon laughed until he choked, ending that topic.

Tony glared, forgetting for the moment that it was Torwell who had studied the marbles. Jon was overplaying his role, threatening them with exposure.

"We will leave you to the port," said Miss Vale, gesturing for her crutch.

"That isn't necessary," protested Tony, taking her arm. "We would prefer your conversation this evening, if that is agreeable. We do not often have the pleasure of genteel company." Adding a graceful compliment for her beauty, he led her haltingly to the drawing room.

Then cursed. He had expected Jon to step aside now that Miss Vale had taken him into aversion, yet the message seemed to have bounced off his cousin's thick head. The moment they reached the drawing room, Jon pounced.

"We are on our way to a house party," he said, grabbing Miss Vale's hand from Tony's arm and shoving her onto a couch. He joined her, crowding close enough that his leg pressed against hers. "I look forward to meeting the other guests, though they can hardly be as entertaining as those at the last gathering. What delectable ladies!" He smacked his lips as if in memory, but his face was beet red.

Tony took a chair on Miss Vale's other side, grateful that Miss Merideth was speaking with the butler. Miss Vale was staring at the floor, but her companion would surely question that blush. He was wondering about it himself. At three-and-thirty, even Jon was no longer a callow youth. He might not have personal experience, but he'd heard enough frank discussion at school to dispel any embarrassment.

A footman carried in the port.

Miss Merideth joined them, touching Jon's arm. "Mr. Linden, perhaps—"

"In a minute." He shrugged her off, tossed down half a glass of port, then continued his story. "Wonderfully diverting party. Every night better than the last. Too bad how it ended, though. House fire. We'd hardly crawled into bed when it started. Place went up like a torch." He leaned closer, lowering his voice. "Devereaux did it. Drunk. Knocked a lamp onto the bed curtains—or maybe it was onto Polly's gown. You wouldn't believe the shouting and shcreaming."

"My goodness." Miss Vale cringed away from him, one hand clutched to her heart.

"Not to worry. We all escaped, but few could grab even a sheet to protect their modesty." His laughter filled the room. "One sweet little thing t-tripped and fell right into my armsh."

"Linden! That is not what He meant by *love thy neighbor*." But Tony was fighting to keep a grin off his face. Dear Lord! Where had Jon come up with such a fable? Miss Vale had wedged herself into a corner in a bid to escape. Miss Merideth was staring in horrified fascination. "Sometimes he forgets his audience," he said soothingly, briefly touching Miss Vale's hand, leaving Miss Merideth to deal with Jon. "I have never found fire an appropriate subject for drawing rooms. Our chandler died in one only last year."

"Tragic," said Miss Vale as Miss Merideth tugged Jon upright.

"Very, though at least his family escaped."

" 'Twas his own fault." Jon had escaped Miss Merideth's grip. He sagged against Miss Vale's shoulder, staring down her bodice. "For real tragedy, talk to my friend Cullum. Devil of a fellow, but one of the unluckiesht I know. Why, only last week, his butler tripped over a doorshtop. Bumped the wine man into the cellar. Broke a hundred bottles of brandy. Merchant wouldn't deliver more until he'd been paid. Damned shame. Made for a dull dinner that night. Couldn't find a d-decent d-drink until we reached the c-cock pit."

Wine! Ignoring Miss Vale's white face, Tony stared at Jon. An empty port glass hung crookedly from his slack fingers. He'd consumed at least six glasses of wine at dinner—Jon, who rarely finished even one, claiming he'd no head for drink.

"Know where we went from there?" Jon demanded loudly as he slumped farther. His head landed on her bosom, his tongue lolling out to lick the exposed flesh.

"N-no."

"Christ!" Tony muttered. This was working too well. At this rate, they would be sleeping in the stables and on the road by dawn.

Miss Merideth glared at him.

He'd hardly registered that he must have spoken aloud, when his gaze again slammed into that memorable bosom, draining the blood from his brain. But he had to rescue Jon.

"Christ—" he repeated, louder, shoving Jon upright, which brought his eyes closer to Miss Merideth's assets, "—tells us it is not good for man to be alone, but this much togetherness is not appropriate to drawing rooms. A gentleman need not disclose all his social contacts. Remember that only the righteous flourish, so refrain from seeking out the unholy and hide your own light under a basket of fish—" God! He was rambling. He couldn't think. What the devil was he trying to say? And how would a vicar say it? "—in the Garden of Gethsemene."

Face burning, he abruptly ceased talking. He'd thought nothing could possibly make him blush, but Miss Merideth's glare had done it. Clearly he had lost all control of his thoughts. Even Jon was silent, and furrows creased Miss Vale's forehead.

But Miss Merideth was the dangerous one. He had to divert her attention. She was remarkably sharp for a female. And he had better brush up on his Bible as soon as he escaped this room. Surely there was an appropriate passage that would keep Jon in line.

"Even the devil cites Scripture for his purpose," he muttered, searching desperately for inspiration. His eyes probed the shadows.

"My God!" he exclaimed, lunging toward the corner. Reverently, he lifted the bronze statue sitting on an open escritoire.

"Minerva. And a remarkable rendition of her. Where did Sir Winton get it?"

Miss Merideth had followed him. "It is mine."

"Then where did *you* get it? This is Roman work. And ancient Roman, at that. Third century. Possibly fourth."

"I know. I fo—" Her eyes widened. "My God! You are *Anthony* Torwell."

"Yes, but—" His voice froze. His card said only A. Torwell. How could she know the full name, unless—

"I've read several of your papers. Your description of the Roman fortifications near York is fascinating."

"You read antiquarian articles?"

"You needn't sound so shocked," she snapped. "I am perfectly capable of understanding them."

He took a deep breath. It wasn't her words that shocked him, but the awe in her face. Worship was not a reaction he inspired in others. But he had vowed to tell the truth about everything but his name, and it was too late to deny his identity, anyway. Reconciling his two lives would happen sooner than he'd planned.

Panic danced along his nerves, leaving him vulnerable. His reputation rarely bothered him because he knew it was false. But the respect he received from other antiquarians was always tinged with questions about whether it would continue once they knew the truth. Now that he must reveal that truth, it felt like a reckless violation of his soul. No more security. Never again could Tony Linden deflect criticism with the mental shield of *if he only knew the real me* . . .

"Forgive me, Miss Merideth. I have no doubt that you are an intelligent woman. I was surprised, not incredulous, for I know few gentlemen who are interested in the past. Never have I encountered a lady knowledgeable about the subject. So where did you find Minerva?"

She bit her lip, closely scanning his face before replying. "In the Roman temple I am excavating."

Chapter Four

Alex watched, fascinated, as emotions flew across Torwell's face. Excitement. Shock. Fear—that couldn't be right. Suspicion. And finally back to interest and suppressed excitement.

Why hadn't she been born a man? A gentleman could have approached Torwell in a straightforward manner, explained his interest, and requested information and guidance.

But she was hampered by society's ingrained belief that ladies were incompetent widgeons who could not even stroll about the grounds without assistance, let alone excavate a Roman temple and correctly evaluate what they found.

Stupid! How could you let a moment of euphoria override all sense? He is a man, with a man's arrogance.

She shivered. Revealing her activities was reckless. Would he scoff at her? Worse, would he spread tales about the silly woman who thought she was an antiquarian? One hint would bring her father home to investigate.

She gripped the back of a chair to hide her tremors.

"How did you clean Minerva?" he asked.

A most unusual man. Rather than jump to conclusions, he had decided to test her skill. "Vinegar baths and scrubbing with mallow-root brushes. I feared that using anything stronger might harm her. Fortunately, she wasn't badly encrusted."

Her pounding heart was making her lightheaded, though at least the tremors had passed. She stroked a finger along the patina coating one slender arm as hope battled fear. Would the celebrated Anthony Torwell share his expertise with a mere female? Would he keep the site a secret? Would leaving Minerva in the drawing room last night bring her luck or unmitigated disaster? So wrapped in thought was she that his voice made her jump.

"What else have you found?"

"Bits of tile. Worked stone that was probably part of the walls. Some chips that may have been pottery bowls." She wanted to show him her workroom, but she could not leave Sarah alone with the lecherous Linden. Especially since she was supposed to be Sarah's companion. "Miss Vale has provided a small room in the old wing as work space. Perhaps you would care to see it before you leave."

"After breakfast. And I would appreciate a look at the temple." His crooked smile nearly melted her bones. What the devil was a vicar doing with a smile like that? And why was a vicar digging up ruins?

She had heard of Anthony Torwell long before she found the temple. He was considered the foremost authority on Roman England, his stature so great that she had thought him the same age as Lord Mitchell. If Mitchell had not been tied to his estate by gout, she would have approached Torwell with her questions. But despite avoiding public appearances, he remained active in the field.

"How does a vicar find so much time for excavation?"

Shock flashed across his face so quickly she nearly missed it. But another of those devastating smiles drove the memory from her mind. "Curates can be quite useful. But how much time does a companion have for digging?"

"As much as I need. We rarely have callers. The valley is rather isolated. In fact, the lane terminates at a tenant farm only a mile past the gate." She raised her brows to show him that Linden's ruse was more than obvious.

His eyes blinked, proving he got the message. "We took a wrong turn."

"Then I must be grateful. Would you mind answering a few questions in the morning?"

"Not at all, if you will answer mine." With a final caress

down Minerva's spine, he returned to the others, murmured something in Linden's ear that brought an unlikely flush to the rake's cheeks, then resumed his seat, turning that magical smile onto Sarah.

Alex caressed Minerva in turn. He was fortunate to have a curate—as was his parish, if the curate was interested in his calling. Too many men took holy orders from necessity rather than choice. It was obvious that Torwell was one of them. Her own vicar was another. He spent most of his time contemplating Greek philosophy, offering little help to his flock.

Sarah's flaming cheeks cooled under Torwell's influence. Only then did Alex realize that temper had raised that vivid color.

She berated herself. In the excitement of identifying him, she had left Sarah at Linden's mercy. What devilment had he been up to while her back was turned? Torwell might know—whatever he had said had turned Linden quiet as a church mouse—but she could not ask without drawing attention to her dereliction of duty. After setting Sarah up as a supposed heiress, she must protect her.

As for Linden, it was obvious that he had little contact with well-born ladies. No wonder he was barred from the strictest drawing rooms. Between his boorish manners and lecherous inclinations, she had grave doubts about accepting him. Never had she met anyone who could change so quickly from dull to obnoxious and back.

You haven't really given him a chance, her conscience pointed out.

Which was true. She'd actually encouraged some of his wilder tales at dinner. And her eyes had kept straying to Torwell. Had she unconsciously suspected his identity even then?

Murch carried in the coffee tray.

Abandoning Minerva, she returned to Linden's side. Torwell continued a humorous story, distracting Sarah's attention. Linden had fallen asleep, an occasional snore emanating from his open mouth.

What a lout.

Torwell flashed another of those smiles, drawing a matching response from Sarah that deepened her dimples. He touched her hand in a gesture of intimacy.

Alex frowned. Was he really covering Linden's vulgar manners, or did he think to win the fortune for himself? Vicars rarely earned enough to support the digging Torwell did. A curate might free his time, but it would also reduce his income. Since he was related to Linden, he could justify taking over the estate—on grounds that Linden did not deserve it, if nothing else. He'd certainly monopolized Sarah at dinner. Perhaps he was smitten by her beauty and thought to rescue her from his villainous cousin.

But this was no time to brood. She had to make her own decision. Turning to Linden, she jostled his arm, meeting his bleary eyes. "I heard of your father's misfortune, Mr. Linden. Are your parents all right?"

"As well as can be expected, no thanks to you." But the flash of pain crossing his face relaxed her. A man who felt his parents' woe could not be all bad.

"Miss Vale knew nothing of the encounter until long afterward," she continued. "I trust you are not planning to retaliate."

"I—I—" His face flushed.

Torwell suddenly towered over her. "What my cousin is trying to put into words is the question that has bedeviled him since he learned the facts four days ago: What kind of people would toss his mother onto the road without a penny to her name?"

"Wha—" Sarah blanched.

"If that is why you staged an accident on our doorstep, you came to the wrong door." Alex rose, glaring at Torwell. "I—we were as appalled as you, but Miss Vale's solicitor confirms that she has no power to change the agreement under which Lord Linden and Sir Winton formed the trust. She wrote to the London bankers who administer it, but they have not yet replied."

"He had expected to see Sir Winton." Torwell's voice was quieter.

"Then he must go to London. Sir Winton is recovering from a broken leg."

"Divine retribution?" His eyes twinkled.

"One might consider it so."

Linden suddenly groaned. "Tiring day. Good night." Lurching to his feet, he made a grotesque bow, then staggered toward the hall, more than a little green.

So much for deciding anything tonight. She stifled a grimace. He must have been half-seas over when he arrived. She'd been congratulating herself that the notorious drunkard had consumed only six glasses of wine at dinner, but she'd not considered other sources. No wonder he seemed so coarse and clumsy. He was nearly unconscious from imbibing several bottles of spirits. Pray God he would reach his room before losing it.

"I, too, have had enough excitement," said Sarah, collecting her crutch.

Alex delayed her until Linden could escape. She wasn't sure if Sarah knew why he'd left so abruptly, but the last thing Sarah needed was to tangle with a drunken libertine. Gentlemen three sheets to the wind assumed that all females were harlots—as she'd learned from dealing with her father's friends. She'd had to slam Abernathy's head into a door to discourage him on his last visit. Thank God she outweighed him.

Finally, she turned to Torwell. "Unless you must help your cousin, would you care to see my workroom?" With Linden drunk as a lord, she need not fear for Sarah's virtue tonight. Only time would reveal how common this situation was. In the meantime, she was free to indulge her own interests.

"Simms will see after him. Lead on."

She took the proffered arm, directing him to a former still room in the old wing. Rough shelves covered two walls. She had moved an old desk against a third. The locked trunk sat unobtrusively in the corner.

Torwell walked slowly along the shelves, fitting stone fragments together to clarify a chiseled phrase, fingering a curved piece of roof tile, part of a bowl, a rotted piece of brass that might have been anything from a belt buckle to a bit of armor.

"How much of the site have you bared?"

"Very little, if my calculations are correct. I've uncovered a quarter of the temple, but test holes indicate a larger structure nearby—possibly a villa."

"A rich site, then." His eyes gleamed. "I've found less than this on entire digs. Any coins?"

"A few, all fitting the parameters elucidated in your treatise on using coins found at military encampments to date the stages of the Roman conquest." She opened the trunk, thrilled when his eyes blazed a brilliant green. If the great Torwell was excited, then she hadn't exaggerated the importance of her work.

Squatting beside her, he picked up a seated clay figurine. "A Celtic mother goddess." His finger stroked gently over the babe in the woman's lap. "A rather archaic form, so it probably predates the Roman era by several centuries."

"There is an earlier structure beneath the temple. I thought it was Druid until I found this last week. Now I wonder."

"Druids served as priests for all the gods. And more. They formed the upper class of their society, acting as rulers, lawmakers, and judges—or so I believe. The few references from Roman times indicate that Druids held absolute authority over every aspect of life."

"My references say nothing of that."

"I'm not surprised. Few people care what preceded the Normans, let alone the Romans." He scanned her small shelf of books. "Quite an extensive collection."

"It is?" She couldn't keep the surprise from her voice.

"Interest in ancient societies arose very recently. Even today, most people care only for treasure." His eyes narrowed as he picked up a gold coin from the reign of Diocletian and Maximian. "Most money was issued locally, like these—" He pointed to a few worn bits of silver. "—so only an officer would have owned Roman coins. Minerva is also of Roman origin. Whoever lived here had to be high ranking."

"This area was one of the designated retirement centers."

"But outposts like Britain were rarely commanded by men from Rome itself. Most came from Gaul or the German states. Or Spain." He stood. "You've an exceptional site. I am amazed that a man of Sir Winton's reputation has allowed a female access to it, and more amazed that he has not sold the better artifacts."

"It is Miss Vale who allows me to excavate," she said carefully. "Sir Winton is unaware of my activities. He is rarely at home and ignores his daughter when he is."

"An interesting problem. What do you plan to do with this?" He gestured toward the trunk.

"Study the artifacts. Since nothing is mine, my only motive is to learn as much as possible about the site and the people who lived there—which is why I do not wish to inform Sir Winton. He would destroy anything he could not sell in his search for what he could."

He nodded, then turned briskly to business. "What do you know of excavation techniques?"

The abrupt question startled her. "I read your paper on the subject, and I studied everything I could find on the period. So far, I've exposed only the temple, which I suspect was deliberately sited atop the earlier shrine."

"Interesting hypothesis."

"I thought so. Replacing existing priests would shift power into Roman hands, reducing Druidic influence while allowing people to visit the site. Perhaps they mixed elements of various rites, making it easier for the locals to accept the new order. Pilgrims could pretend to worship the new gods while actually following the old. Within a generation or two, it would no longer be pretense."

He raised his brows. "I've heard that suggestion before."

"From Lord Mitchell, perhaps?" She enjoyed his jump. "But I doubt expediency played a role here. A villa owner would care nothing about local beliefs. The site is large enough to indicate wealth, so he probably built a temple for his personal use. Locating it there might have been a convenient way to erase the older gods."

"Technique?" he repeated, his eyes drilling into hers.

Mentally shrugging, she pulled a sheaf of papers from the desk. "I surveyed the site before starting," she began, handing him a map marked into squares. "I sketch everything before removing it, noting depth, orientation, and condition. The site occupies a clearing in the home wood, but few people go there. Not only is it private land, but legend claims the wood is both sacred and haunted. Old Peter swears he's seen ghostly priests looming out of the fog. Most of the staff know I am digging, but none have come out to see my work. They have no interest in broken stones."

"And you keep everything of value hidden."

"Exactly."

He looked up from her map. "This looks like Mitchell's style."

She could feel her face heat. "I asked him for suggestions after finding Minerva."

"He actually agreed to help you?"

"You needn't sound so shocked. He has no idea I am a lowly female," she snapped, tired of having to justify her intelligence. "His response goes to our vicar. You are not the only churchman interested in history."

"Forgive me," he begged, with another of those crooked smiles. "You are obviously competent—more so than others I could name. I will become accustomed to the idea in time."

"Is it so astounding?"

"Not really. Many London intellectuals are women—though I know of none interested in antiquity." He scanned two of her sketches before frowning. "You knew I heard that theory from Mitchell because you suggested it to him."

She nodded.

"He claimed it arose during discussions with his assistant."

"I'm flattered that he would rate me so highly, though he did ask me to present it to the Antiquarian Society. I've been trying to figure out how."

"Have someone read your paper for you. That's what I always do. Barely half the papers are presented in person," he said absently, brow furrowed over her most recent sketch. "What is this?"

"I've no idea." She pulled out the twisted piece of bronze. "I was hoping you could identify it."

He turned the piece in his hands. "It is worked, not cast. Beautiful piece." He turned it, much as she had done. "Where have I seen this shape?"

He was obviously talking to himself, so she merely watched his face twist as his thoughts raced.

"Ah. I believe it is a surgeon's tool. The angles improve its leverage. It was used to lift broken bones into position for setting or to hold a wound open while bone chips were removed. The sketch I saw had only one rod, but this probably belonged to a military doctor. The shared handle would make his kit lighter to carry into the field. Where did it come from?"

"Here." She pointed to the map. "It was atop a dressed stone, but I've no idea what portion of the villa this might have been, or even if it was inside or out. Though test pits indicate the site is large, I have not uncovered enough to develop a floor plan."

"May I visit the site in the morning?" He must have read her objections, because he continued. "Miss Vale will be perfectly safe. Linden's behavior has never come close to his reputation. And I doubt he will rise before noon, in any event."

"We must return by noon, then."

"Unnecessary. I promise, on my honor as a gentleman, that my cousin will do nothing to disturb Miss Vale."

For some reason, she believed him. "Very well. Breakfast will be out by seven, in the same room as dinner."

His smile widened, sending shivers down her back. What the devil was wrong with her? No man was trustworthy. Not even a vicar, no matter how revered he was in antiquarian circles. She could not allow a smile to deflect her caution, especially from so enigmatic a man.

As she headed up to her room, away from his overwhelming intensity, she revised some long-standing impressions of Mr. Anthony Torwell. His age was not the only surprise. His man-

ner was just as unexpected. Torwell was known as a recluse, so
she had expected him to be a shy, scholarly man.

But he wasn't. Despite a certain wariness—probably due to
his cousin's condition—he was at ease in a drawing room. His
looks and manners would make him welcome anywhere. To say
nothing of an understated charm and crooked smile that could
convince the weak-willed that black was white. So why did he
avoid public appearances?

Tony slowly circled the clearing, fighting to hide his growing excitement. He was a guest. This wasn't his site.

The area was at least two hundred feet long and half that
wide, larger and richer than anything he had excavated in ten
years of work. Hardly a surprise. By avoiding the great estates,
he eliminated most of the desirable locations that might hold
villas. Digging in towns was impossible unless something
turned up while constructing new buildings. So most of his
work was at military encampments or small sites on marginal
land.

Yearning filled him as he gazed at the wealth of stone she
had already unearthed. Yet most of the clearing was untouched.
And completing its exploration was beyond the abilities of one
person.

She had made a good start, but it would take her years to finish. Maintaining secrecy that long would be impossible. Sooner
or later a servant would let something slip, or a dare would send
a boy into the haunted wood, or Sir Winton would ride out
some bright morning on a whim.

Few trees dotted the clearing, proving that the remains were
close to the surface, allowing only grass and shallow-rooted
shrubs to flourish. He hoped the floors remained intact, though
the likelihood was remote. But if he could find a mosaic . . .

He thrust the dream aside. Wishing for the moon was pointless. And this wasn't his site.

Evidence of worked stone was everywhere, though only tu-
tored eyes would spot the chisel marks that decorated broken
bits. But too much usable stone remained in the temple to be-

lieve that it had been abandoned. Roman buildings had been a valuable source of material for centuries, offering quality stone that required little or no dressing.

He scanned the horizon. The valley was bounded by steep hills and sharp cliffs. A stream meandered through its center. Forest covered this portion of the floor, sloping gently toward the water.

At a guess, the nearest cliff had collapsed, burying the villa in mud and rock. That would make the site even richer—and bigger—for many of the furnishings would have slid toward the stream. An unexpected burial would offer a unique glimpse of a time he could usually study only in brief flashes.

He shivered. Just so must Winckelmann have felt when he first beheld the treasures being unearthed at Pompeii and Herculaneum. The man's *Unpublished Relics of Antiquity* had exerted a profound influence on his own life ever since he'd discovered it at age fifteen.

Miss Merideth had probably stumbled onto this site when erosion exposed the temple, but why would she have recognized the stones as significant? Few people could identify dressed stone even when it was not covered in dirt and moss.

Her comments had become increasingly terse as they approached the clearing, as if she were nervous, though that seemed unlikely. If Mitchell thought her good enough to submit a paper, then she was already more knowledgeable than half the members of the Antiquarian Society. She must know that.

Lady Luck was finally shining on him. The villa provided the perfect excuse to stay until Miss Vale agreed to wed him. Sir Winton could not return for weeks, so he need not rush his courtship. Miss Vale accepted her companion's interest in antiquity, which boded well for the future—she would understand his own frequent absences.

Jon would be relieved that he could abandon last night's antics.

"Have you permission to cut any trees?" he asked, noting two that might have to come down.

"The steward will take care of it once I ask him."

"Sir Winton lets his steward take orders from you?"

She paled. "He knows nothing of estate affairs. The steward does whatever is necessary."

He saw the fear in her eyes. "Do you understand the gravity of keeping this a secret? Sir Winton could transport you for disturbing his property without permission."

"Miss Vale and the steward are aware of my activities," she said, turning away. "They agreed to let me study the artifacts before revealing anything, lest Sir Winton dispose of them to cover his latest gaming debts."

"It's your risk. But I would hate to see a serious scholar ruined." Shrugging, he resumed his study of the site.

If a landslide had buried the villa, it would have swept the roof and at least part of the walls toward the stream—and many of the furnishings. He studied the cliffs, but time had erased any sign of the slip. It could have come from any of several spots, each crossing the clearing in a different direction. Turning the other way, he headed for the stream.

It meandered through the trees a hundred yards away. Ignoring the damage to his boots, he clambered into the water, working his way first upstream, then down as he studied the bank.

"What are you doing?" Miss Merideth finally asked.

"Looking for traces of the villa. Not only are there too many dressed stones remaining, but Minerva would have been removed from the site if it had been abandoned or looted. Nothing in such perfect condition would have been left behind, which means the villa was probably buried in a mudslide. Finding the direction of the flow will make it easier to excavate the rubble."

"Why didn't you say so? I dug a roof tile from the bank several months ago."

She headed upstream, leaving him to slip and splash through the water as best he could. They rounded a wide bend before she finally stopped.

"It was here," she said, pointing. "About two feet from the top."

"You are sure?"

"Quite." She pointed to a length of black wool looped around the branch of a nearby tree. It was above eye level, invisible to anyone who was not looking for it.

"Have you found other pieces along the stream?" His voice was colder than he liked, but he was mentally kicking himself. Underestimating her was not a mistake he would make again. She might have drawn her maps à la Mitchell, but her site organization followed his own treatise on the subject. Even though she had admitted reading it and was good enough that Mitchell claimed her as an assistant, he had not truly accepted her expertise. *Idiot!*

"Nothing useful. I found five pieces of worked stone in the stream—including those bits with the inscription—but I've no idea where they originated. Only that one piece of tile has come to light."

"Only one that was recognizably tile," he countered. He had been scraping away at the bank while she spoke and now pulled out a thumbnail-sized bit. "Much of the tile will look like that—chips and shards that bear no resemblance to a roof."

"Good heavens. This stuff is everywhere."

He nodded absently, staring back toward the cliffs. "This isn't right. For a slide to move in this direction, it would have had to originate there." He pointed toward a low mound. "If something big enough to spread this far had collapsed, the site would be buried under at least twenty feet of muck." He pulled himself up the bank. "Show me your test holes."

She started to speak, then snapped her mouth shut and turned away. Only then did he realize how condescending he sounded. But she gave him no chance to apologize, slipping through the woods until she reached the edge of the clearing.

"This is the farthest from the temple I've dug. Rain has washed new debris into the hole, but about three feet down is a paving stone—actually the joint between two paving stones." She moved thirty feet farther, near a tree. "I found nothing here, though it might be the garden portion of a courtyard."

"Or the space between buildings. Or a place where the floor

is gone—trees don't do well in shallow soil, which means most of this clearing is either paved or thick with rubble."

She shrugged.

"I apologize for snapping at you, Miss Merideth," he said, turning her to face him, then dropping his hands when her expressive eyes stirred new traces of lust. "I am accustomed to digging alone, with at most a single servant to help. It will take me a day or two to get used to having another antiquarian around. That in no way reflects on you. It merely exposes my habit of slipping into brown studies so I forget whom I am addressing."

"As do I." She smiled. "Do you really think the entire clearing is paved?"

"Perhaps. The closer stone is to the surface, the smaller the plants that grow above it. Look at the hills. They are composed of rock with a thin layer of soil, supporting only grasses and shrubs. But the valley is richer, capable of sustaining trees—except here."

"Obvious, now that you've pointed it out. But if part of that hill collapsed, much of the fall must have been rock. So perhaps the villa is smaller than you think."

"I doubt it. Whatever rock fell from the hill would have spread from its base at least as far as the stream. Yet we are surrounded by forest—except here. From that, I conclude that the rock from the fall is well mixed with soil or at least is sufficiently broken that roots can find a way through." He shivered, for the words reminded him that a lack of trees might mean the floors remained intact.

"Excellent point. As for the other test holes, I found a foundation just there." She pointed to a depression ten feet away. "And another over here." A frown creased her forehead. "Why would someone build a villa this large in so isolated a place?"

"It is too soon to tell how big it was. And there would have been outbuildings—granaries, barns, stables. Someone who owned the entire valley could support a large villa—Vale House is larger, for example, and there are other Roman sites this size." He raised his brow.

She immediately pounced on his exaggeration. "One other. Singular. Near Severston. But it was inhabited and expanded for centuries, eventually running to six wings, the last two built by Saxons, one only a century before William the Conqueror destroyed it." She gestured. "If this was buried during the Roman era, there would have been no time for such expansion."

"True, though we have no evidence of the rank or fortune of Severston's various owners. Much of it may have fallen into disrepair long before the end, and it may have been of average size to begin with. One need only look at today's estates. Linden Park has been expanded repeatedly since before Elizabeth's reign, yet it seems tiny when compared to Blenheim Palace, which was built only a century ago."

"Good point. So we assume it is a villa."

"No. We keep open minds. It might be a temple complex, or even a small town. Have you dug beyond the shrine?"

She nodded. "I found nothing in two pits. Once I discovered foundations in this direction, I concentrated here."

The clouds that had glowered all morning opened up.

Tony studied them, then shrugged. "This won't stop any time soon. May I see your maps again?"

"Of course." She led him back to the workroom.

An hour later, he finished his perusal. "The temple is not only built on a rise, but it is closer to the surface. Thus its hill would have been more prominent before the slide."

"Did the Druids build their shrines on hilltops?"

"Someti—" A squeal interrupted his response. Surprised— Miss Merideth had claimed that the wing was unused—he opened the door.

A maid clung to a very red-faced Jon, her mouth nuzzling his neck as she pulled his head lower. The neck of her gown hung open, exposing one breast. His hands dug into her hips.

Chapter Five

Tony frowned as Miss Merideth squeezed past him into the hall.

"Were you looking for me, Mary?" she asked the maid, her voice dripping ice.

Jon's face turned even redder.

The girl jumped aside, hands frantically straightening her gown. Her mouth opened, but she contented herself with nodding.

Tony nearly chuckled. Obviously Mary had not realized anyone else was here. Had she intended to poke through Miss Merideth's workroom, or had she merely followed the rakish Mr. Linden, looking for a little slap and tickle? He would stake anything that Jon's hands had not undone her gown.

"Well?" Miss Merideth's voice could freeze water.

"C-cook wants to know how many for dinner. And Mr. Murch was askin' for you."

"I will show Linden the garden," said Tony. Miss Merideth would be occupied for some time. At the very least, she must report this incident to Miss Vale, for he suspected the girl was stretching the truth. And he needed to discuss the change in plans with Jon.

Miss Merideth flashed him a grateful smile before accompanying the maid away.

Tony remained silent until they were well beyond the house. Jon's color had faded back to green.

"What are you doing out of bed?" he finally asked. "I cannot imagine that Simms let you up. You look like death incarnate."

Jon groaned. "This was all his fault, so I sent him away. He added brandy to that posset last night, though I'd been very specific about what to put in it."

He would have to speak to the man. Simms had definite ideas about treating ailments, but he must accept that Jon could not tolerate wine.

"And I had to get out of that room before the smell set me going again," Jon finished with a shudder.

"I trust you will refrain from drinking for the remainder of our stay."

"Absolutely."

"Good. Now suppose you explain why you were mauling the maid. You are overplaying your role."

"I did nothing," protested Jon. "The girl attacked me!"

"You didn't look unwilling." But he couldn't help grinning. Jon needed to broaden his horizons.

He blushed. "I was *trying* to pry her loose."

"Why? She'd make a comfortable armful."

"How can you say that?"

"Experience. I'm not a rake, but neither am I a saint. If a willing wench throws herself into my arms, I see no need to shove her aside."

Jon choked, stamping away, then back.

"Is there something about her I don't know?"

"She's touched in the head."

Tony turned a laugh into a cough.

Jon glared. "I was exploring the house, choosing the older areas so I would not meet anyone, but she must have followed me. Before I even knew she was there, she shoved my hand down her—her—" He couldn't force the word out. "Then she grabbed me around the neck and kissed me!"

"A serious indiscretion, to be sure." Hilarity threatened his composure. Jon's outrage was priceless, but laughter would not improve his temper. "Consider this an opportunity to expand your education, Cousin. She is no different than a hundred other maids eager to increase their vails, and she looks like she'd show you a rollicking good time. I've met her sort before. Think of it as one of the benefits of being a rake."

"I couldn't." His face had paled alarmingly.

"Relax, Jon. If you are not interested, simply tell her so."

"How?" A new blush spread across his face.

"Claim you are doing penance for a life of sin." It was time to change the subject, before Jon either swooned or cast up his accounts from all this emotion. "You need not play your role so blatantly. In fact, now that we've established you as a boorish lout who revels in light-skirts, you can become more genteel. An occasional lapse will keep up your image. But I've arranged for us to remain indefinitely, so you must do nothing to change Miss Vale's mind."

"How did you manage that? I was sure that we would be gone today after you revealed our purpose last night."

"*You* revealed it. I merely covered for you."

"Yes, well . . ." He again flushed. "So why are they letting us stay. They must know we are after Linden Park."

"Undoubtedly. Miss Merideth is smarter than most men. She probably divined our purpose the moment she heard the Linden name."

"Yet she agreed to keep us here? She hovers over Miss Vale like a mother hen."

"I noticed." It was an apt description. Miss Merideth was a foot taller than her employer. "I had to promise that you would behave, so perhaps you should overdo the pious act tonight. Make a show of not drinking. Move a table between your chair and Miss Vale's. Prove that you are determined to behave, but that good behavior is so unusual, you don't trust yourself."

Jon groaned.

"How hard can that be?"

He groaned louder. "If this stomach doesn't settle down, I won't be joining you tonight." He swallowed several times. "At least tell me how you are keeping us here."

"That was easy. Miss Merideth is excavating a Roman temple. She recognized me as Anthony Torwell and begged me to help. The woman has read every word I've written and has her site organized exactly like mine. She's incredible. Even Mitchell is more interested in treasure than study."

"She sounds like your sort of female."

He stifled his instinctive agreement. "Hardly. I'm merely flattered by her interest. And the site is breathtaking. I've never had access to a better one."

"Just don't forget why we are here."

"Never. I cannot allow Father's stupidity to hurt Mother. Miss Merideth is no different than any other student confronted by a potential mentor. She is anxious to learn as much as possible, but few books exist on the subject, so only personal contact will further her education. If playing tutor gives me an opportunity to court Miss Vale properly, without rushing, then I will teach Miss Merideth whatever she wants to know."

Jon nodded, but his face remained dubious.

"It will work," he insisted, suppressing the image of her awed face when she'd realized his identity. He must not let the adoration go to his head, for she would have reacted the same way toward Mitchell or any other antiquarian who walked into her drawing room. "But you must be careful. Do you recall anything of Miss Vale?"

"Not much. She pulled away whenever possible, and Miss Merideth kept distracting me. I doubt the woman believed anything I said, though. Her mind is as sharp as yours."

"But she will ascribe any mistakes to drunkenness—she harbors no illusions about your condition last night. Miss Vale is more conventional. If anything, she is shyer than I expected. And warier. I doubt she is accustomed to a gentleman's attention. Sir Winton probably keeps her out of sight when he's entertaining. His friends are not above plucking so pretty a blossom when in their cups. I think you scared her."

Jon paled.

"That was not a complaint, for it accomplished our purpose. But now that we have established your identity, we must avoid pushing too hard," he continued. "Play the rake just enough to avoid suspicion, but she has only a companion her own age for protection, so do nothing that might ruin her in the eyes of society."

"You will be there to keep me on the right path."

"In the evenings. I will be out most days."

"Out?" He shook his head. "Of course, you will be out. And Miss Merideth with you. So how can she chaperon Miss Vale?"

"Damn!" He paced the garden, running his hands through his hair. "You will have to avoid her during the day."

"How?"

"You can always help with the digging."

"You must be joking. You know I have no interest in buried treasure." His brow furrowed. "But who will chaperon you if I don't? Miss Vale can hardly join you."

This was getting too complicated. "We need no chaperon. No one will think twice about an antiquarian vicar assisting a paid companion, assuming they even hear of it. She is keeping the project a secret. As for Miss Vale, surely a neighbor lady can join us for a few days. I just hope it isn't anyone I know."

Jon stripped the leaves from a branch. "You could always tell the truth."

"And get us tossed out on the road? Miss Vale is sweet enough to sympathize with Mother's plight, but Miss Merideth would never stand for such a deception. I have a sinking feeling that her opinions carry a great deal of weight." He sighed, recalling how the maid had brought the household problems to her. She probably oversaw the staff, for he'd seen no evidence of a housekeeper. "Damn me for a fool. Why the devil did I ever create that plagued reputation?"

"I can't blame you entirely," said Jon, leading the way toward the house. "Uncle Robert's strictures would try a saint— and you were never a saint. Speaking of which," he added, "watch your own tongue. What you know about the Bible wouldn't fill half a page. I nearly exploded trying to keep a straight face last night."

"That bad?"

"Worse." He chuckled. "I'd swear I heard as much Shakespeare as King James."

Heat crept up Tony's face, for another childhood rebellion had been avoiding church. And the nunneries he knew were hardly religious enclaves. But Jon didn't need to hear about that. "Why don't you lie down for a while?" he said when they arrived on the terrace. "I want to check something."

As soon as Jon was gone, he returned to Miss Merideth's workroom for a closer look at the stones. But the carving was too abbreviated to accurately date the site. All he could say for sure was that the destruction had occurred after the reign of Diocletian and Maximian, sometime during the last century of Roman rule—unless a high-ranking Roman had remained behind when the legions departed.

Alex ordered Mary back to work, then joined Sarah in the drawing room, staying by the window to keep an eye on their visitors. The men were strolling through the garden, deep in talk. Was Torwell chastising his cousin for dallying with a maid?

Not that Mary would object to his attentions. She was the most forward girl on the staff, often slipping off to the stables. Perhaps it was time to let her go. Heaven knew her mind was rarely on her work. Keeping her could send the wrong message to the other servants.

Yet dismissing her could cause new problems. What if she took revenge by revealing the villa?

She sighed. When she'd started this project, it had seemed simple enough. Excavating a small temple would take two, maybe three months.

But the site was larger than she had ever dreamed. It was larger than she'd thought even a day ago. If Torwell was right, it might extend clear to the stream. Keeping a dig secret for years would be impossible.

"Will you accept Linden?" asked Sarah.

Alex turned away from the window. "I don't know. I've been too busy today to think about it."

"Busy?"

"Torwell is a renowned antiquarian and the foremost scholar

on Roman England. He is very excited about the temple, so I must extend this charade for a few days."

"Why? He can work with Alex Vale as easily as Miss Merideth." Sarah's needle flashed in the sunlight.

"No, he can't," she said slowly, realizing that her supposed insignificance would have affected Torwell's impressions. "No gentleman believes a lady is capable of thought. At the moment, he accepts me because I am a companion. Oddities are allowed to those in service."

"Fustian."

"Not at all. Besides, if I wed Linden, I must leave Vale House." Which was a point against this match. Abandoning a temple was possible, but how could she turn her back on an entire villa? Yet turning him down would send him away, and his cousin with him. So she had to postpone any decision. "Torwell will join me at the villa each day, but how are we to protect you?"

"I need no protection," protested Sarah.

"Of course you do. Linden is an unconscionable rakehell. Even had we known nothing about him, his behavior last night was rude, crude, and altogether disgusting." He had not made it to his room, though at least he'd directed most of the mess into the ginger jar on the hall table—from great practice, she had no doubt. "And I found him entwined with Mary just now, confirming what we've heard for years. No one is safe with him, especially you. He thinks you are the key to regaining his inheritance."

"We never should have started this."

"But we did, and I have no intention of confessing just yet. I need time to decide whether it is possible to live with Linden— if you press right now, I will refuse him." Sarah closed her mouth and glowered. "I will see him only in the evening, for I cannot pass up this opportunity to learn from Torwell. Few people have even met him, for he leaves his study only to excavate in remote areas. Becoming his protégée could lead to acceptance by others. His stature is great enough that people would follow his lead, despite my gender."

Sarah snorted. "Pull your head out of the clouds, Alex. No man would risk his reputation by championing a female—especially one who has tricked him. He may be knowledgeable, but by your own admission, he is reclusive and thus has no personal friends among antiquarians."

Flinching, she admitted that Sarah was right. A glance out the window confirmed that the gentlemen still stood in the garden. Torwell was clearly frustrated. Was Linden refusing to cooperate? He had been sure he could control his cousin.

"Even discounting Torwell, I need more time, Sarah. If this were anyone but Linden, I would insist that he leave. His manners are appalling, and his language is worse. If he can insult a potential bride when he is trying to turn her up sweet, how will he behave once he has achieved his goal?"

"Very well, we will continue the ruse until tomorrow."

"Longer. He will be suffering the aftereffects of wine today. And even if he behaves tonight, that proves nothing. I must watch him for two or three days, at the very least. And I need Torwell's assistance to make up for the time I lost to Father's visits. So we must protect you."

"Linden will not force me," insisted Sarah. "Nor will he do anything to harm you once you're wed. You need not fear accepting him."

"What makes you think that? He angered you badly enough last night. What did he say?"

"Nothing in particular. Just flirtatious compliments."

"Yet you insist he will not use force?"

She shrugged. "There is something about his eyes. They indicate uncertainty. Or perhaps he is merely flustered. But no matter what he is like on the surface, underneath, he is kind."

"Maybe." Sarah had always possessed an uncanny ability to judge people. "But I would discount whatever impressions you formed last night. The man was drunk as a lord even before they arrived. You saw him. He could hardly stay on his feet."

"Who can blame him? Most men drown themselves in wine when fate deals them a blow. Losing everything he was taught

to expect must have been devastating. He may be seeking re-
dress, but his heart is not in it. He will not harm me."

"But we cannot take chances. You must have a chaperon. No
matter how unlikely you think my chances, I cannot pass up an
opportunity to win Torwell's support, so you will be alone with
Linden much of the time."

"You are not thinking, Alex. Name one person that we could
invite into this house right now. Who would condone this charade? Who would agree to hide your excavation?"

Alex took a turn about the room. Who indeed? No one from
the village would share a roof with Linden, and none would
keep her secrets. The neighbors already disapproved her mannish forthrightness and bluestocking education. They would
immediately summon her father if they learned of this latest
start. In retrospect, she could hardly believe it herself.

"Bessie," she finally said, naming her maid. "She can remain
in the corner and sew, but at least we will have preserved the
proprieties." And it might remind Linden to behave himself.

The situation was ridiculous, though she had no one to blame
but herself. Sarah was right. Even if she won Torwell's respect
as an antiquarian, it would likely disappear the moment she
confessed her identity—which was yet another reason to learn
as much as possible now. Why couldn't they have met under
different circumstances?

And how could she prevent Linden from assaulting Sarah
while in the throes of another drunken revel? No matter how
kind his eyes might be, wine deadened the conscience.

Sarah was too naïve and tenderhearted for her own good.

But they must make the best of it. Bessie would stay with
Sarah day and night. And Murch must remain nearby whenever
Linden was up.

"No, no, no," said Linden, slapping his palm across the top
of his glass. "No wine for me tonight. I am not in the mood. Not
at all. Perhaps a drop of lemonade will do. Or water. Yes, water
it will be. Nectar of the gods. Purity for the spirit."

Alex cringed. As grateful as she was that Torwell's admonishments were working, she was not at all sure that a pious Linden was any improvement.

It had started in the drawing room before dinner. He had arrived before Torwell, raising a flash of fear that infuriated her. But she had nearly laughed when he stopped at least eight feet away from where she and Sarah were talking.

"Goood e-ven-ing, Miss Vale, Miss Merideth," he'd said, drawing out the words in a very deep voice as he offered a stiff bow to each in turn. His heels clicked together.

"We are pleased that you could join us," said Sarah.

"And I am delighted to be a guest in your home." His precise enunciation grated on her nerves.

Torwell arrived, his relaxed charm a welcome relief. He bent over Sarah's hand, that crooked smile triggering her dimples, then turned to salute her own fingers as well. No one had ever treated her like a lady, and she found the experience oddly moving.

When she next looked at Linden, she choked. He had chosen a chair near her escritoire, positioning a table and a footstool between him and the room. He sat bolt upright, both hands tucked firmly under his thighs.

Sarah was staring in astonishment.

His own eyes remained fixed on the doorway. But as she watched, they flicked briefly toward Sarah, and he licked his lips.

The scamp.

Torwell escorted Sarah to dinner. Once they were out of sight, Linden offered his arm, but he kept so much distance between them that she had to lean sideways to reach it. Now he was making a theatrical production out of draining his water glass.

"I must thank you for allowing us to remain for a few days," Torwell said to Sarah, flashing one of his killer smiles. "Miss Merideth's work is quite intriguing."

"She enjoys it." But Sarah's attention was on the covetous gaze Linden was casting on Torwell's wineglass. He wrenched his eyes away when he caught her looking.

"My dearest lo—" Linden snapped his mouth shut, cooled his tone, then tried again, his eyes now fixed on Sarah's plate. "You have done my cousin a great service, Miss Vale. He rarely encounters sites that stir his senses. We thank you so very, very much."

Alex bit her tongue when his eyes lifted to Sarah's bosom and widened. He raised them to her face, smiled and winked, then ostentatiously returned to his dinner.

Sarah blushed.

Torwell hurried to distract her.

Alex had to take a huge bite of bitter fish to keep from laughing aloud. What a rogue!

She kept Linden's attention firmly on her for the rest of the meal, but she couldn't believe a word he said. When he stopped to think, his conversation was amazingly prissy. The rest of the time he had to frequently backtrack, stumbling to turn lurid comments into innocuous ones, contradicting himself until he was stammering through quagmires of convoluted logic that would not deceive an infant—which served him right. He should know better than to try passing himself off as a saint.

"Will you join us in the drawing room this evening?" asked Sarah over the dessert course.

"We would be delighted," said Torwell.

"Excellent. Since we are four, perhaps we can try a hand or two of whist."

Linden choked, spraying water across the table. "I couldn't," he gasped, a hand to his brow. "The memories!" His other hand fluttered in distress. "Mother's misery. Father's shame. I will never play cards again."

"I thought he lost at dice," Alex said dryly.

Linden pulled out a lacy handkerchief to wipe droplets from his sleeve. "Cards. Dice. A friendly wager at the races. What is the difference? My life will never be the same."

"Doing it too brown," she murmured.

He ignored the aside, though his eyes blinked, proving that he'd heard. "Perhaps an evening of reading aloud would interest you." He gazed soulfully into Sarah's eyes. "My dear cousin has been after me this age and more to refresh my acquaintance with the Bible."

This time it was Torwell who choked, a condition that returned a quarter hour later when Linden opened the Bible, seemingly at random, and began reading. "*King Solomon loved many strange women. He had seven hundred wives and three hundred concubines*." And in an aside, "Those were the days."

Many times a rogue!

"I have never been so diverted in my life." Sarah laughed as they compared notes that evening. "Grab him quick, Alex. He is a delight."

"How can you say so? He is deliberately mocking us."

"You wrong him," insisted Sarah. "No man can blush at will. Were you watching when I caught him peeking at my bodice. The look on his face! Like a small boy caught with his eye to a hole in the maids' wall."

"Do not be naïve, Sarah. Lucy Perkins can produce a blush any time she wants."

"Only because she practices the art just as assiduously as flirting with fans or shedding heartrending tears. Can you imagine a rakehell spending hours before a mirror practicing a skill that would get him laughed out of his clubs?"

"When you put it that way . . ." She giggled.

"While his sense of humor is certainly wicked, he is not the man his reputation describes, Alex. I suspect that he has amused himself by perpetrating a monumental fraud upon the *ton*. You know how people always jump on the worst rumors, then defend their opinions to the death even in the face of incontrovertible evidence to the contrary."

"Perhaps." Not that she believed it. He was playing games, all right, but with them. She could see why he had a reputation for charm. When not in his cups, his antics were quite diverting. Yet Sarah was too sheltered to recognize that it was only an act. She wished her father had not tied up Linden Park. If not for the demands of justice, she would never consider this al-

liance. A man who would stoop to one game would play others
that might not be as harmless.

"Let's establish the site's boundaries today," suggested Tony
as he tethered their horses in the clearing.

"We know the boundaries—the clearing itself and the forest
as far as the stream." Miss Merideth waved toward the spot
where she had dug out the tile.

"That is merely a guess." He waited while she unlocked the
tool shed, then pulled out a spade for each of them. "That tile
may have been an anomaly. We cannot know where debris settled without looking. Think about it. The clearing is here." He
drew an oval on the ground to represent it, adding a line for the
cliffs to the north and a curve where the stream curved from
east to south. "A slide from the cliffs should have carried detritus straight south, yet you found the tile to the east. So either
we are wrong about the villa's demise or the disaster was more
complicated than we know. Since the debris field should contain interesting artifacts, we must know where to look, which
requires marking the bounds of the site."

"So what do you propose?"

"Test holes ringing the clearing, starting about fifty feet out.
If anything turns up, even bits of tile, mark it and move on.
Once we get directions established, we can refine the search."

"Tree roots," she muttered.

"Welcome to the frustration of studying the past, Miss
Merideth." Temper threaded his voice, though he knew he
should not be snapping at her. "You've been spoiled. Most people dig for years without unearthing a single artifact as good as
those you've found here."

"That's not—"

"Ask the groundskeeper for an ax tomorrow," he said,
clamping control over his tone. His irritation was not her fault.
He was still furious at Jon's latest performance. It hadn't been
necessary to play the buffoon. He'd drawn as much derision as
he'd done with drunken excess. Miss Merideth had not been
impressed. If, as he suspected, she was the real ruler of the

household, they would be out on the road the moment she decided Linden was dangerous.

But that was better left until later. Assigning her to a spot that
he hoped would contain few roots, he started his own test hole
a hundred feet away.

"Tile shard," she called within minutes.

"Mark it." He watched her move to a new location, then continued his own hole.

Two hours later, they stopped for lemonade while he added
the latest results to a rough sketch of the site. "Thank God for
tile." The chips were so abundant they had already accomplished more than he'd expected to do in a full day. Only a foot
of soil covered the slide field.

"What would destroy it so thoroughly?" she asked.

"Tons of rock, though I'm hoping for some other explanation. Tons of rock would also destroy walls, floors, and furnishings. Perhaps the tile was of poor quality—low firing
temperature, impurities in the clay, something like that."

"One could hope. Where now?"

"We'll start a new ring, fifty feet out from the first."

"Right." She turned away, catching her skirt in a shrub.
"Devil take this thing," she muttered, tugging it loose. "Always
in the way."

"So wear pantaloons."

"Right." She met his eyes, refusing to apologize for either
her language or her sarcasm. "The dressmaker fell into hyster-
ics when I asked for a pair."

"And Sir Winton's would never fit," he finished, casting a
measuring glance over her very fine physique. Her father was
several inches shorter, with legs like a stork. "But mine should.
I'll send a pair to your room tonight."

"Miss Vale would never approve."

Though she tried to sound dismissive, he could see the longing in her eyes. He shrugged. "Do as you wish, but there is
nothing to stop you from wearing them under your habit skirt—
Princess Charlotte does exactly that with lacy pantalets, by all
accounts. You can leave the skirt in the shed while you work."

She paced, muttering something about hating deceptions.

"It's your decision, Miss Merideth. I was only trying to help."

"I know." She sighed. "And I appreciate it. But having to sneak about is frustrating. You've no idea how difficult it is for females to be serious."

"True. One thing I've never tried to do is impersonate a female." He grinned.

"Don't jest. I hate jokes at my expense. Especially when they are not funny. Why do men work so hard to keep women from using their minds?"

"Probably because few women are capable of rational thought." He held up a hand to silence her. "Notice I said *few*, not *none*. You are obviously an exception."

"Thank you. Just as you are also an exception. Most men are naught but selfish schemers willing to do or say anything in pursuit of their own interests. I despise deceit."

He recoiled. Fortunately, she was turned away and didn't see.

Selfish.

Schemer.

Deceit.

The words reverberated in his head.

But you are not deceiving her. You really are Torwell. And you do respect her abilities.

Yet he was also Linden, who had arrived at Vale House under false pretenses and was determined to coerce Miss Vale into marriage so he could recover his inheritance.

"Let's dig holes," he grumbled, seeing no way out of the one he was rapidly sinking into. His head hurt.

Chapter Six

Three days later, Tony paused to survey the site. They had dug dozens of test holes and several trenches, finally gaining a reasonable picture of its size. Miss Merideth had been right about the temple. It marked the western boundary of the dig. And nothing turned up north of the clearing.

East and south were another matter. A huge fan of detritus stretched from the clearing east to the stream. A second fan spread south, stopping just short of the water. Its origin was obvious, but he had yet to devise an acceptable explanation for the eastern flow.

His eyes paused, for Miss Merideth had bent over to pluck something from her latest test hole, her borrowed pantaloons outlining a remarkably fine derriere. The expected wave of lust slammed through his loins, just as it did every time he looked her way. Working with a female offered some delightful benefits.

Frustrating benefits, he conceded. Suggesting pantaloons had been incredibly stupid, and contributing a pair of his own wasn't much better. They stretched across shapely hips like a second skin before skimming the longest legs he'd ever seen. He hadn't had a decent night's sleep since giving them to her.

Warm afternoons made it worse. It was bad enough watching her remove her skirt. But since she accepted him as a harmless antiquarian, she also removed her habit coat whenever the work made her hot. Like yesterday. The thin cambric shirt he'd given her left nothing to the imagination, for she didn't wear a corset. If the sun hit just right . . .

He'd had to move well away to keep his hands from touching.

Concentrate on business. She is too high-born for dalliance.

His conscience was right. Her mother had been a lady, and her vicar father had been a baronet's son—bolstering Jon's plea that he refrain from Biblical quotations. It also explained her suspicion that first evening.

Damn her for being so voluptuous. And so intriguing. She was the first person he'd met—man or woman—who shared so many of his interests. She promised to become a close friend, if he could keep his baser instincts under control. Perhaps he should look up that maid. Perpetual arousal made digging difficult.

But he had no interest in the maid.

He forced his eyes to complete their circuit of the site.

"Where was the entrance?" he muttered, mentally matching the maps they had completed last evening to the uneven ground, most of which was hidden by forest.

"Did you say something?" She tossed the piece back into the hole and joined him.

"I am trying to orient the buildings. Where would the main entrance have been?"

"Near the temple?"

"No. If this was a villa, the temple would be private. If it was a town, we are probably dealing with dozens of individual structures. If it was a religious complex, they would want pilgrims to pass through other buildings before reaching the temple."

"Why?"

"To collect tribute. It may have been in the form of coins, offerings, or gifts, but no one reached the sanctuary without paying. And the complex would have contained accommodations."

"That sounds huge."

"In some places it was, though if this were a major center, some mention would have turned up elsewhere. But whether this was a villa or temple, the approach would have been from there." He walked toward the edge of the clearing, then shook his head. "Too many trees."

"What are you looking for?"

"The shape of the land. I know it has changed considerably, but the place must have been reached by a lane. Knowing where it ran would make it easier to find the entrance. I'd like to start excavating there, for it was likely quite ornate." He refused to utter the word *mosaic*, though it echoed in his mind.

"You could always climb a tree."

He heard the joke in her voice, but her words triggered an idea. Grabbing her hand, he headed for the cliff.

"Where are we going?" she gasped.

"Up."

It wasn't far, though they had to push through tangled bushes that covered the talus slope. The cliff face offered plenty of holds. Within minutes, they had scrambled to a ledge halfway up.

"Look," he said, turning her to face the valley.

She trembled, so he kept his hands on her waist. Many people disliked heights—a fact he should have remembered sooner.

Liar, taunted his conscience.

Very well. Fear of heights made a convenient excuse, but he could not have removed his hands if he'd tried. Her heat burned through his gloves, raising images of stroking sleek flesh and kissing the ear that hovered tantalizing inches from his mouth.

"Where would the road have been?" he asked, forcing disinterest into his tone even as he prayed that she would interpret his hoarseness as exertion from the climb.

"Along the stream."

They could see over most of the trees. Vale House stood on a rise in the distance. The stream meandered between fields before disappearing into the trees, though its breadth allowed them to follow its course even there. Their horses were tethered in the clearing.

"So the approach was along the stream. But that is not where they placed the buildings."

"The shrine was already here."

"That would certainly influence locating a temple complex."

"Are you saying it would not affect a villa?"

"No, I'm not." He tried to empty his mind of lust so he could think, but not until he moved an arm's length away did he manage it. "We'll assume, for the moment, that this was a villa. A wealthy Roman gained ownership of this valley. Maybe he bought it, or won it, or was awarded it for service to the empire. It could have been as early as the first century or as late as the fourth. Perhaps it still contained the old shrine, or maybe someone had already replaced it with a temple. But now he plans to add a house. He wants it sheltered from the elements—the worst storms come out of the north and west—but he also needs easy access to roads, for he will wish to visit Glevum on occasion."

"I see." She peered into the clearing, comparing it with the surrounding land. "It looks so different from up here."

"And different now than then. The shrine was on a hill."

"So the road probably skirted that hill to reach the villa. It may even have followed an ancient footpath serving the shrine."

"I wonder . . ." He straightened, staring at the clearing. "Do you see lines down there?"

"No—" She inhaled in a quick gasp. "Maybe. But there is nothing there. I've checked every foot of that clearing."

"Look again. They are faint, but I see three lines." His heart was pounding in his throat, for two of those lines came together in a square corner.

"A trick of nature," she said, shrugging. "That is merely the boundary between two kinds of grass, one dry, the other still green."

"Perhaps—if you can explain why that boundary is so straight. Suppose a wall lies just below the surface."

"Why stop there? Perhaps your mythical wall marks the entrance hall."

He grinned. "It's as good a reason as any for starting there.

The spot is in the center of the clearing. An entrance would be flanked on each side by rooms and lead back to the atrium."

"Maybe you are right." She was catching his excitement. "That largest tree is positioned in line with your wall, and it probably grows in the atrium."

"Then let's get started. If we can find an intact floor, it may tell us what this place was."

"Mosaics." She headed down the cliff, not waiting for him to steady her.

He cursed her for uttering the word and thus tempting bad luck. "Finding more than fragments would be rare indeed."

Not until they reached the clearing did he realize the significance of her sure-footed descent. If she was not afraid of heights, then she must have trembled from his touch.

You fool! He had been so focused on his own purpose—and so disturbed by his growing desire for the delectable Miss Merideth—that he had not considered her situation. To a lady's companion, the appearance of an unmarried vicar who shared her interests must seem like a gift from the gods.

He had to prevent her from forming a *tendre*, for he could never offer for her. Miss Vale was the antithesis of her companion—petite, shy, boringly conformable—but he must wed her if he was to protect his family. His mother deserved a roof over her head. And once he owned Linden Park, he could force his father to let her participate in the accepted activities of their class.

He sighed. The reminder of what was at stake was necessary. To protect her employer, Miss Merideth drew Jon away whenever possible. Thus he had ample opportunity to become acquainted with his hostess. But he rarely enjoyed conversing with her.

Miss Vale was a typical society maid, unschooled beyond mastering those feminine frivolities he always found insipid. Her only virtue was eschewing the usual selfish chatter about her plans, her clothes, and the number of compliments she received from other gentlemen. She rarely spoke of others, either, not even her companion. In fact, she had little to say about anything.

But he had no choice, he reminded himself again. He could always spend more time on excavations.

In the meantime, he must nip Miss Merideth's infatuation in the bud.

They passed the remainder of the afternoon digging. He kept his voice abrupt, uttering nothing beyond necessary instructions. And he remained as far from her as possible, on the excuse that two trenches were twice as likely to find the entrance.

Much of the rock they removed was residue from the slide, but enough dressed stone turned up to satisfy him. A foundation did, indeed, lie along the line. But no sign remained of what it had once supported.

He was about to mention the time—if they did not leave, they would be late for dinner—when Miss Merideth gasped.

"Did you find something?"

"I don't know. Whatever I just struck does not sound like rock." She scooped out more soil, then scraped with her hands. "It's only another roof tile." Discouragement filled her voice.

"We're not likely to find another Minerva," he snapped, stifling his pain at her shocked face. *It's necessary*, that irritating voice reminded him. But far from pleasant.

"Of course not." But her shock changed to interest as she finished freeing the piece. "It seems larger than the other one."

He peered over her shoulder, then leaned closer. "It looks like a flue tile from the hypocaust." Excitement drove his resolutions away as one finger scraped away clinging soil. "See the ridge along this edge and the groove in the other? A matching tile would fit atop it, forming a closed pipe that would bring hot air from the furnaces into the hypocaust beneath each room, heating the farthest reaches of the building. At least we know this wasn't a barn. And it tells us where the floor level is likely to be. Congratulations."

She smiled up at him. "I wonder if other tiles are here."

"Tomorrow. It's time for dinner."

He pulled her to her feet, then gathered up their tools, locking them in the shed. He did not watch her don her skirt. Nor did he help her mount. And he scolded himself all the way back to the house.

Her smile hinted at more than simple pleasure over a careless compliment. How could he discourage her, while still treating her with the respect he owed a colleague?

Tony enjoyed dinner even less than usual, discouraged by his lack of progress with Miss Vale. Despite turning to him even before Miss Merideth drew Jon's attention, he suspected she was using him only to avoid Jon. Did she care at all? His fabled charm wasn't working. She treated him no differently than when he'd arrived. Or was she pretending not to care because she knew Miss Merideth hoped to catch him?

His head spun. Why had he embarked on this stupid charade anyway? Every day it grew harder to remember what he was doing and why. He could no longer relax with Miss Merideth. Miss Vale remained shy, refusing to discuss anything personal. He wanted to pack up and leave.

But he couldn't.

If he failed to recover the Park, his mother would suffer. So would the family dependents. Not only did Miss Vale lack the strength of character to demand a role in administering her dowry, but Sir Winton might well regret losing so lucrative an estate, forcing his daughter into wedding someone he could dominate. But that would cause even worse problems for the Park's dependents.

It was too late to confess and start with a clean slate. Changing course would alienate both ladies. And his original reasoning still held. Tony Linden's reputation dominated every interaction. Miss Vale's maid and butler hovered over her during the day, prompting Jon to limit his afternoon conversations to a single hour lest he unduly disrupt the household. Miss Merideth worked hard to keep Jon away from her employer in the evenings. A footman patrolled the ladies' wing at night. He had to believe that they were tolerating Tony Linden's presence only to keep Torwell around.

"Is it true that ladies have more freedom in London than in the country?" Miss Vale asked, pulling him from his thoughts. "Mr. Linden was telling me the most diverting stories this afternoon."

"I'm sure he was." Here was another problem. Though he'd often teased Jon about leading a monastic life, he'd never expected such complete ignorance. Nor had he known that Jon possessed the imagination to fill voids in experience with improbable tales. "That depends on how you define freedom. While London offers opportunities, it also sets traps for the unwary."

"What do you mean?" She widened her blue eyes, reminding him too sharply of the flirtatious chits who staged come-outs every Season.

"Many activities are found only in town," he said carefully. "Exhibitions, for example; the opera; the royal theater; gardens like Kew or Vauxhall. And society entertains constantly, with dozens of events scheduled every day. With so much variety, people are free to amuse themselves however they wish. In the country, one can choose only to accept an invitation or remain at home."

"And that choice is possible only if one has an invitation to consider."

He nodded, cursing himself for offering this particular example. By now, he hardly noticed her foot, but he suspected that few invitations arrived at Vale House. There had been no callers in the time he'd been there.

"But what do you mean by traps?" she asked.

"It is frightfully easy to tarnish one's reputation. Actions that draw only a raised brow in the country—galloping one's horse or walking unescorted, for example—can invite cuts and even ostracism in town."

"Walking alone?"

He nodded. "It creates an opportunity for unwanted advances, and can be downright dangerous. London is the largest city in the world. Mayfair may be opulent and beautiful, but there are places that I would not go at high noon accompanied by a dozen Bow Street runners. And some of them adjoin Mayfair."

She effected an artistic—and totally false—shiver. "Since no one of sense would go there, they hardly matter. Surely a lady can walk a short distance along her own street without escort. Yet Mr. Linden insists that is not possible."

"Since he lives in London, you must believe him," he said, grateful that Jon had said something sensible for once. "Appearance matters far more than truth. A lady walking alone is inviting advances. Whether she would accept them is irrelevant. Allowing the opportunity is not acceptable."

"You are sure?"

"Very. I have visited London often enough to know its customs," he said, determined to keep his lies to a minimum. She was slow to form an attachment. The longer the masquerade lasted, the harder revealing it would become. Every lie would make it worse.

Later, he admonished himself. Having embarked on this game, he could only play out the hand. "Oxford students often visit London, and I have conducted business there more recently."

"Then you must be familiar with St. Paul's." Her smile deepened her dimples, but he hardly noticed. Temper flashing in brown eyes was more enticing. "Is it as awe-inspiring as I have heard?"

"More." He gazed up as though overcome, but his mind was frantically trying to recall his one visit to the cathedral—at age ten, when his tutor had dragged him there. Twenty-two years had dimmed those memories. And he had paid little attention, even then, for the trip had been his father's idea. Exposure to London cathedrals was supposed to inspire piety and discourage pranks. It hadn't.

"It is like nothing you will have seen," he said finally, trying to inject enthusiasm into his words. Why hadn't she directed this question to Jon? He probably recalled every detail. "St. Paul's is as different from a village church as Hampton Court is from a tenant cottage. Wouldn't you say so, Cousin?" he asked

Jon, who was floundering through a convoluted explanation directed at Miss Merideth. She had a knack for leading him into the most confused tales anyone ever heard. If this kept up, Jon might blurt out the truth merely to escape.

He had to conclude his courtship before things grew worse.

"About what?" Jon asked, relief lighting his eyes.

"St. Paul's. It is difficult to describe it to someone familiar only with a parish church."

"It is impressive," he agreed, then shrugged and added, "if you like that sort of thing. My own taste runs to Jackson's Saloon and Cribb's Parlor."

"What are those?" asked Miss Vale.

"Nothing you need concern yourself with," Tony answered shortly, signaling the footman for more wine.

"Drinking and gaming houses, I suppose," said Miss Merideth, glaring from him to Jon. She seemed piqued that his interruption had rescued Jon from their conversation.

"I—" Jon's eyes begged for help. He'd probably forgotten which was which.

He sighed. "Not exactly, though plenty of wagers have been made at Cribb's. Both he and Jackson are retired boxers. Cribb opened a taproom that appeals to fighters and those who enjoy the sport. Jackson teaches boxing, mostly to gentlemen. Linden enjoys going a few rounds, but he's not a true follower of the Fancy."

She shrugged, drawing Jon back into conversation.

Tony couldn't follow their low-voiced exchange. He and Jon must start comparing notes each night. The longer they talked privately with the ladies, the more likely they would say something wrong.

Alex hid her irritation as she turned back to Linden. She was tired of having Torwell jump in to cover his cousin's slips. He swore that Linden's reputation was misleading, yet his vigilance made her nervous. Might the man be even worse than rumor claimed?

She shivered. Sarah was demanding that she resume her own

identity, agreeing to postpone the confession for another day only after a heated argument. But confession must go hand-in-hand with accepting Linden—if she could do so. How could she wed a man she didn't trust? Torwell would not be there to protect her.

And that was good, she reminded herself. He treated her as a colleague, which had clearly gone to her head. In the euphoria of having a digging partner, she had forgotten that she remained stuck inside this ungainly woman's body—as today's encounter had proved. What had she been thinking?

She'd climbed that cliff a hundred times as a child, so she'd been shocked that the scramble left her breathless. Fool! Double a fool. The pause to catch her breath had stretched until Torwell had grown tired and turned her around for himself. She'd nearly swooned from the jolt of heat that surged from his hands. She cursed.

He'd spotted her reaction, of course. He'd been curt and aloof ever since. It needed no intelligence to know why. Fearing that she was infatuated, he was doing everything possible to discourage her. Not only had she placed him in an untenable position, since he couldn't abandon his cousin, but she had diminished her chances of being accepted as an antiquarian.

Damn him! And damn every other man on earth. They all believed that women were incompetent. Torwell had momentarily forgotten her gender, but only because she had successfully become a man in his eyes—completing her share of the work without protest, giving as good as she got in debates pertaining to the site or the Romans, even wearing the same clothes so her female garments would not hamper her movements. Yet there were still differences. She lacked the strength to shift large stones. And she'd turned breathless from a brisk scramble.

He'd noticed.

How could he believe she was attracted to him? Yes, he made a striking figure—especially when the sun caught those green eyes. And his smile could melt granite. But he would turn on her in an instant if it would benefit him, just like every other man. Even the most debauched were conceited fools who considered themselves superior to the most gifted female.

If only she didn't have to waste time with Linden. Not only was he less interesting than his cousin, but attending him every evening reminded Torwell of her gender. Maybe men were right to claim that partnerships were impossible. Even the tiniest incident could be misinterpreted. Like this one: She had shivered because she hadn't realized until he touched her how chill the air had grown. That was all. His hand had been hot.

But she had to admit that working with him had distracted her from her purpose. Justice demanded marriage to Linden, but she had yet to decide if she could tolerate him. He was nothing like what she'd expected, which increased her confusion.

Linden launched another improbable tale of good deeds and pure thoughts that reminded her of his second evening in the drawing room. Bible reading, indeed. He'd trotted out every lascivious verse she'd ever heard—and a few she hadn't, though she'd later verified that all were real.

Rogue.

How could anyone know who he really was? He shifted from drunken boor to lascivious rake to dedicated puritan without warning. She couldn't tell if his roles offered glimpses into a complicated man or if they merely mocked the world while cloaking his true self.

Bessie claimed that he divided his days between the library—a strange activity for so debauched a man, unless he was working on the brandy decanter—and walking about the grounds. Though bawdiness often slipped into his conversation, he had made no attempt to seduce Sarah. Perhaps Mary was keeping him entertained, though if that were true, she was being unusually discreet about it.

Torwell's vigilance only added to her nervousness. He kept one eye on Linden, no matter what else he was doing. How could she trust a man who needed such surveillance?

But Torwell also had a stake in her decision, she realized. He had grown up at Linden Park and was second in line for the title—that viscountcy could descend through the female line in the absence of a male heir. And he might easily lose his parish if the Park fell into the wrong hands, making it difficult to continue his excavations.

But she could hardly wed Linden merely to finance Torwell's digs. So far, she disliked all of Linden's faces. He showed little of Torwell's charm, and her conscience kept raising uncomfortable questions. Such as how a man as crass as Linden could enjoy such success with the ladies.

In vino veritas. Fury over having to offer for a stranger—and one closely related to his father's nemesis—would account for his drunkenness on arrival. So his truest character had emerged that first night. Could she live with that lascivious bore? Despite Sarah's insistence that he was sweet, the girl had never met a man like Linden.

She shivered, recalling rumors that he could become vicious.

One way to learn his true character was to confess her deceit. His reaction would reveal much, for he behaved very differently with her than with Sarah. He talked easily with Sarah, often drawing smiles. But with her, he rarely uttered a complete sentence without backing up or appealing to Torwell for help. Since she couldn't believe she made him nervous, he must dislike wasting his time with an antidote—further evidence that wedding him might be a huge mistake; he could tolerate Sarah, but wanted nothing to do with her.

Her father never hid the fact that she was unacceptable. No gentleman would willingly choose a tall, mannish wife possessing a sharp tongue and bluestocking education. Torwell might work with her on the excavation, but he had made it clear that afternoon that he would not tolerate missishness or flirtation.

Torwell's enchantment with Sarah was growing. And it was real. She no longer believed him capable of coveting his cousin's inheritance. Were the men toying with having Torwell wed Sarah, then turn the dowry over to Linden? Or were both of them infatuated?

Petite, beautiful Sarah. Sweet, accomplished Sarah. If she weren't crippled, she would be the toast of London.

Appalled by her bitter thoughts, Alex straightened. This was getting her nowhere. She had accepted her limitations years ago, which was another reason she had vowed never to wed. Why had her father suddenly remembered her existence?

Linden wanted the money, so he would cheerfully change allegiance once she revealed her identity. Sarah might enjoy life as a vicar's wife, particularly with a man who showed no disgust over her foot. They must discuss it. But first, she had to decide whether she could live with Linden. Why did he have to be so venal?

Tony paced his room, waiting for Simms. Not that he needed help with his clothing. It would not do for a mere vicar to be too well dressed.

It was his courtship that was tattered. So far his plan was progressing more slowly than he had imagined was possible.

And whose fault is that?

He threaded his fingers into his hair.

He had never dreamed of finding a site as promising as the villa. Despite having no authority to excavate, he could not pass up the opportunity. But that left little time for courtship. Evenings in the drawing room grew more stilted every day. He knew duchesses who employed less aloof formality than Miss Vale did. The more he pressed, the more elusive she grew. Some nights he suspected her mind had fled the room entirely.

Not until that very evening had he realized the problem. Both ladies gave most of their attention to Jon. Even as Miss Vale spoke with him, half her mind was watching Jon's exchanges with Miss Merideth, ready to pounce should he do anything gauche.

The charade was working too well. They had created a monster that demanded the attention of everyone in the room. And rather than turn to him for help or comfort, Miss Vale relied on her companion. Such loyalty was laudable, but it did not further his cause.

Yet he was as guilty as they. Part of his own mind remained alert, ready to intervene if Jon's antics got out of hand. He should have considered this scheme more thoroughly before proposing it. But it was too late to change course.

The most lowering thought was that his basic assumptions might be wrong. Though he had always secured any woman he wanted, he now suspected that none had cared a whit for him. Torwell rarely encountered females, and Tony Linden had carried his lurid reputation since age fifteen. Young girls craved playing with fire. Wives and widows sought the excitement of bedding his notoriety. Courtesans fawned over anyone willing to pay. Did any actually know him?

His father's admonitions circled through his mind. *Worthless . . . No decent person can want you . . . Failure . . .*

Banishing the voice was impossible. He wanted to believe the complaints were baseless, but no one saw his core more clearly than his own sire, who had uttered similar sentiments long before rebellion had fashioned his false image. So perhaps he was incapable of attracting women in his own guise. That fabled charm might only be the mystique of the forbidden. He certainly lacked a history of good judgment.

Miss Merideth was a case in point. She had acted nothing like an infatuated miss tonight. So that shiver had probably been disgust rather than desire. She had pointedly avoided him since returning to the house, and not just because she was keeping Jon away from Miss Vale.

His treacherous mind returned to that encounter on the ledge. Her body was perfect. Tall enough that he needn't fear hurting her. Voluptuous enough that he fought a daily battle to keep his hands from cradling those magnificent breasts. Or stroking the shapely legs. Or burying his fingers in her glorious hair.

Flames licked his groin. Thinking had been difficult since he'd first set eyes on the woman. She even invaded his dreams, making his nights a torture. A Siren. An Amazon. Why had fate decreed that he must court Miss Vale when so delectable a woman was available?

He snorted. His real problem was that she was *not* available. And she never would be.

Simms finally arrived.

Tony pulled his mind back to business. "I need to spend more time with Miss Vale, preferably away from the house. Is there an excursion I can suggest?"

He would make no progress until he could separate Miss Vale from the others, especially Miss Merideth. If he left Simms with Jon, she could forget her companion and concentrate on him.

Whether she could like him was another question. If he found her insipid, what did she think of him? He was beginning to doubt she would ever care. So where did that leave his plan?

Simms interrupted these glum thoughts. "The village fair is in two days, in conjunction with the annual harvest festival. The servants are excited. There is to be a fortune teller, a puppet show, and several traveling peddlers. The ladies generally attend."

"I wonder why they have said nothing." But the conclusion was obvious. They did not believe their visitors would be interested in a village festival—or at least they doubted the London rakehell would be. He sighed, dismissing Simms.

Many of his excavations had concluded near harvest time, so he had sampled several country fairs. But few of his acquaintances would condescend to attend such vulgar fetes. His interests never matched those espoused by society. Now he feared he was so different that no one of breeding could accept him.

It was a depressing thought. Would his mother suffer because he could not attract the interest of one sheltered cripple?

Idiot! Don't be so maudlin.

Determined to do his best, he told Jon that they would escort the ladies to the fair.

Jon relaxed. "It's about time. You've let this continue far too long already."

"I agree. And I believe she will respond once we are alone. So we must become separated."

Jon nodded. Within minutes, they had formed plans for every possible contingency.

Chapter Seven

For once, Alex beat Torwell to the breakfast room, though he usually rose even earlier than she did. Eating before sunrise increased their excavation time—an important consideration as the year raced toward winter.

But today he was late.

She relaxed, grateful for the respite. Last night's reflections had straightened her priorities. Sarah was right. Postponing her confession was merely making it harder. And working with Torwell was an inadequate excuse. By now, he knew her well enough to accept her expertise. Once she was wed, Linden could go to London to terminate the trust, leaving Torwell here to continue work on the villa and pursue his courtship of Sarah.

It was time to decide her future. She needed an hour alone with Linden, without distractions. Since he slept late, she would leave the site early, joining Sarah in the drawing room. When he arrived, Sarah could plead business and leave. If their tête-à-tête went well, she would confess.

Convincing Torwell to continue working alone should be easy. He was fascinated by the villa and as excited as she when anything interesting turned up—which defined her real problem, she admitted in chagrin. Did she have the determination to leave him there and risk missing the thrill of a new discovery? Seeing an artifact later was not the same as actually finding it.

Pay attention to priorities. Ending this nonsense is your most pressing concern.

Cursing, she slashed at her ham, sending a strip spinning across the table when her knife slipped.

"Good morning," Torwell said from the doorway, eyes laughing as they followed the track of the ham.

She muttered a greeting, furious that he had seen that display of temper. And appalled that the sight of him recalled yesterday's silliness so clearly.

"Linden tells me the village fair is tomorrow." He took his usual seat, accepting a heaped plate from the footman. "What time will it start?"

"You wish to attend?" The question burst out on a squeak of surprise before she could stop it.

"Of course. Celebrating the harvest is important to any community. Ignoring the festivities would imply disdain for the tenants' labor—especially this year. The harvest is the poorest I've ever seen."

"No one can argue that. Even the grazing is bad, hurting dairy production."

"So we will attend. I've always enjoyed fairs." He grinned. "My favorite was one in Cumberland several years ago. For only half a shilling, one could watch the Amazing Merland produce an astonishing number of eggs from an empty bag."

"Eggs?"

"Nearly three dozen, all fresh, yet I looked in the bag before he began, and it was empty. Quite a wizard. I doubt your fair can top that, but there will be other wonders. Miss Vale can hardly enjoy sitting in the drawing room every day. She will think us the most boring of company."

She swore under her breath. Even settling with Linden would not allow her to attend the fair. She could not appear in public with a man if she wanted to keep digging. Her father would hear of it and send an agent to investigate, which could reveal the villa.

But Sarah could go.

"Miss Vale will undoubtedly enjoy an outing," she said slowly, ignoring the voice urging her to stop and think. Sarah loved the fair and had used it in her most recent argument for terminating their deceit. "But you need not sacrifice your time to accompany her. I am anxious to excavate as much as possible before winter." Even as the words left her mouth, she kicked herself for ignoring that mental warning. How could she return before dinner after making a statement like that? Never had she felt so unbalanced.

"I understand, but it is no sacrifice. I love fairs and look forward to the outing."

She was neatly trapped. "Very well. We will leave at two."

Torwell turned the conversation to the villa. She automatically answered, but thoughts and curses raged through her mind.

She must decide about Linden before dinner. Yes or no. She had no further time for study. Once she revealed her identity, they could plan the next step. Linden would agree to keep his presence secret. Neither man would want to deal with the spate of invitations that would arrive once the neighbors learned they were here. And Torwell would give up the fair to protect the villa from her father.

She offered a bland reply to his latest question. It had seemed so simple in the beginning—hide her identity for a day or two until she decided whether she could live with Linden. And it would have worked if she had not lost her head over Torwell.

How stupid could she be? Even a moment's thought could have prevented this mess. When Torwell had spotted Minerva, she should have claimed that it had been in the family for centuries. Instead, she had admitted to digging it up, then compounded the error by showing Torwell the villa. In her eagerness to learn, she had lost sight of the central fact of his life.

He was Linden's cousin. If she wed Linden, she would see him often, so there was no urgency about their partnership—or hadn't been until now.

If only she had stopped to think! Whatever Linden's faults— and he had plenty—he accepted her interest in antiquity, just as he accepted Torwell's. Unlike most men, he would not object to her continued interest in the subject. She had played her hand very badly. A moment of reflection would have convinced her to deal with Linden first. Now, she risked losing everything.

Linden confused her more each day, for his behavior was as inconsistent as his conversation. He had actually avoided Sarah last night. Perhaps he'd agreed to let Torwell have her. Why else would he have dragged the supposed companion off to the portrait gallery, leaving Torwell and Sarah alone?

Her initial fear had been ravishment—if Mary wasn't entertaining him, he must be growing desperate—but he'd only questioned her about the pictures. Did he find her so repulsive that he would not even flirt? Yet the change in his behavior raised disturbing images. If he'd arranged to recover the dowry without having to wed, he would be even angrier to discover that Sarah didn't control it.

For God's sake, Alex. Quit shilly-shallying. You sound like a brainless widgeon!

True. Thinking was pointless. Every new delay made her position worse. Torwell swore that Linden was better than gossip implied. She believed him—her hand trembled at the admission that she trusted him; never before had she trusted any man—so tonight she must confess. If he offered, she must accept. They would probably wed immediately.

Pain doubled her over.

Tony chopped at a root intruding into his trench. Once he merged his two identities, he could hire assistants to do the heaviest digging. Removing the centuries of dirt and debris that covered Roman sites was boring work that offered little reward.

Miss Merideth had been abstracted since breakfast, leaving him to his unproductive thoughts. Though digging had always been a time for pleasant contemplation, today it seemed dull. He'd become accustomed to her enthusiasm.

In the week they had worked together, she had been full of questions. And argument, he admitted, suppressing a grin. Several times she had scoffed at his pontifical remarks. And her logic was often right.

But today, she was quiet. Too quiet. Lines creased her brow, as though she carried the weight of the universe on her shoulders. He had tried to draw her out, hoping he could put a smile back on her face, but she had deflected his concern. He would not ask again.

Which was good, he reminded himself, forcing his thoughts back to business. The villa was distracting him. He needed to remember that marriage could actually increase his access to Vale House. He would even have Miss Merideth's assistance—though that was a double-edged sword, he admitted as that familiar wave of lust washed over him. But time would remedy that, so his only problem would be to keep Sir Winton from selling artifacts before he had a chance to study them.

Today would be his last day of digging until spring. Tomorrow he would escort Miss Vale to the festival, draw her away from the others, then propose. Putting off the inevitable was pointless. He would not confess until shortly before the wedding, adding at least four more days to the deceit, so the longer he dragged out his courtship, the more difficult that confession would become.

She would make an acceptable wife, he reminded himself, driving a spade deep enough to strike a rock—at least he hoped it was a rock. Temper was making him careless.

She would do. She was pretty and sweet. And capable of running a household—he'd revised his impressions on that score; Miss Merideth spent most of her time at the villa, so Miss Vale had to be overseeing the staff. Her foot did not bother him. If anything, it accounted for her sweet temper. Most diamonds had become selfish, greedy harridans by the time they reached London. He didn't want a wife who would make constant demands on him.

Yet his heart sank lower as he ticked off each asset, for they paled against her one glaring fault. She was the most insipid woman he had ever met. Even his mother, who was thoroughly under his father's thumb, displayed more spirit. In one way, it was good—he need never fret that she would object to his absences. But he wanted a home that would welcome him, not one that would oppress him with dullness. Could she provide it? His heart already recoiled at having to escort her tomorrow.

But perhaps he was doing her an injustice. She must prefer his company, for she had willingly abandoned Jon whenever he tried to attract her attention. His neglect was his own fault. He often found himself debating with Miss Merideth when he should have been courting Miss Vale. Even Jon had noticed, pointedly removing Miss Merideth from the drawing room last evening so he could get on with business.

Hardening his determination, he wrestled the latest rock out of the trench. Tonight he would remain at Miss Vale's side, ignoring the others completely. Tomorrow he would propose.

"No more reneging, Tony." Jon returned a book to the library shelf. "You vowed to finish it today, and I will hold you to that. I can no longer keep up this pretense. I've forgotten many of my early claims, a fact Miss Merideth has noticed. Miss Vale politely ignores my contradictions, but even she has frowned at me more than once. All these lies are keeping me awake at night."

"Forgive me for placing you in so unbearable a position." He'd imposed on Jon more than enough. "But I have every intention of settling the matter today. When I signal you, draw Miss Merideth away. I need Miss Vale's complete attention. She is too anxious for her companion when we are all together."

"You won't force her."

"Of course not! Though I will do my best to talk her round. Once she agrees to wed me, I will send Simms for a special license. You can marry us when it arrives." He should have picked one up before coming here, but he hadn't thought of it. At the time, he had believed eloping would be necessary to evade Sir Winton.

"Not under false pretenses."

So it was suspicion rather than cold feet that was putting the icy formality into Jon's tone. Or last night's unpleasantness, though he still had no idea what had happened. Jon's conversation with Miss Merideth had suddenly exploded into an argument. Miss Merideth had fled. Miss Vale had followed. But Jon refused to discuss it.

At least he could reassure him on this point. "I wouldn't ask you to condone a lie. An illegal union would cost me everything."

"It's not just that," said Jon with a sigh. "She doesn't deserve the tricks we've played on her. I wish we'd never started."

"So do I, but it will be over soon."

A scream rent the air.

"Miss Vale!" Jon gasped, beating him to the door. Miss

Merideth was already kneeling beside the crumpled form when they reached the hall.

"What happened?" Tony demanded.

"She slipped on the stairs." Her hands remained steady as she examined Miss Vale's good ankle, but she was clearly upset.

Miss Vale struggled into a more modest position, tugging her skirt until it covered her twisted foot. "I don't think it is broken," she said, though she winced from her companion's prodding. "It should be fine in a few minutes."

"Nonsense," snapped Jon. "You must summon a doctor immediately."

"No!"

Tony stared at Miss Merideth, surprised at her vehemence.

Her eyes dropped. "It is merely a sprain," she said more calmly. "If you can carry her into the drawing room, I will examine it more closely. But I suspect that a few days of rest will cure it. We call the doctor only in extreme emergency," she added, meeting his gaze.

"Very well." He understood. A few country doctors were competent physicians whose efforts speeded healing. Others were charlatans whose ministrations inflicted worse damage. Most lay in between. The nearest doctor to his last excavation had been downright dangerous, nearly killing a boy through excessive blood-letting before Tony could bring in a man from Carlisle to set his broken leg.

Scooping Miss Vale into his arms, he carried her to the drawing room couch. Concentrating on protecting her injury allowed him to ignore her slight frame. Comparisons would make duty even harder.

"I will stay with her," said Miss Merideth, drawing him aside. "You and Mr. Linden can leave for town now."

"Not without you."

"Go. She needs to remain under observation for a few hours, but you can do nothing for her, and you wanted to attend the festival. She is embarrassed enough by this accident. That will worsen if she believes her clumsiness ruined your outing."

She was right. However much he wanted to settle his betrothal, he could not do so now. He had sworn not to coerce her, but tending her would damage her reputation, removing any choice about marriage.

Even Jon would accept this new delay. If she must remain quiet for several days, he would see even less of her than before.

Irritated over the postponement—yet lighthearted for the same reason—he bade the ladies farewell, dragging an equally reluctant Jon outside.

Alex stayed at the window until Linden's carriage was out of sight. The accident had provided very lowering insight into both gentlemen's minds.

Linden had shocked her. Not only had he arrived first, but fear had twisted his face. And it had nothing to do with his inheritance, for it remained long after he knew that Sarah had suffered no serious damage. Even after it faded, he'd remained concerned. Was he falling in love with Sarah? What a nasty complication that would be. But it might explain why he had started last night's fight.

For the first time since his arrival, he had refused to move from Sarah's side. She'd plowed ahead with her confession anyway, beginning with the fears that had resulted in her decision to lie. But the moment she'd mentioned his reputation, he'd exploded.

"Why must you harp on my background?" he'd demanded, brown eyes turning harsh in the lamplight. "I am sick and tired of being quizzed by servants. Your employer is satisfied. That is all you need to know." He'd refused to listen to another word, just as every other man did. So she'd given up. He was in no mood to forgive anything.

Only now did she understand. His quest had changed. Having formed an attachment to Sarah, talking to the companion was a waste of his valuable time.

She clenched her fists.

But why, then, had he dragged her off to the gallery two nights ago? And why talk to her more than to Sarah? He'd made no mention of marriage. Sarah still described him as confused and irritated, not symptoms of a man courting a woman he loved. And why let Torwell carry Sarah to the couch? Was he trying so hard to distance himself from his reputation that he dared not touch anyone?

Instead of trying to explain, she should have announced her deceit and been done with it. Now she was left with new concerns. He would take it even harder if she had led him to love the wrong lady. Even if Torwell were willing to wed her and transfer everything back to Linden, she would lose. Torwell preferred Sarah, too.

Her head spun.

Torwell's infatuation added to her confusion. A blind man could see that he wanted Sarah, so why was Linden dragging his feet? Until last night, he had willingly allowed Torwell to cut him out.

They were gone.

"Are you all right?" she asked, turning back to the room.

"Of course. I did not really fall."

She sighed in relief, for she hadn't been sure. "Then you are a far better actress than I am. I could have sworn you took a genuine tumble. Forgive me for putting you through this, but after last night, I didn't know what else to do."

"It is nothing. But you must confess tonight. I will not be there to divide his attention, so you will have no excuses. Surely you know that he is a decent man."

"Better than I thought, yes. But how much? A reputation of that magnitude does not grow from a young man's wild oats."

"Alex! Indecision is not like you. Trust me. I have spent many hours with him. Youthful indiscretion may have started it, but others keep the tale alive for their own purposes. You must know that society is slow to forgive. He could be ten years past a problem and still find it a millstone round his neck."

"True." She frowned. "But his behavior is not as benign as he would have us believe. He is playacting much of the time."

"No."

"Face facts, Sarah. You saw him last week—meek and mild, even as he leered down your gown."

"Alex!" She blushed.

"He does exactly what he wants, even when pretending to do the opposite." Her tone hardened as she realized that last night's fight had also been deliberate, driving her from the drawing room so he needn't bother with her.

"You exaggerate." Sarah's quiet voice cut through the haze of anger. "And unless you condone your father's cheating, you have little choice."

"I had already decided to accept him," she admitted. "The problem is confessing this ridiculous deceit. I never meant it to last this long. By now, I fear he will wash his hands of us when he learns the truth."

"He cannot afford to," Sarah said stoutly. "His reasons for pursuing this match are far stronger than yours. No matter how badly you behave, he must wed you. But if you let this drag on much longer, he may make you pay for the humiliation. Tell them the truth when they return."

"Only if I can get Linden alone." She couldn't watch Torwell's respect die. It would, of course, but she could not face him while it happened. "Tomorrow I will send Torwell to the villa alone, then give Linden a tour of the estate—you will need to rest. I will tell him then." She would drive him to the orchard. Faced with a three-mile hike home if he fled, he would listen until she had finished speaking.

"Very well. But that must be the end. No more procrastinating." Rising from the couch, she headed upstairs to her room.

Alex sighed, relieved that Sarah's limp was no more pronounced than usual.

Tomorrow.

And in the meantime, she would discover how Linden behaved when he was not pretending to be a saint.

She summoned Murch. "I want you to observe our guests, particularly Linden. I wish to know what he does."

"Yes, Miss Alex." But his face was troubled. He started to speak, but thought better of it.

"You needn't chastise me for adding a new deceit to the old," she said, interpreting his look. "I will finish it tomorrow."

He nodded. "Remaining silent about the bits of stone you

find in the wood is a small thing, but the staff is unaccustomed to secrets. Someone is bound to slip."

She caught up on the household accounts while searching for an approach that would earn Linden's forgiveness. How had she backed herself into so demeaning a corner? She must have been mad.

But the past could not be changed, so she must deal with the consequences.

Murch returned before dark.

"The gentlemen are back," he reported. "They did not introduce themselves to the villagers and made no mention of Vale House. When the innkeeper asked where they were staying, Mr. Torwell claimed they were headed for Gloucester and had merely stopped on a whim. They sampled gingerbread and sweetmeats, enjoyed the entertainment, and paid close attention to the horses offered for sale. The blacksmith's daughter seemed interested in Mr. Torwell, but he ignored her. The Mason girl flirted with Mr. Linden, without drawing a response. Perhaps they are concerned about Miss Sarah's injury, for they left before the feasting commenced, claiming a wish to reach Gloucester before dark. And they seem eager to protect your reputation, for they did indeed head for the post road, using back lanes to return here."

"Thank you, Murch."

Now what? Perhaps Linden really had outgrown whatever wildness had produced his reputation. Or maybe the men had remained on good behavior, knowing that news of any slip would reach to Vale House.

Stupid, Alex. Very stupid. Of course they would not revert to form so close to her home. Half the servants had attended the fair today. The rest would go this evening. Linden was determined to appear a saint, even making his cousin tell the lies about their business.

So her cowardice had produced only a new deceit. She should have called both men into the hall this morning and announced her identity. Now it would be even harder. How could she begin? *Please accept my most humble apologies, Mr. Linden. But believing you to be a monster, I hid behind my companion's skirts . . .*

That would never do. *Knowing you meant to offer for me, I pretended to be someone else until I decided that I could tolerate you . . .*

Worse. That put her in the position of proposing. Such a breach of propriety was as bad as her deception. And what if he refused? The image of his face bent over a supposedly injured Sarah smote her heart.

Fearing you would compromise me, I diverted your attention to a cripple . . .

Impossible. Even in the face of his reputation, her assumptions were insulting. How was she to do this?

Jon chewed his dinner in peace. For once, he could enjoy the food, for his companions had not said a word since sitting down.

He wasn't concerned about Miss Merideth. She might remain piqued over last night's outburst—he'd been so frustrated by her pressure that he'd wanted only to escape—or her silence might be guilt over Miss Vale's fall. But her troubles were temporary.

Tony presented a more serious problem, for he was suffering one of his moods.

He would never blame Tony for being moody. Uncle Thomas had tried every way he could think of to break his spirit—unreasonable punishments, heavy-handed discipline, punitive orders, setting a host of spies to watch his every move, blatantly favoring the nephew over the son . . .

It was a miracle that Tony had survived. He was probably the only boy in school who welcomed the harsh discipline as an improvement over living at home. At least school punishments were rarely malicious.

But despite Tony's usual equanimity, frustration sometimes overwhelmed him. Blue-devils would move in, bringing a blackness of spirit that might last for days. During those periods, he would withdraw into himself, brooding until the pressure exploded in a frenzy of activity.

As a child, the moods would often break in an outburst of disobedience—like the summer that had created his reputation.

As an adult, they usually drove him to a frenzy of work. Tony would move a mountain of rock tomorrow.

The cause this time was obvious. Tony's world had been reeling for two weeks. Only loyalty to Aunt Mary had forced him to pursue marriage to a lady who already bored him.

Jon shuddered, imagining Miss Vale's future. Tony would never deliberately hurt anyone, but she would not enjoy living with a man who had never wanted her. No matter how kind he tried to be, she would know the truth. And since his benevolence would include protecting her from the society that loathed him, she would remain isolated.

Not that Tony was thinking that far ahead. After finally pushing himself into concluding the distasteful business, fate had stepped in, postponing it yet again. He would be reeling from frustration, from fear that the delay would threaten him with exposure, and from new doubts about marrying Miss Vale.

Refusing a serving of cabbage, Jon chewed on a piece of beef.

He wished he knew how to help Tony through these dark periods, but he'd had no success in twenty-three years of trying. At least Miss Merideth would force him back to the house tomorrow before he was too exhausted to move.

Tony's youthful disobedience had created only minor trouble, some of which he'd helped cover up. But this penchant for overwork raised a fear he had lived with for ten years. The day he'd discovered it had been the most frightening of his life . . .

He'd awakened early that morning, overwhelmed by a powerful urge to visit Tony, who was excavating a small villa a day's ride from Linden Park. Dismissing it as nonsense, he had gone about his business. But by noon, the feeling was too strong to ignore. Somehow, he knew Tony was in trouble.

It was midnight when he'd reached the inn to find that Tony hadn't returned. Dawn was breaking by the time he had located the site, illuminating Tony's unconscious body sprawled in a trench, a shovel still clutched in his hand, his brow feverish from the night air. He'd remained delirious for days. Even after he recovered, he never explained why he'd nearly worked himself to death. But Jon knew. He'd found an eight-page rant from

Uncle Thomas scattered on the floor when he had hauled Tony's limp body up to his room . . .

"Will you join me in the drawing room this evening?" asked Miss Merideth, interrupting Jon's memories.

"Not tonight." Tony emptied his wineglass. "I want to get an early start tomorrow."

"Retiring is an excellent idea," Jon agreed, though manners made him offer an arm to Miss Merideth.

Tony was already mounting the stairs when they reached the hall. Miss Merideth's hand prevented him from following.

"Miss Vale will be confined to bed for a day or two," she said woodenly. "You would enjoy a tour of the estate tomorrow. We have been neglecting you."

"Not at all. Do not change your plans on my account. Ton-Torwell will need your assistance."

"He is quite accustomed to working alone."

"But he should not—" He stopped, unable to mention Tony's mood without revealing why the day had been so frustrating.

How could he discourage her? Miss Merideth was a conscientious companion, who would do whatever she could to entertain her employer's guests. From her perspective, he was the higher ranking, and thus her most pressing problem. The only way he could convince her to care for Tony was to disappear.

"I appreciate your offer, Miss Merideth," he said, dropping her arm as he faced her. "And I will enjoy a tour another day. But I will not be here tomorrow. I had meant to call on a friend while I was in the area. Miss Vale's injury gives me the opportunity to do so without insult. I will return in three days." That would give Tony time to complete his business.

"But—" Her face changed from surprise to resignation. "I wish you a pleasant journey."

"Thank you. Please see that Torwell does not work overlong while I am gone." Without waiting to hear the question hovering on her lips, he turned upstairs.

Giving Simms the job of relaying his sudden change of plans to Tony, he climbed into bed. How far must he go to be certain that the Vale House staff would not hear news of him?

Chapter Eight

Tony exchanged his spade for a trowel, gently scraping soil from around the latest stone. Miss Vale had not left her room since falling four days ago. It had taken him two days to work off the frustration raised by the collapse of his plans. Turning up nothing but broken flue tiles and bits of brick hadn't helped. They were digging through a hypocaust, but there was no sign of the floor that had once overlaid it.

He shook his head. This stone had not been worked. Heaving it aside, he drove the spade into the ground.

Jon's absence was just as frustrating. Simms had immediately reported the change of plans. Dear innocent Jon. He had overlooked one important point in his scheming. The honorable Tony Linden would hardly leave his valet behind when paying a call. But disappearing for a few days was a good idea. They could all relax once Linden's reputation departed. So he had sent Jon and Simms to London for the special license. By the time they returned, he should have settled with Miss Vale.

His other frustration had been losing a day of digging. He'd enjoyed the festival, of course, but an honest look at the future showed that he had no guarantee of access to this site once Sir Winton discovered his identity. The baronet would probably disown his daughter for thwarting him. So he would have preferred spending the day investigating the questions teasing his mind.

Perhaps Miss Vale would consider staying here a while after marriage, so he could continue work, though that would mean digging into winter and risking criminal charges if Sir Winton discovered him.

Stupid! He snorted, admitting that the idea was impossible. Unless he took possession of the trust before the month was up, his parents must leave Linden Park.

So he must settle with Miss Vale. But she had not yet appeared. Miss Merideth swore she was improving, but needed further rest. Supposedly she would join them for dinner tonight. If Jon had encountered no trouble on the road—and no opposition from the Archbishop's staff—he might also be back.

Miss Merideth leaned over her trench, drawing his eyes to her delectable backside. Keeping his hands to himself was becoming more difficult every day—which was why he was angling his trenches farther from hers.

Not now, he reminded his baser instincts as heat stirred his groin. Cursing himself for suggesting she wear pantaloons, he sauntered closer. "Find something?"

"Not really." She sounded discouraged. "Another chunk of the cliff."

He helped her dig it out. A jumble of broken bricks lay beneath it.

"Another support pillar for the floor?"

"Exactly, though more of this one survived," he murmured, making a quick sketch before pulling the pieces loose.

"This is the same color as the tiles," she said, turning one in her hand.

"Probably from the same kiln." He scanned the slope, his eyes narrowing when they reached the stakes marking the debris fan. "Brick. I've been—"

"Look!" she interrupted.

A flash of blue caught the sunlight as she pulled another brick loose. She grabbed a trowel, scraping away soil in a sudden frenzy.

"Easy, Miss Merideth. There is no need to rush. It isn't going anywhere." But his heart had speeded up. He jumped into the trench, helping her deepen it around the find, barely noticing when his arm brushed hers.

An hour later, they collapsed in exhaustion. His excitement had risen and fallen too many times to count.

"Definitely mosaic tiles," he said, poking through a mound of colored chips.

"But not one remains attached, though some of the bricks show traces of mortar." She picked up a handful of chips. "So many colors. The picture must have been beautiful. Too bad the floor shattered in the slide."

"I'm not sure it did." He pointed at the tiles. "Not only are they loose, but they are all square."

"Square?"

He nodded. "Artists kept stocks of colored stone trimmed into square rods. They sliced the rods into tiles when they prepared for a job. Further shaping and polishing occurred on site as the tiles were set."

"Do you mean these were not yet set?"

"I suspect so. Perhaps this room belonged to a mosaic artist hired to decorate a floor or repair an existing one. If the building was still under construction, that would explain why we've found only the hypocaust."

"You are contradicting yourself. No artist would live or work in a room without a floor, nor would he be called in before the floor was laid. And I doubt that a villa this large was built at one time. Perhaps this was a new wing. If the artist was working elsewhere, the slide could have carried his supplies here."

"Excellent points," he admitted, recalling the thought he'd set aside an hour ago. "And they bolster the feeling that I've been approaching this puzzle wrong from the beginning."

"How?" Her eyes radiated surprise.

"All the other sites I've excavated were abandoned, so no personal items remained. Building materials had been appropriated for other projects until only the foundations were left. Centuries of dirt and debris had buried them, but they were basically intact."

"I see what you mean," she said slowly. "If this site was buried by a slide, then even the foundations would have been damaged or destroyed."

"True, but that is not what I meant. A site that was buried in a sudden catastrophe is richer in artifacts than an abandoned one. Like Minerva. But it also means that the walls remained, mixed with the foundation stones. Brick. While the Romans used stone for temples and large public buildings, smaller ones were built of brick atop a stone foundation—which is why abandoned sites never have walls. Brick is easy to transport and can be reused in other structures."

"What is your point?"

"If you shatter brick and tile into pieces the size we see here, they look very much alike. In fact, brick breaks more easily than tile. It is not fired. But if the rubble is mostly brick, then I've greatly overestimated the size of the roof."

"So the building may have been small? But what does that do to your theory that the entire clearing was paved? We've found remnants of the hypocaust in several places."

"True, but they may have paved large areas of courtyard. What I'm more concerned about is this absence of floors. If the slide came down hard enough to destroy them, then we might be better off exploring the debris fan."

"Why? So far we've found nothing but shards there." She pointed toward the temple. "Minerva was undamaged, so the slide could not have destroyed everything. We might have better luck starting at the temple and working back toward the villa."

"That would take forever. Perhaps we should expand trenches along known foundations."

"Which will also take time. If this was a new wing, then the original villa lies between here and the temple. Why not start at the midpoint? Maybe we'll turn up the entrance."

He climbed out of the trench, staring from the cliff to the debris fan. "That is a possibility, but I think we need a new approach entirely. Let's start at the beginning. I've never liked all that debris to the east. It is not in line with any hill, so something must have deflected at least part of the slide. A heavy stone building might have done it, but I cannot imagine brick holding up long enough."

"It would depend on how much of the cliff came down," she countered. "Maybe this was a series of small falls instead of one big one."

"Small ones might pile against the walls until they finally buckled, but the force of the collapse would hardly destroy floors. Nor would it sweep possessions away from the site."

"The owner might have had time to salvage his belongings."

Running his hands through his hair, he paced the clearing. "How does a slide behave? I've been assuming that the cliff crumbled, flowed into the valley, and swept everything away, but I've never actually seen a slide. Let's try an experiment." He stopped next to a three-foot-deep trench they had dug several days earlier. Rain had softened its walls, making them unstable. Portions had already collapsed, piling dirt, clods, and pebbles in the bottom.

"These look like the talus slopes at the foot of the cliff," he said, pointing. "What will happen in the next slide?"

"The new debris will make the mound higher."

"Let's see . . ." He crumbled the top of the wall, letting dirt tumble down in a series of small falls.

She nodded. "The mound grows larger with each fall."

"But there is not enough material to spread much beyond the original mound," he said, frowning. "And if we use the same scale as the cliff, the villa would have been over here." He pointed to a spot near the other side of the trench. "So the entire cliff must have failed."

He loosened more of the bank with his trowel, starting several inches back from the edge, careful to keep the chunk intact until he had freed a large piece of the face.

It fell as a block, shattering when it hit the mound. This time the soil did not pile up. Debris rolled in a wave across the trench floor, leaving the mound lower than before.

"Interesting," Miss Merideth said, crouching to examine the slide. "Not only did it sweep earlier falls along with it, but it did not spread uniformly."

Excitement tingled, as it always did when he solved a puzzle. "When it started spreading, the front edge of the wave was the deepest, which would cause serious damage to anything it hit—like the villa. It must have shattered the walls, rolling and crunching everything as it swept toward the river."

"But not everywhere. This is what I meant by lacking uniformity. Wherever the front of the wave was thick, it spread far from the impact point, yet in other places, it hardly cleared the original mound. Look at the edge of the flow. This tongue passes your hypothetical villa, while only inches away, the flow stopped well short. So just because we found no floor here, we cannot conclude that all the floors are gone."

"Ever the optimist."

"Why not? Minerva survived without a scratch. And she remained in the temple."

"Good point. So we will start a new search. Your suggestion was as good as any. Perhaps it will yield the entrance." He headed for the spot. "I'll start at this point. You work there, and we'll meet in the center."

Only after he drove in his spade did he admit that positioning the trenches this way had more to do with enjoying the sight of Miss Merideth bent over a shovel than with maps of the clearing.

Tonight!

Yes, he must see Miss Vale alone tonight. He was running out of time. So far, no one had revealed his impersonation, but that was due only to luck. Several acquaintances lived nearby. Any of them might have been at the village fair the other day.

Jon could distract Miss Merideth, if he was back. Otherwise, he would send her on an errand. But he must conclude this business tonight. If everything fell into place, he could be a married man by morning.

A cloud engulfed the sun, which accounted for his sudden shiver.

Tony was leading both ladies into the dining room when Jon returned.

"Welcome back, sir," said Miss Vale, blushing. "I trust you had a good journey. How is your friend?"

"Q-quite well. My felicitations on your recovery. I had feared to find you still suffering."

"It was only a trifling sprain, sir. You refine too much."

"Hardly," said Tony, easily reading the question in Jon's eyes. "This is the first time she has left her room since falling." He nearly mentioned long evenings with both of them absent, but Miss Merideth was on his other arm. He could hardly insult her—especially since he had enjoyed their spirited discussions.

"Then I shan't keep you standing." Jon nodded at each lady in turn. "If you will excuse me, I must retire."

"Nonsense," said Miss Vale, abandoning Tony to take Jon's arm. "You needn't change into evening dress or eat in your room. Join us for dinner. You can tell us about your trip."

Tony met Jon's panicky eyes, glee over his cousin's discomfort overcoming irritation that Miss Vale had seemed uncommonly pleased at his return. "Yes, do join us, Linden. We would love to know how Wilkerson is keeping," he added, naming a schoolmate Jon despised, who now lived in Yorkshire. Wilkerson was an unwed lump of a man who had trouble recalling his own name. But he took umbrage at anyone who thought him slow, and had once beaten Jon quite soundly for refusing to drink with him.

"He is quite well, though surprised to see me."

"I can imagine. And his wife? Charlotte, I believe." He ignored Miss Merideth's flinch, though he cursed her acuity. She also heard the strain in Jon's voice.

"Cassandra," said Jon, falling into the spirit. "I saw little of her, for her oldest was suffering quite loudly from croup."

"They have two sons—or is it three?"

"Two, plus twin daughters. You really should spend less time poking about ruins, Cousin. You are losing track of the years."

"But he is doing such fascinating research," said Miss Merideth, frowning at their banter.

"Croup can be very alarming," said Miss Vale, drawing Jon's attention as he seated her at the table. "How is she treating it? I do hope someone has showed her the efficacy of steam."

"Wilkerson mentioned steam, so I am sure she knows," said

Jon, patting her hand before turning to his soup. He had resumed his own manner in the days away.

Tony frowned, irritated at how the evening had begun. Jon was undoubtedly exhausted—to London and back in four days was a grueling journey—but that was no excuse for ignoring their situation. He had missed every hint that he should take himself off, and now had forgotten his role as Tony Linden. Disaster loomed. Miss Merideth was staring, clearly suspicious of this new character. A single slip could destroy everything.

But he could only pray that Jon kept his wits about him, for Miss Vale was quizzing him closely about his journey, clearly reveling in a new topic of conversation. She ignored his own attempts to speak with her.

He finally fell quiet, alternating between blue-devils over what might be his last hours as a bachelor and chuckles over the fictional tales of Wilkerson's highly precocious offspring. Where had Jon's imagination come from?

Only after dessert was served did Miss Merideth finally give him a chance to set his plans into motion. When she distracted Jon's attention, Tony leaned closer to Miss Vale.

"Let us retire to the music room," he suggested softly. "I have heard much praise for your skill—if you feel up to playing. Your ankle must protest this activity," he added, knowing his assumption would force a denial.

"It is quite recovered." She smiled. "I could have come down last evening, but we chose to take no chance of another fall."

"I would have carried you down had I known," he said warmly. "As my cousin often reminds me, too much devotion to ruins must make me quite boring. But you are a delight to the senses. Do you also sing?"

"Only if you will join me. Preferably both of you," she added, turning to Jon. "I am a trifle out of practice."

"Delighted." Jon's agreement was out before he noted Tony's scowl. "Miss Merideth?"

"I will listen. My voice is unsuited to song," she said, shrugging.

Tony hid his disappointment. He had hoped a love song or

two would lead into a proposal. Jon should have retired on the excuse of weariness, but the opportunity might yet arise. If Miss Merideth did not sing, she would likely leave before the evening was concluded. Jon would follow.

Alex accepted Linden's arm for the trek to the music room. Torwell's abandonment irritated her more than she cared to admit. She had grown accustomed to their nightly tête-à-têtes. He was so different from her father's boisterous friends, whose conversation rarely moved beyond gaming, gossip, and wenching.

But Torwell willingly discussed any subject, from estate problems and her frustration at having no influence to correct them, to living conditions of the lower classes, to history, scientific experiments, ideas, and a host of other topics. He did not care if she disagreed with him, willingly conceding points when her arguments were more persuasive, treating her as an equal capable of thinking for herself.

But those evenings were now gone. He had merely been filling time until Sarah reappeared. In the thrill of discovery, she had forgotten that he had formed a *tendre* for Sarah before that staged fall. Thus there would be no more stimulating conversations. He kept his mind firmly on digging while they worked.

Fool! she admonished herself. Despite knowing she must attach Linden, she had begun to think of Torwell as her special friend. But like other gentlemen, he was willing to pass the evening with her only when he had nothing better to do, treating her no different than he would his colleagues or the men he might meet at a club.

She hadn't missed his irritation when Linden returned, with his greater claim to Sarah's attention. Nor had she missed the disapproving frown he'd tossed Linden's way at dinner.

But that was good, she reminded herself sharply. Once she confessed her identity, Torwell could wed Sarah without creating a rift with his cousin. And Sarah would benefit. She deserved a steady, trustworthy husband. Whatever Linden's personal feelings, he would wed the fortune. His attraction to Sarah would not have lasted anyway.

She released Linden's arm so he could join Sarah at the harpsichord.

Everyone would be happy. Linden would recover his inheritance. Sarah would have a husband she could respect. Torwell would make a love match. And she could continue working with him on excavations. He had accepted her as a partner.

Or had he?

She frowned. Torwell had no authority to dig at Vale House. The owner did not even know the site existed. Since she had invited him to participate, he might think that flattering her was the only way he could dig there.

It was so obvious that she berated herself for not having considered it earlier. Lord Mitchell accepted her ideas only because he thought they came from a man. Torwell was humoring her because pretense was the only way he could investigate the site.

She picked up a sketch pad, using it as an excuse to settle far from the others. The strains of a Robert Burns ballad drifted through the room. It was one of his sadder songs, striking a chord deep in her breast, though she rarely identified with music.

Her pencil captured the image on paper. Sarah, seated at the keyboard. Torwell and Linden standing behind her, one on each side. But it was Torwell's hand that rested on Sarah's shoulder, and Torwell's cheek that brushed hers whenever he leaned forward to turn a page. His rich voice sent shivers down her spine. All three were turned half away from her, emphasizing the gulf that had always stood between her and the world.

Her life in a capsule.

She shook away the thought, but the truth hung starkly before her. Even a musical evening among friends left her standing apart, a freak amidst her own class. Her voice was strident enough at any time, but it sounded like a raven's when she tried to sing. The fingers that could patiently sketch a long-buried artifact tied themselves into knots if they came within touching distance of a keyboard. Music was so far beyond her that she could rarely enjoy even listening to it.

Ladies were accomplished musicians. She was incompetent. It was yet another reason her father had never considered her a lady. She was abnormal, unable to get along with her peers. The only time she was truly comfortable was when her mind was in the past.

The music came to an end, accompanied by laughter. Linden suggested a new song.

"Not suitable," Torwell said, frowning. "How about that red rose piece?"

Sarah shuffled pages.

"Perfect," Torwell said, draping himself around her shoulders as he reached down to strike a key. "*My love is like a red, red rose,*" he began singing, bestowing a heated look on her when he caught her eye.

Sarah's fingers hit an uncharacteristic number of wrong notes. Linden joined in, but his face resembled a thundercloud.

Alex tore her eyes from the tableau, her fingers producing a new sketch, this one of Minerva thrusting a lance through Torwell's heart. She should have known better than to accept him as a friend. He was no different from a thousand other schemers. How could she have trusted him?

She'd been wrong about his intentions. The look in his eye as he gazed at Sarah was exactly like the one he'd used on the mosaic tiles that very afternoon—disappointment at failing to find what he truly wanted mixed with determination to take whatever he could get. Linden looked exactly the same. Neither wanted marriage, but somehow, Linden must have forced Torwell to rescue the family—probably by letting him keep the estate. It would remove his responsibilities to the church while providing support for his excavations.

Her masquerade allowed her to spot motives she might otherwise have missed. Torwell was pretending affection for Sarah. So was Linden, of course, but at least his motives were clear. Once she revealed her identity, both would switch their allegiance to her. Torwell might even claim undying love on the basis of their shared interest in the Romans. How could she have trusted him? Thank heaven she'd planned to tell Linden in private. Living with an honest reprobate would be easier than with a sneak.

She was cold.

Though no fire had been lit in here, she knew the room was not to blame. She must draw Linden off alone and confess. Immediately. And once he knew the truth, she could not allow him near Torwell until they settled the question of marriage.

She rose. At least an hour had passed since dinner. Murch could chaperon Sarah while she and Linden spoke.

"Is your ankle fatiguing you, Miss Vale?" Torwell asked. "Perhaps we should move into the drawing room where it is warmer."

"That won't be necessary," said Sarah. "Merideth will help me upstairs. It has been a most pleasant evening, but I should rest."

Alex sighed. Something had pushed Sarah into flight, so she would have to go along with it long enough to find out the facts. They must also discuss Torwell. She could find Linden later.

Ignoring the gentlemen's glowers, she helped Sarah from the room.

"Be careful of Torwell," she said the moment they reached the stairs. "He is as dangerous as Linden, possibly more so. They have agreed to split the fortune, with Torwell taking the bride. Perhaps he hopes to gain control of the villa."

"You cannot be serious. He is all that is amiable."

"Do not let his charm deceive you. I've watched his eyes. He is determined to have you. Guard yourself. I sense great determination beneath his surface. That is one man who will take what he wants, and to hell with the consequences."

"Alex!" Sarah cast a reproachful look over her shoulder. "You know how cursing distresses me. You are allowing your emotions to subvert your intellect. Mr. Torwell is all that is proper. He pays me court only to plead his cousin's case, as you would know if jealousy were not blinding your senses."

"Jealousy!" She recoiled. "He has well and truly pulled the wool over your eyes."

"As I thought. You overreact to hide the truth even from yourself, but I have seen the way you look at him—and how he looks at you, with hopeless longing clouding his eyes. I can only suppose you've treated him to one of your tirades against men. You had best examine your heart, lest you find yourself wed to one man while loving another."

"That is quite enough, Sarah." Fury replaced her shock. "I have no interest in Torwell beyond a mutual love for antiquity. I thought to protect you by repeating what I've learned of the man, for I will settle with Linden as soon as possible. In the meantime, lock your door and avoid any contact with Torwell. You would hardly enjoy being forcibly tied to a man who hates you for not having the dowry."

Chapter Nine

Tony awoke before dawn with a raging headache. A largely sleepless night had contributed, but the real cause was the admission that his scheme was doomed to failure.

Last night had been a disaster. He had done everything he could to convey his interest—touching her, whispering compliments in her ear whenever he turned a page, suggesting the most romantic songs he knew. She had reacted, displaying what he first thought was nervous anticipation. Not until she refused his escort to the drawing room had he realized that she was afraid rather than titillated.

Why? He'd mulled the question all night. Yet every possibility raised more questions.

He shook his head, then wished he had been more careful.

Perhaps fresh air would clear his mind. Shrugging into his work clothes, he headed into the Park.

The autumn air had a decided bite to it this morning, but he did not mind. Emptying his head of Miss Vale, Miss Merideth, and even the villa they were excavating, he concentrated on dawn's play across bronze and gold trees, on a flock of waterfowl arrowing south for the winter, on the musical flow of the stream bubbling along its rocky bed . . .

The pain gradually eased behind his eyes. By the time he turned back, it was gone. He could finally think.

Miss Vale was sheltered, an innocent with little experience of the world. Yet he could not believe that his courtship had scared her. The time period he had originally envisioned might have, but he had been here for nearly a fortnight. And he had hardly pressed.

Had she realized that Jon was going to keep Miss Merideth in the music room, so they would be alone? Some girls panicked at such a situation, but only if they expected either unwanted advances or an unwanted proposal. Neither applied to Miss Vale. She believed he was a vicar. After spending so much time with a supposed rakehell, attended only by a lady's maid, she would hardly cavil about him. He was an innocuous character, his only oddity an interest in antiquity. Since she'd encouraged her companion to follow the same pursuit, she would not object to him. And unless she knew his true identity, she would hardly expect an offer.

Miss Merideth.

He swore. Surely Miss Vale wasn't playing matchmaker for her companion! He would have to set her straight on that score. Miss Merideth had made her own disinterest abundantly clear. And he had no choice in the matter.

Appalled . . . she has no power to change the agreement . . .

"Devil take it!" he swore, suddenly recalling Miss Merideth's words. He'd hardly heeded them at the time and hadn't thought of them since.

The answer had been staring him in the face from the beginning, but he had been too stupid to see it. She had been appalled at what her father had done to his. Perhaps she even suspected chicanery about the game, but investigating the trust had proved that she could not even allow his parents to remain in residence. So she had realized that wedding him was the only way to soften the blow, even if she must accept his reputation in the process.

But she didn't know that he was the one she must wed.

Cursing himself for every stupidity known to man, he shook his head. Hiding his identity had been the worst possible approach. Yet how could he have known that her sense of justice would override even his abominable reputation? It hinted at depths of character he had not suspected.

No wonder she willingly spent time with Jon. And this explained those odd looks she had given him—and her efforts to avoid him last night. Whatever her personal feelings, she had decided to accept Tony Linden. She was probably confused because Tony Linden had made no offer. In the meantime, she was suppressing any attraction to Torwell.

He briefly toyed with negotiating a proxy marriage that would postpone revealing the truth until they had both irrevocably taken the step they had already planned. But that would add yet another layer of deceit, making the ultimate denouement even worse.

So he had to reveal his identity, beg her forgiveness, and hope she would not respond by washing her hands of the entire Linden family. And he could not postpone his confession. For good or ill, he must see her as soon as possible. Since she rarely arose until noon, he could do no digging today.

So he would avoid breakfast. Miss Merideth was astute enough to recognize that something was wrong. He could not risk others learning the truth until he had confessed to his hostess.

If only he had not started this!

"Mornin', Mr. Torwell," called the head groom as he passed the stable. "You're up and about even earlier than usual. Shall I saddle Orpheus?"

"Not just yet. I must deal with other business before riding out."

"Lord Bushnell, I suppose. Miss Vale will be upset when he arrives."

"She has said nothing about a new guest," said Tony cautiously, but his mind was racing. Meeting an acquaintance was a risk he'd ignored in recent days. Not that Bushnell was a friend. Far from it. What would so debauched a man be doing at Vale House?

"You've been out a good long time, then. The innkeeper's lad brought the letter an hour ago. Lord Bushnell always stops here on his way to London, as do most of Sir Winton's friends."

"Even when he is not in residence?"

The groom shrugged. "They are always welcomed."

The implication was obvious. "Do you mean that Sir Winton invites his rackety friends to make use of his house, even when no one is here but his innocent daughter?"

"It isn't my place to judge, though I can understand why a vicar might object." Shifting his eyes to scan the stable yard, he lowered his voice. "But between the two of us, I expect Sir Winton would be right pleased if someone compromised the girl badly enough to get her off his hands. She has sworn for years that she would never wed, and he's found no one willing to take on a barely dowered harridan. Making her an heiress is his final try."

Harridan? Tony bit back a sharp retort. Miss Vale must put on quite an act if her father considered her so. Maybe the groom hoped a nice vicar would take her on to protect her from worse. He must know that nothing would keep her single much longer, and he could like Linden's reputation no better than anyone else did.

This gave a new urgency to his confession. He must see Miss Vale the moment she arose. Simms could send word via her maid to meet him before breakfast. Everything must be settled before Bushnell arrived.

Head again pounding, he started for the house. The more he considered this new problem, the worse it seemed.

Bushnell was poison. Though not the most revolting of Sir Winton's friends, he was not an appropriate visitor to an innocent maiden. Miss Merideth was hardly old enough to be a suitable chaperon, especially when confronted by lecherous rogues. What the devil had Sir Winton been thinking?

Of course, his own stay at Vale House was just as irregular, particularly with Jon away for so long. But he had every intention of wedding her.

No wonder so many area gentlemen considered her ineligible. Entertaining Sir Winton's friends had to have tarnished her image.

Keep your mind on business.

Sighing, he glared at a busy squirrel. Jon must wed them before Bushnell arrived, so the man would find nothing even marginally disreputable. He was a consummate gossip, who put the worst interpretation on every story he told.

She has sworn for years that she would never wed . . . He shuddered. Was that why she was being so cautious? Perhaps she was waging a mental war between rectifying an injustice and reneging on a long-standing vow. After all, her reasons for considering this match were far weaker than his.

Why she eschewed marriage was harder to grasp. If it had been Miss Merideth, he could understand, for marriage would make pursuing her interests even more difficult. Never mind that she was more competent than most of those who would laugh in her face.

But Miss Vale had much to gain. She was under the thumb of a father who disdained her. She would never be unconventional enough to set up her own establishment, so why avoid marriage? Had she suffered some insult at the hands of her father's rackety friends?

Don't invent trouble. The day would be difficult enough without setting new obstacles in his path.

"A word, sir," said Murch when he reached the house.

Tony nodded.

"One of Sir Winton's friends will be arriving today," the butler began. "I must ask that you not mention the excavation. Sir Winton would never approve of his dau—the work. Since his friends always report everything they see or hear, it is best to remain discreet."

"I understand. When may we expect him?"

"Within the hour, if he follows his usual habit."

Tony must have let shock show on his face, for Murch continued. "Sir Winton encourages friends to call without warning. Their courtesy notices often arrive after they do."

Damn! That explained why the innkeeper had sent the letter to Vale House at dawn instead of waiting for the footman to collect it.

But his own plans were now futile. He could hardly barge into her room, awaken her, confess, propose, and wed her within an hour. Yet he could not allow Bushnell to expose him.

"How long will this friend remain?"

"One night, as a rule."

"There will be no problem, then," he said. "One of my school friends will pass through Gloucester this evening. Under normal circumstances, it would be rude to leave at a moment's notice, but Miss Vale might prefer that we retire during this call."

"Perhaps, though Lord Bushnell will learn of your visit." His voice was unusually dry. "I presume that Mr. Linden will accompany you?"

"He will be pleased to renew an old acquaintance. We will return in two days."

"Excellent."

Tony wrote notes to Miss Merideth and Miss Vale, then woke Jon. "We are leaving immediately," he said, tossing a valise onto the bed.

"Did she turn you down?"

"No. Bushnell will be here shortly. I can't let him expose me."

"Christ on a crutch! Why don't you just tell her the truth? Running away will only make it worse."

"Damnation! I am not running away." He fought his temper under control. "Sometimes a strategic retreat is necessary if one is to win the war. Bushnell has vices even my reputation does not embrace. Unless you wish to force Miss Vale into wedding me right now—rousting her out of bed to do so—we must leave."

"I don't understand." But he was dressing.

"If he finds me under this roof, unwed, he will destroy Miss Vale's reputation. Society will consider her a whore within the week. Nothing will deter him, for he loves inflicting pain on anyone weaker than he is." Especially Tony Linden. They'd been enemies since the night he'd responded to terrified screams at Madame LaFleur's, rescuing one of the girls from Bushnell's beating. Bushnell had been banned from the premises, taking revenge by spreading new rumors that accused him of vicious brutality.

"Dear Lord!"

"Exactly, so make haste. His carriage is coming up the drive."

He returned to his room, changing his plans yet again as he tossed items into his own valise. Adding a postscript to Miss Vale's note, he sent a footman to request that two horses meet them outside the kitchen, then led Jon down the servants' stairs. Murch might assume he was protecting his hostess, but he was also saving himself. Bushnell's malicious twist on this debacle would make it impossible to redeem his reputation.

Alex picked at her breakfast, furious at herself for not settling with Linden last night. Now she would be exposed, and in a way that would humiliate him.

Bushnell's letter lay by her plate. She hated him even more than her father's other friends. He was sneaky, with a sanctimonious facade that belied his own rackety behavior. And he treated her like an ignorant child. His lectures on manners made her so angry that she often behaved rudely just to annoy him.

Was it possible to confront Linden before Bushnell arrived? Maybe she should crawl into his bed, then summon Torwell to wed them where they lay.

She blushed.

Torwell would never accept her as a serious antiquarian after that. Where was he this morning? He should have arrived for breakfast by now.

Murch appeared in the doorway, his grave expression proving that it was too late. She had lost all control of the situation.

"Lord Bushnell has arrived, Miss Alex. I have put him in the drawing room."

"What am I to tell Linden, Murch?" She bit her lip.

"You will tell him the entire truth the moment he returns."

"Returns?" Hope nearly choked her.

Murch adopted his remotest pose. "I spoke with Mr. Torwell a short time ago, reminding him that Sir Winton is unaware of your endeavors. He immediately recalled that a friend is passing through Gloucester today. He and Mr. Linden wish to meet him."

"He is gone?"

"Nearly." Murch nodded toward the window, which over-looked the back lawn and kitchen garden. Torwell and Linden were cantering toward the trees. "He left these."

Dazed, Alex accepted two notes, one directed to Miss Merideth, the other to Miss Vale. They were formal and nearly identical.

> *. . . leaving for two days as I would not wish to embarrass you. Those disposed to gossip—such as Lord Bushnell— would not ask whether our presence threatens your modesty. He rarely looks beyond his own impressions and gleefully spreads malice about those he disapproves. Linden knows all too well how damaging false tales can be. We will do everything possible to protect you from scurrilous innuendo.*

A postscript to Miss Merideth's letter said that he would use this opportunity to visit a colleague whose extensive collection of manuscripts included a book of legends compiled by a tenth-century monk. While most were clearly myths, some provided clues to ancient sites and practices. Perhaps he could find information related to her excavation.

Miss Vale's postscript thanked her for the loan of two horses.

She grinned. Cheeky devil. Loan of her horses, indeed. But she was too delighted at this unexpected reprieve to take umbrage.

Two days. She would write out a confession and practice it. The moment Linden returned, she would see him. In the meantime, she must deal with Bushnell.

Obviously Torwell knew him. Just as obviously, he despised him—she had to admire his taste. Thus she would do well to keep both gentlemen out of the discussion.

But that hope died a quick death.

"How could you allow that wastrel into the house, Alex?" demanded Bushnell the moment she entered the drawing room.

Alex glared, even less pleased to see him than usual. He hadn't even offered a greeting or his usual apology for arriving without warning. Well, if he was willing to abandon any pretense of manners, she saw no reason to be polite. "Who might you mean?"

"Linden, of course. I was appalled to see his carriage in the stable yard. Winton will be outraged to learn that you spoke to the man. He will doubtless lock you in the cellar for inviting so evil a person inside."

"Mr. Linden's coach broke a wheel near the gates, injuring one of his horses—not that it is any of your business. But since you would have me offer refuge only to people with spotless reputations, I must ask you to leave."

"This is not your home," sputtered Bushnell. "And Linden is the business of every man of sense. The man is a pariah—a drunken gamester whose acquaintances are unfit for any drawing room."

"I saw no evidence of drinking during his brief stay," she lied.

"You are so naïve, I doubt you would recognize unsavory behavior if it slapped you in the face."

Temper flashing, she strode close enough to tower over him—he was a good foot shorter. "You have no call to take advantage of Father's generosity by sticking your nose into my business. I do recognize vice, my lord. Father's gaming is many times worse than Linden's reputed play. As is his drinking. But I welcome your warning against Linden's acquaintances. Since you know him so well, I now have another reason for asking you to leave."

Bushnell choked, then paced to the window to escape her intimidation. "You are more sheltered than I believed. I should not have mentioned his acquaintances. They have no place in genteel conversation."

"Ah. You meant his bits of muslin." She nearly laughed at the look on his face. "I may live in the country, but that does not make me ignorant. Again, I must chastise you. How can you condemn any man for enjoying the ladies? I doubt there is a gentleman in London who didn't cut a swath through the muslin company in his youth—and many still do. I have not heard that fidelity is considered a virtue in our class. Your wife has certainly turned a blind eye to your own sport."

The choking increased, turning his face purple. "He has subverted the last vestige of your manners. Where is he? I'll give him the thrashing he so richly deserves."

"Gone."

"But—"

"His carriage? He arranged for repairs, but remained only until his companion recovered from the incident. He will collect the carriage on his return."

"Companion?"

She really should not tease him, but the temptation was too great. She was heartily sick of having him chastise her several times a year. Behaving never discouraged him. Perhaps deliberate rudeness might do some good. "A most charming companion. We became quite close."

Bushnell collapsed into a chair, his face suddenly ashen. "Close?" He nearly strangled himself forcing the word out.

"Quite. We share so many interests." She paused a long moment, then cocked her head. "Your journey has wearied you, I see. Since you prose so often about proper manners, only utter exhaustion would have prompted you to sit while I remain on my feet. Perhaps some brandy would be in order."

He swallowed most of the glass before finding his voice. "What am I to tell Winton?"

"You could try the truth: His daughter is capable of conducting her own affairs. Or you could mind your own business and say nothing."

"You are absurd," he snapped, fury leaping into his eyes. "No female is capable of rational thought, as you prove every time you open your mouth. Where is Linden? I will inform him that he is not welcome to return."

"Visiting a friend."

"He has no friends."

"It is his companion's friend, my lord. Now, if you will excuse me, I have household matters to see to. If you had demonstrated even one of the social graces you are so fond of espousing, you would have warned me of your arrival so I could properly entertain you—but we have had this discussion before. You persist in behaving as a boorish lout."

She turned to leave.

"When will Linden return?" he demanded.

"I've no idea, though I suspect it will be some weeks. The party sounded quite delightful."

Walking out on him felt good. Watching horror spread over his face had been even more satisfying. And learning that he was a coward at heart—he had nearly swooned when she'd loomed over him—was downright exhilarating. For years, her father's friends had turned up to scrutinize her behavior—one reason he rarely returned home was because he received so many reports on her conduct.

She was tired of playing dutiful daughter for wastrels and gamesters. And she was doubly tired of people telling her what to think. How long could she milk his misunderstanding before revealing the truth? She hadn't had this much fun in years.

"Warn Sarah to stay abed until dinner," she murmured to Murch as she headed for her workroom—Bushnell was insulted if he had to face a cripple in the drawing room. Murch would need no other reminders. He would have heard every word of her exchange. The staff hated Bushnell's servants enough to follow Murch's lead. And he would already have locked her guests' rooms.

The fun continued through dinner. Murch readily answered Bushnell's questions, but he referred to Torwell only as Linden's companion. The rest of the staff said little, their reticence prolonging the joke by making it appear that the companion was too scandalous to discuss, or that they were too shocked to talk about it.

Sarah also helped, rhapsodizing about Linden's sweet nature and expounding on his charm, wit, and magnanimity until Bushnell nearly fell into an apoplectic fit.

Not until breakfast did she relent. Bushnell was heading for London within the hour. It would not do to have her father storm home to bar the gates. His leg might be improved enough for carriage travel.

"I have ordered Murch to deny admittance to Linden if he dares to return," Bushnell informed her as he filled his plate with ham and kidneys—the footman who normally served meals was pointedly absent.

"You have no authority over my staff," she said stiffly.

"Someone of sense must take charge," he countered. "Anyone who allows a light-skirt into the house belongs in Bedlam."

"Light-skirt?" She laughed heartily. "It is you who belongs in Bedlam, sir. Carousing with Father has addled your wits—if you had any left after so many debauches in opium dens." She met his furious glare. "I warned you I was not sheltered. You are not the only one who revels in carrying tales, my lord. Father is free with news of his friends. I've heard many stories about you, including full details of that contretemps that barred you for life from Madame LaFleur's brothel."

He ignored her aside. "Do not think that changing stories will save you. You clearly stated that Linden brought a companion with him."

"And you thought he brought his mistress? Your mind is mired in vice, sir. How can a gentleman assume that a lady would speak thusly? You insult me. You insult Mr. Linden. And you especially insult Mr. Anthony, who is spending several weeks with a school friend, studying his collection of religious manuscripts. His parishioners would be horrified by your suspicions."

"Parishioners?" His face was purpling again. If the man did not learn to control himself, he would likely die of a fit.

"He is vicar to a parish in Lincolnshire—quite revered, as I understand it. I've seldom met a man more dedicated to his work. He will be sorry to have missed you, for he is always in search of souls worth saving."

"I am amazed that he would waste his time on Linden."

"Really? I am amazed at how easily you deceive yourself by jumping to ridiculous and wholly unwarranted conclusions. I must question what other baseless notions you might hold, particularly about Mr. Linden, who strikes me as the sort of man who might mention your failings to your face. Are you pursuing a personal quarrel? I cannot envision a reasonable gentleman railing so forcefully against someone I found quite charming."

"Ingrate!"

"I owe you nothing, sir. Your officious interference has been the bane of my existence. Since you have such poor judgment, I prefer to follow my own instincts rather than listen to your sensational scandal. I trust you will have a good journey to London. Perhaps you will spare my delicate sensibilities in future by calling only when Father is in residence. I may have no authority to deny you his roof, but I am displeased at the liberties you have taken with my staff. And am I appalled at your determination to order my life. Next time you suffer this urge to be fatherly, stay home long enough to set up your nursery—or take charge of the bastards with which you have already littered the landscape."

"Alexandra!" His eyes protruded from a purple face.

"You are doing it again. If you do not enjoy my company, then avoid it. I see no need to display exquisite manners before a man who has none. That would place me at a disadvantage, in the same way a greenling is helpless against a card sharp."

He whitened, confirming her suspicions that he was a cheat. "You can be sure that your father will hear of this," he said, rising.

"You can be sure that he will hear of your insults. But I no longer care what he thinks, so your threats are empty. He has more to lose from annoying me than he could ever gain by locking me up. You seem to forget that I am of age, and have been for some time. Good day, sir."

It was true, she realized as she strode from the room, giving him no chance to respond. And her father would surely have realized it by now. In turning the Linden fortune over to her, he had lost any access to it—until she wed.

Her euphoria over routing Bushnell faded. The fortune was out of reach until she married. Thus Sir Winton had a strong incentive to find her a weak-willed husband. It would allow him to dip into the funds whenever he ran short.

She should not have insulted Bushnell. Always before, she had played the role of untutored rustic with her father's friends, being obnoxious enough to discourage any interest, but stopping short of presenting a challenge they would be compelled to meet. More than one considered himself an irresistible lover. But this time she had revealed her determination. If Sir Winton recognized that, he might take steps to force obedience—like locking her into a room with whichever man he chose, and leaving her there until she was obviously increasing.

Or killing her. She had not asked what would happen to the trust if she died unwed.

She must settle with Linden the moment he returned. She could only hope he really did have a special license in his pocket. Her father could be here in four days.

Blue-devils banished the last of her euphoria as she headed to the villa. The confrontation with Bushnell had raised the memory of all her dealings with gentlemen, and not just those sent by her father. Belligerence was her usual style—scoffing at statements, slipping cant phrases and even mild curses into her speech, intruding into conversations involving money or crops or the latest mill, as if trying to prove she knew as much as they.

Which she did.

She had carried her aversions too far. While it was true that she had vowed never to wed, her aggressiveness pushed men so far away that even friendship was impossible. And she was the loser, as the past fortnight showed. By adopting an agreeable role with Linden, she had set the stage for her growing friendship with Torwell.

If it continued. He might never forgive her deceit.

Thoroughly out of sorts, she dragged out her tools and resumed her original excavation of the temple. Continuing the work they had started two days ago was too depressing.

Chapter Ten

"Send for Simms," shouted Tony when Murch opened the Vale House door. He helped a moaning Jon from his horse, then caught him when his legs gave out.

"Drunk?" asked Murch, grabbing Jon's other arm. He had flung an order over his shoulder, then raced at unbutlerly speed to help.

"Bad fish. I warned him not to eat it."

Jon choked, then vomited onto the drive. Little remained in his stomach, but that did not mitigate the violence of the attack.

"How long has he been like this?" asked Murch.

"An hour. I wasn't sure we'd make it back."

They maneuvered him up the steps and into the hall, where he sagged onto a chair.

"He's in for an unpleasant day," observed Murch as Simms hurried in.

"At least." He shook Jon's arm. "Wake up, Linden. One more flight of stairs."

Jon groaned.

"We will have to carry him, sir." Simms shrugged.

Half an hour passed before they finished stripping Jon and tucking him into bed. His stomach rebelled again before they finished.

Tony sighed. This was not how he had envisioned his return. But even more urgent than settling with Miss Vale were his questions about Bushnell. He had meant to stop first at the stables to make sure the baron was gone, but Jon's illness had made that impossible. And he also wondered how Miss Vale had survived the visit.

Bushnell might be a friend of Sir Winton, but his bad reputation was well earned. In addition to the usual vices, the man was an opium-eater, which made his behavior quite unpredictable.

"Is Lord Bushnell still here?" he finally asked Murch.

"He stayed only the one night." He paused, then continued. "I was not sorry to see his backside, sir. He was even more officious than usual."

"Violent?"

"No. I've never known him to turn violent."

Seeing the question in Murch's eye, Tony pressed on. The Vale affairs would soon be his business. "Is Sir Winton aware that Bushnell craves opium?"

"He has said nothing to me." But his eyes darkened with fury.

"His need grows stronger every year, leading to unpredictable and often violent outbursts. He's injured several people in London, a fact society ignores, for his victims are from the lower classes—so far. It is only a matter of time before he turns on one of his peers."

"He will not be welcomed here again, on Miss Vale's orders. Thank you for providing a reason that Sir Winton cannot dispute."

"Where is she today?"

Murch's response died as Miss Vale burst into the room, maid in tow. Jon was rolling about in new pain.

"Miss Vale," Tony began, but she brushed past him with only a distracted smile.

"Try to relax, Mr. Linden," she said, snatching the cloth Simms was using to wipe Jon's sweating brow. Crowding the valet aside, she bent over the patient. "How frequent are his attacks?"

Tony answered. "A quarter hour. Perhaps a little longer."

"Has he had laudanum?"

"No. It always makes him ill."

Jon's face had been flushing and paling in rapid succession. Now he erupted in a new attack that Simms barely caught in the basin.

"Lie back," said Miss Vale softly, adding soothing sounds as she again wiped his face. The maid produced a cup. "Drink this—slowly. It will calm you."

"Come along, sir," said Murch, distracting Tony from the improbable scene. "Mr. Linden is in good hands. They are experienced with nursing."

"But—" He shook his head. He'd considered Miss Vale an insipid innocent, but she hadn't turned a hair at Jon's display. He'd been right. She had depths he didn't know.

But he would have no opportunity to speak with her before dinner.

"Is Miss Merideth working today?"

Murch nodded.

"I will join her. Send word if Linden's condition worsens."

He doubted it would. He'd suffered from bad food often enough to know that Jon would be confined to bed until tomorrow, but he should be recovered by then.

"Mr. Torwell!" Alex was shocked at the pleasure washing over her as he dismounted in the clearing. "We did not expect you until dinner. Are your friends well?"

"Quite, though I learned nothing about your site. But that itself is useful. If this had been a temple complex, or even a town, some reference would surely have survived. So it was likely a villa."

"What brings you back so early?" she asked, wrenching her thoughts from the way his eyes blazed green in the sun.

"I promised to return today, and I always keep my word—though this time that meant rushing before that fish Linden insisted on for breakfast caught up with him."

"Oh, no!"

"Afraid so. I left him tied to a basin, with Miss Vale, her maid, and Simms in attendance." His voice turned it into a joke, though the man must be suffering.

But this meant she could not speak to Linden until tomorrow. Unconscionably pleased, she climbed out of her trench. "He is in good hands, then. Look what I found this morning." She held out a bit of brass.

"A buckle. That's the best discovery in days." Gathering his own tools, he set to work.

Two hours later, Alex glanced up from a jumble of broken tile. She had returned to the trench they'd started two days ago, pushing it forward. Though flues and clumps of bricks turned up in large numbers, some still holding traces of plaster that hinted they had once formed a wall, she'd found no trace of the floor. And even undamaged tiles no longer raised enough excitement to keep her mind on work. Torwell was too great a distraction.

At first, he had talked about his trip, repeating several impious tales and sarcastic remarks he'd found in the old monk's journal. She'd laughed, even at the earthier ones. But he'd been silent for nearly an hour now. As their trenches inched closer together, she became too aware of his coat stretching across shoulders powerful enough to wrestle rocks from the ground that she couldn't budge. Of the narrow waist and lean hips that had once filled the very clothes she wore. Of muscular legs that added shape to even the loosest work pantaloons.

What the devil was wrong with her? She never noticed men's physiques, and certainly should not notice Torwell's. Working with him would become extremely uncomfortable.

She was merely unsettled from the strain of preparing to meet Linden, she assured herself. And she was warm because the day was unseasonably mild. Removing her jacket, she returned to work.

It did no good. Within minutes, her eyes were again riveted on Torwell. Exertion had also made him toss his jacket aside. He never wore waistcoats while digging. Muscles rippled as he heaved another stone out of the way. She could feel her hands sliding across that wavy surface.

Hard resilience.

That's what it felt like. She blushed, recalling how her hands rested on his shoulders whenever he helped her dismount. Three days ago her foot had caught in the stirrup, throwing all her weight against him as she slid down that masculine chest— hard, hot, unbelievably virile . . .

Odd sensations tightened her breasts.

Jealousy blinding your senses . . .

Cheeks flaming, she drove her spade into the trench.

Stupid fool! Stronger epithets filled her mind. Sarah was right. She'd formed a *tendre* for the man. Somehow he'd slipped past her defenses and . . .

No. It wasn't his fault. She was the one who had let him in. How could she have been so foolish?

The situation had just become impossibly complicated. Working together must cease, for she could never hide her infatuation. But the real harm would be to Linden. He was known for escorting beautiful women. It was bad enough to saddle him with a towering, mannish redhead who would be unwelcome in society. It was unconscionable to force a wife on him who was attracted to another. And not just any other, but his own cousin, a man who was central in his life. How could she have been so stupid? She, who had sworn to avoid all men.

The spade scraped stone, but this time the surface felt different. Gasping, she exchanged it for a trowel, wrenching her mind back to the excavation. In her agitation, she had deepened the trench well below its previous level.

"My God!"

"What!"

"Mosaic." Rubbing removed the last sheen of dirt, revealing a bed of cream and brown tiles forming intertwining lines.

Torwell squeezed in beside her. "Dear Lord!" He dug into the walls, widening her hole. "I wonder how much is undamaged."

"Or what room this was. Would this design be in an entrance hall, or is this the family quarters? Perhaps that first trench was a storeroom rather than a new wing."

"Or the slave quarters."

Her eyes jerked up. "I forgot that even here the Romans used slaves."

"Most civilizations have done so. Only now are people admitting that it is wrong. But slavery was not a permanent condition in the Roman empire. Many slaves were eventually freed. Some even achieved positions of influence."

"Which doesn't make the practice right."

He grinned. "A reformer. I should have known." His eyes dropped back to the tile. "Let's see what we've got here . . ." They had exposed two feet of floor, intact.

"Beautiful, but I thought Roman mosaics formed pictures." She kept her voice carefully neutral. His grin had nearly made her swoon. This had to be their last day together. He wouldn't want her assistance once he learned the truth anyway.

"They did, but most also include a border. The floors commonly found in this area have very complex borders. In fact, this reminds me of the inner frame at Woodchester. That mosaic starts with an outer band of line work. Inside is a wider band of square panels, each displaying a different geometric pattern, though they are so damaged that the actual designs are difficult to follow. Inside that is the picture. They are quite different from the mosaics found in Lincolnshire, which rarely have more than one narrow frame."

"You wrote a paper expounding regional variations, as I recall."

"Which you read. I'll try not to repeat myself." He gazed at the mosaic, awe clearly lighting his face. "This might be a variation of the Woodchester design—if it's in a room. Mitchell once postulated that wealthy Romans used mosaic even on paths in courtyards."

He was already widening the trench, tunneling into its side to follow the floor. She did the same in the other direction. At least this discovery was exciting enough to distract her from his nearness.

"This is so similar to the Woodchester floor that it could well be by the same artist," murmured Torwell, more to himself than to her. "I can't believe its condition. This fragment alone is in better shape than the best piece there. How was it spared?"

The question set her mind working. Only distraction had

caused her to dig so deep. But she'd turned up an undamaged floor, so their conclusions about the original ground level must be wrong. Yet those ideas had been based on the volume of hypocaust remnants they'd found at higher levels. Were there two villas, or had the slide churned debris until depth had no meaning?

She glanced toward the cliffs. Perhaps the complex had extended farther to the north, with the slide scraping away even the foundations of the first buildings it encountered, then dumping them atop the buildings that had filled what was now the clearing.

Jon awoke, afraid to blink lest it set his stomach roiling. Never again would he ignore Tony's suspicions about food.

Pain sliced through his abdomen, but this time it settled into a dull ache similar to those spawned by overexertion.

"Good. You're awake."

Miss Vale. His face heated at the memory of her hand on his brow as he retched his insides out, again and again. Why the devil had Tony allowed her into his bedchamber? Squeezing his eyes shut, he tried to pretend she wasn't there. Never had he been in so compromising a position.

"Drink this." A soft hand turned his head. "Come on. I know you can hear me. This will make you feel better."

"What is it?"

"Peppermint tea."

Aunt Mary had used peppermint tea. Cracking one eye, he opened his mouth. She spooned in tea, washing away the foul taste. Peppermint curled warmly in his stomach, easing the ache.

"Thank you," he murmured when he finished.

"I believe he can manage a little more, Bessie."

The words jerked his eyes wide open.

Bessie pulled a kettle from the fire, adding liquid to his cup. Simms sat in the corner, stitching up the shirt he'd ripped leaping off his horse when the first attack hit yesterday. Miss Vale had pulled a chair closer to his bed and was reaching out to wipe a cool cloth over his forehead. He'd not had such an audience for sleeping since that bout of influenza when he was fourteen.

His blush deepened.

"Are you feverish?" she asked, touching his brow.

Not the way she meant, though he was burning from head to toe. "Merely embarrassed." But the admission brought on a new wave of heat. Finding a pretty girl in his bedchamber would never embarrass Tony Linden.

"You needn't be. This is not the first time I've treated a victim of bad food."

"Really? Nursing is not a usual occupation for a single lady."

Delicate pink touched her cheeks. "Perhaps not, but our doctor is so incompetent that I've had little choice. Tenants often need help, as do the villagers."

"That is true, regardless of the doctor's skill," he mumbled. "Many people cannot afford professional fees, and some cannot even pay an apothecary. Aun-Mother sees after as many as possible." Which wasn't as many as she would like. Uncle Thomas did not want her gallivanting about the countryside.

His eyes sagged shut as he continued. "Poor Mrs. Watts might have died last winter without help. She was widowed many years ago, but her portion barely covers her barest needs. We found her half-frozen in February, suffering a serious ague, and with coal enough for only the meanest cooking fire. I brought her home until she recovered, then organized the neighbors to call on her regularly." His voice fell as he slid toward sleep. But remembering his fury at Uncle Thomas roused him. The man had actually berated him for allowing the woman to recover at the vicarage. She was on the list of those he disapproved, because she occasionally played loo for pennies with other village widows.

"We have widows in that position, as well," said Miss Vale, pulling him out of his thoughts.

He'd better pay attention. Tony would be furious if he revealed the truth by prattling overmuch—and rightly so. Only his own stubbornness had put him in this bed. And it must have prevented Tony from confessing—again. He'd probably gone out to his digging.

He glanced at the window. Sunlight. So the charade must continued a few hours longer.

She was watching him, a frown creasing her forehead.

She certainly was easy on the eyes. And relaxing to talk to. Their daily chats delighted him, for she was the first woman he'd ever met who didn't make him trip over his own feet—except for that first night.

He blushed to recall his gauche behavior. Tony had assumed he was playacting, but that was untrue. He'd been terrified, unable to admit his failings, yet knowing they would come out. He froze around strangers, unable to think or behave in any normal way. Even with people he knew, he could never relax with females unless they were very young or very old. From the moment Tony had broached this masquerade, he'd known that he could never manage the role. Yet he'd had to try, for Aunt Mary's sake.

In desperation, he had gulped wine, trying to banish his fears—and paid dearly for the stupidity. Yet even after he'd made a complete ass of himself, Miss Vale accepted him. He no longer felt awkward or backward with her. She radiated contentment, relaxing anyone nearby.

Tony had better take very good care of her, and not just materially. He would not sit by and allow his cousin to ignore her. She deserved to be cherished.

Sir Winton's descriptions echoed in his ears. *Freak. Deformed. Unnatural.* When Tony had repeated them, he hadn't believed that anyone could describe his own child in such terms. Even Uncle Thomas had never gone that far. For all the man's tirades, he loved his son.

But Miss Merideth had confirmed that Sir Winton despised the clubfoot and refused to even eat with the girl. Murch had said the same thing. How could anyone turn against someone so warm and caring? And how could anyone become warm and caring with a father who despised her?

"Miss Horton has the same problem," Miss Vale said.

He'd missed quite a bit of conversation. "But you will take care of her," he murmured.

"As best I can."

"What would you recommend for rheumatism? I know several people who suffer from it."

She sighed. "Nothing relieves it for long, but I've had positive results using powders of devil bit—the root of the devil's claw—and a tonic containing willow bark tea and St. John's wort. Soaking the hands in warm water helps local stiffness," she added unnecessarily. Everyone knew that effect.

His eyelids grew heavier. "How long until Ton–Torwell returns?"

"Two or three hours, at least. You know they always use every minute of daylight." She picked up a piece of needlework and settled back into her chair. "Did you enjoy visiting Mr. Torwell's friend?"

"Very much. Both of them." She made a soothing picture that banished the last of his embarrassment.

"Were they traveling together?"

"No." He blinked, forcing his mind off the needle sparkling between long, elegant fingers. "The second lives near Gloucester. His library contains records from an ancient abbey. Torwell had hoped to find references to the temple Miss Merideth is excavating, but his brief search was unsuccessful."

They talked for at least an hour. He took pains to describe Tony in the best possible light. She would need that image to counter the shock of learning Tony's identity. With luck everything would be settled by evening, including the wedding.

The special license was in his valise. Getting it had been easy once he'd found the information the application required. But he'd had to search half the library to learn Miss Vale's full name. Sir Winton did not keep the family Bible in plain view.

Alexandra Merideth Vale. A pretty name for a beautiful lady. Her family must follow the same custom as his—using the mother's family name as one of the child's Christian names.

Anthony Torwell Linden.

Jonathan Concord Linden.

Alexandra Merideth Vale. So Miss Merideth's father would have been Lady Vale's brother. The portrait in the gallery must depict a young Lady Vale, for she bore a startling resemblance to Miss Merideth. Family likenesses were often quite strong . . .

He slept.

Tony gouged his tunnel deeper, feeling for the uneven surface of mosaic tiles. His other hand scooped the loosened soil into the trench behind him.

He was having trouble breathing. The more they uncovered, the more complex the design appeared. And it was in better shape than anything he'd ever seen. The villa's size had not been his only miscalculation. Mud must have flowed inside before its collapse, cushioning the floors. Or at least this one . . .

That would account for the double fan, he realized, pausing to shovel the accumulated dirt from the trench. Heavy rainfall could wash vast quantities of mud from the hills. The temple had been on a rise that might have deflected the flow through the villa. Even if it were liquid enough to leave walls intact, it would have piled mud and debris in every corner and carried possessions away. It might even have filled the hypocaust and knocked down rickety outbuildings, battering bricks into dust as it tumbled downhill. Stone walls surrounding the grounds could have deflected everything toward the east. Had the paving stones in the test hole actually been the top of a wall?

Then the hill itself had collapsed, dropping mud and rock straight onto the hapless villa, folding the northern edges atop more protected areas—much like his test slide had scraped away some of the mound. But most of the debris would have been swept straight south.

At least part of this room had been deep in mud by then. A foot of soil lay between the mosaic and the artifacts they had been uncovering. How much of the floor had survived?

His mind raced with the implications of this discovery. Once word leaked out—as it was bound to—the estate would be overrun with scholars, fortune hunters, and the curious. Sir Winton would dig out the floor and sell it to the highest bidder.

That might be the best solution for its ultimate preservation, of course, for protecting it here would be nearly impossible. Unscrupulous people had been known to sneak onto a site and chip away sections of mosaic, especially mosaic of this quality. Even guards were not immune to greed.

The artist had been an exquisite craftsman. Many mosaics were quite crude, especially in the border areas. But not this one.

His fingers jammed against stone. Had he hit the foundation of the wall that had once enclosed this room, or a bit of debris?

Shifting to allow as much light as possible into the hole, he brushed the floor. More design, but in a simpler pattern. Brown and red. Probably the outer frame. Thus the stone would be a foundation block.

"I just hit the wall," he announced, abandoning his digging, "so unless this was a walkway, the center of the room is on your side." As soon as they had a better idea of the room's size, they could stake out the edges and work their way in. With luck, mud had filled the hypocaust without damaging the floor supports. But even if this was the only intact piece, it was the find of a lifetime.

"The pattern is changing," she confirmed. Instead of tunneling as he had done, she had been shaving the trench walls.

"To brown and red?"

But the question was unnecessary, for he was already clearing loose soil from the mosaic. It was a room. And, at least at this point, the floor was unbroken.

He worked back along the trench, deepening it to this new level. When he'd cleared enough space to work, he turned toward the room's center. Occasionally, he brushed against Miss Merideth's arm or leg, but he hardly noticed in the excitement of uncovering a masterpiece. He *did* note how his donated shirt clung to her breasts, though. But even that could not distract him for long.

An hour later, he stared at the result. "Incredible."

A cat snarled, one paw poised to strike, though its body was still buried. A circular frame curved beneath the second paw.

"The corner panel," he said softly.

"Corner panel?" Awe thickened her voice. Her eyes never strayed from the mosaic.

He used the point of his trowel to carve a quick sketch into the trench wall. "Rooms in the Glevum region were usually square. The brown and red outer frame I found would have run along the edge, about a foot wide. The panel frame is two feet wide, forming a square that should contain the circular main picture, also framed." He pointed at the frame under the cat's paw. "These triangular sections filled the corners between the circle and the square. Judging from the curve, this room might be as much as eighteen feet across. We came in near the center of one wall." He stood, his eyes already noting the probable locations of the other walls. If the entire floor was intact . . .

"The cat looks alive." She stroked the raised paw.

"Exquisite workmanship," he agreed. "I hope the entire mosaic was executed by the same artist."

"Why wouldn't it be?"

"I've seen several mosaics that show different levels of expertise. Maybe an impatient owner hired a dozen workmen— laying mosaic is a slow process. Or perhaps he ran out of money and had to finish with an apprentice. Or the artist may have died, or been lured away by a more influential patron. Or someone might have fixed a damaged floor a century after it had originally been laid. Who knows?"

She stood to gaze around the clearing, seeming not to have heard him. But her hands trembled.

"Are you all right?"

"Yes. No." She shook her head to clear it. "I can't seem to take it in."

"Shock." He grinned as his own euphoria broke free. "This is the best-preserved floor I've ever seen."

"I've never seen a Roman mosaic. I had no idea. The tiles we found the other day gave no hint of their potential."

"They wouldn't. Pieces were shaped as they were laid. And a true artist used gradations in color and even inclusions to heighten the impact of his work."

She again stared at the cat, her smile broadening until it

matched his own grin. Suddenly, she laughed and threw her arms around his shoulders. "It's real. The villa is real. It's fabulous. I can't believe it was just sitting here, waiting for us. I could have found it two days ago if I'd only dug a little deeper."

His own excitement flared, bursting in a wave of exhilaration. He twirled her around, nearly knocking her feet against the trench wall. Without thought, he hugged her closer and kissed her.

The first touch of her lips drove the villa from his mind. Heat rampaged through his body. Scorching heat that burned away memory of every kiss he had savored in thirty-two years of living. Pulling her closer, he prodded her lips, drinking in her taste as she responded. What had started as a simple act of celebration rapidly turned to searing passion.

She tightened arms strengthened by hours of digging, dragging him into her skin. He'd been drooling since the moment she'd removed her jacket, revealing nipples pinched tight from the chill air. Now they dug into his chest, separated only by two thin layers of cambric.

Mine. His hand slid down her hip, kneading, stroking, calling forth the moans that sang like a Siren's song in his ears. Her legs tangled with his, lacking the usual bulk of skirts and petticoats that formed so frustrating a barrier.

Mine, echoed his body as fire swirled into his groin and excitement sizzled along every nerve. He could not be more aroused if she lay naked beneath him.

Not yours! his conscience screamed. He froze.

Alex's emotions had shifted so often in the last hour that she hardly knew what she was doing. Guilt. Pain. Shock. Excitement. Euphoria. When Torwell's mouth crushed into hers, it set off an explosion that drove every rational thought from her mind.

His body was as hard as she'd remembered, and far hotter. He radiated heat, excitement, passion . . .

She clung, amazed to feel almost fragile in his arms. Her hands roamed freely over his back, around his shoulders, into his hair. She opened her mouth to him, the exchange of breath raising desire that weakened her knees.

I actually feel normal!

He was tall enough that kissing was not awkward—for either of them, though that was a stupid thought. He was far too good at this to ever feel awkward. His tongue twisted around hers in an erotic dance that melted her bones. She pressed closer to keep from falling, reveling in the feel of his body, shocked to realize she was grinding against him as if she were trying to crawl inside his skin.

He stiffened.

Dear Lord! She was on the verge of ripping the clothes off a man she could never wed.

She stepped back.

"Forgive me," he begged woodenly. "The excitement of the moment carried me away."

"And me," she said shakily, though all her senses protested the lost contact. "Since I started it, it is I who must beg your pardon. One does not discover so rare a treasure very often."

"True." He retrieved his spade and trowel. "Let's see how much of the cat remains. Then we need to discuss how to protect it."

"From the weather?"

The last trace of pleasure drained from his face. "From men. Do not mention this to anyone, even Miss Vale, until we secure the site. Looters have destroyed even amateurish mosaics. Once word of this leaks, it will become the target of every treasure hunter in England and beyond."

That sobering thought kept her silent for the rest of the afternoon.

He was right to raise the issue, but she could not escape the conclusion that doing so now was deliberate. He had sensed that her reaction transcended mere celebration. As he'd done last week, he was reminding her that they were colleagues only. He had no interest in her as a woman, so unless she got her unruly passions under control, they could not even work together.

A moot point. After tonight, he would never allow her near one of his digs anyway—assuming Linden was recovered enough to receive her.

Chapter Eleven

Alex paced her bedchamber, oblivious to the spectacular sunrise outside her window.

The evening had been a worse disaster than the afternoon. Linden had remained in his room. His valet never left his bedside, so she had no opportunity to talk to him. And Sarah had insisted on sharing his dinner, claiming that he would feel neglected if he had only servants for company. Thus Bessie had also been there.

She should have joined them, she admitted, pounding a well-worn circuit from fireplace to window to dressing table and back. Dining with Torwell had been the most uncomfortable experience of her life. Their stilted conversation—if a few terse exchanges separated by interminable periods of silence could be termed conversation—demonstrated how far she had stepped across the line. Gone were the easy repartee, the sparkling wit, the enjoyable debates when they argued opposite sides of a question. Gone were the smiles, the relaxation, the anticipation of the next day's dig.

Every gesture revived memories she was trying to forget—his hand curling around a wineglass as it had curled into her thigh; his eyes glinting green in the candlelight when he turned to speak with Murch; his tongue sliding along his lip in search of a wayward crumb . . .

Her body had burned with recollection. She'd barely stifled a moan. Thank God his attention had remained firmly on his plate, leaving him unaware of her reaction. She had escaped even before the dessert course, pleading fatigue.

He'd been relieved.

How could she have been so stupid? Throwing herself at him was bad enough—and she could only thank fate that he was an honorable, trustworthy vicar; Linden would have taken advantage of such an opportunity—but losing control of herself was beyond comprehension. She'd nearly ripped his clothes off! He'd been appalled, though he was gentleman enough to take the blame.

Not that it mattered who was at fault. The incident had destroyed their partnership, to say nothing of her peace of mind. She couldn't sleep. Even lying down was impossible, for it brought a surge of memory so strong, she could actually feel him against her—deepening his kisses, crushing her closer, sucking and biting and moaning . . .

Sensation flooded every inch of her body. Groaning with needs she barely understood, she sank to the floor, her head in her hands.

So this was desire. More proof that she was no lady. But perhaps that would appeal to Linden. He preferred the unconventional. How would his kisses affect her? She couldn't imagine anything better than Torwell's, but then until yesterday, she could not have imagined his, either. His technique was lethal.

He sure doesn't kiss like a vicar.

"And how would you know?" she demanded, climbing to her feet. "You have no experience. Stop thinking of Torwell and concentrate on Linden." But she could not imagine kissing Linden. Or even touching him.

"Stupid," she muttered, pacing the floor. "It's the same body—broad shoulders, narrow hips, hard muscles. Same coloring, even." But her mind remained unconvinced. The thought of running her fingers through *his* dark hair left her cold.

Shoving the image aside, she concentrated on the mosaic and on Torwell, the antiquarian. Mortification was no excuse to avoid him. They had business that could not be postponed, no matter how uncomfortable the meeting would be.

Working silently, they had uncovered the rest of the cat, flinching whenever their hands or arms accidentally touched. It was a beautiful piece of work, pristine except for minor damage near its tail.

Awe had filled his face, though he remained as far from her as the trench allowed. She recognized his discomfort, for it mirrored her own.

Desperate to get away, they'd tossed their tools in the shed and galloped back to the house. Thus they'd not yet held that discussion about security.

But she needed his ideas before he left.

As clearly as if he'd told her, she knew he would never visit the villa again. If not for his cousin, he would have fled Vale House last night. Once she confessed to Linden—which was another unpleasant chore that awaited her this morning—Torwell would leave. Only loyalty to Linden would keep him here long enough to preside at the wedding.

Or would it? Even a vicar would have recognized her infatuation during that wild embrace. Was Linden Park worth saddling his cousin with a wife who cared for another?

But the decision would not be his. He was too honest to remain quiet once he learned her identity. So Linden would make his own choice, fully aware of the facts. He had come here intending to wed a stranger, so her own feelings would hardly sway him.

Unless . . . If Linden wanted the entire fortune, why had he said nothing to Sarah? He might have postponed his offer to give Torwell more time at the villa, but that was far from certain. If he had talked Torwell into taking the bride, her confession could send them both fleeing. Torwell had made no attempt to hide his revulsion once he realized who was in his arms, and Linden was clearly having second thoughts about wedding anyone.

Her head spun.

"I am so stupid," she snapped, loathing in her tone. "Why the devil did I ever think this would work?"

Linden was a problem she would address later, for he would not rise for several hours yet. Torwell was more immediate.

He undoubtedly planned to leave today, if only to protect himself from further assault. It would be months, if not years, before they could face each other without remembering.

And cursing.

She rubbed her chest to assuage the pain.

It had been a euphoric moment, which explained his initial response. Men would consort with anyone if the moment was right. But when he calmed enough to recognize her, he had pulled away, flinching in horror. The shock on his face had frozen something in her soul.

He would never have embraced her on his own. And now that he knew she was susceptible to lust, he would stay as far from her as possible.

This time the pain was harsher. Her father had always claimed she was a freak. His charges sounded more damning than ever as she admitted the folly she'd been trying to ignore since Torwell had recoiled from her embrace.

She had fallen in love with him.

"Ass!" she hissed at herself, adding every curse she had heard during a lifetime of living in the shadows while her father and his debauched friends swaggered through the sunlight.

The situation was impossible—more than impossible. She was incapable of inspiring affection in any man. Linden would take her only to recover his fortune, though even he might balk at this point. If he did, would Torwell step in, sacrificing himself to save his family? It would be like him.

Fool!

She was becoming as fanciful as the most pea-brained, moonstruck widgeon. She could never accept Torwell. He might have treated her as a colleague before she'd destroyed even that relationship, but he found her unattractive. She would be happier with Linden. At least neither of them would expect anything from the other.

"Accept it, Alex. You have no future there. The sooner you admit it, the sooner you can get over him. Now pull yourself together and face the morning."

Her reflection stared back from the mirror, convinced that control was impossible.

At least not today. She knew what she must do. Talking to Linden was hopeless. Discussing security with Torwell was worse.

And if Sarah saw her in this state, she would shower her with compassion that would break her down completely.

Donning her riding habit, she slipped down the servants' stairs. Stroud was far enough away to provide a welcome escape from her memories, and she had business there anyway. It would make a pleasant all-day excursion. By the time she returned, she could face Linden.

Tony spent half the night cursing himself. It was natural to embrace a colleague after finding something as spectacular as that mosaic. But the exuberance of the moment was no excuse for kissing her. Never mind that she had responded. She was too innocent to know what she was doing.

But he was far from innocent.

There were so many things wrong with the way he'd devoured her, that he hardly knew where to start. She was an unwed lady closely related to the woman he must wed. She was a colleague for whom he had the deepest respect. How could he have treated her like a light-skirt?

Dinner had been the most uncomfortable meal of his life. He'd tried to find the words to apologize and put their partnership back together. But they wouldn't come. Everything sounded hopelessly stilted or fatuously frivolous or downright insincere.

No surprise there. How could he sound contrite when he wasn't the least sorry? That had been the most exciting encounter of his life. But their partnership was hopelessly compromised. Like the fallen Humpty Dumpty, nothing could put it together again.

He finally fell asleep, not waking until nearly eleven. But that was good. Miss Merideth would be at the villa, so he needn't fear seeing her. Instead, he would seek out Miss Vale, confess his other sins, and place a betrothal between him and temptation before he must face her again.

Girding himself for this new confrontation, he headed for the breakfast room. Jon and Miss Vale were already there.

"Feeling better?" he asked Jon. He'd been too agitated last night to check his cousin's condition.

"Much," said Jon. Yet his breakfast consisted solely of porridge.

"Merideth is in Stroud today," said Miss Vale in response to his greeting. "She urges you to continue the work without her."

"Why did you not accompany her? Winter will soon be here. You won't have many more opportunities before spring."

"I never go to town," she objected, blushing.

"Why? Carriage travel is quite easy."

She shrugged. "Sir W—Father forbids it. Flaunting my deformity before a world I can never enter is rude and pointless."

Jon gasped.

A burning sensation settled in Tony's stomach. "Forgive me for insulting your father, but he lied. You belong in society. His only reason for denying you entrance is a selfish disdain for anyone's needs but his own."

She stared, but shook her head. "He was thinking of me. Enduring stares and whispers is never enjoyable."

"Nonsense!" Jon's objection was so unexpectedly loud, the footman dropped a dish. "Your limp is no worse than Byron's, and he was welcomed into every drawing room in London until his behavior forced him to flee the country."

Her eyes widened. She carefully set her cup aside.

"Do the tenants and villagers stare and whisper?" asked Tony softly. Jon rarely spoke strongly about anything, and his willingness to use a man he loathed as an example was nothing short of astonishing. But Miss Vale's isolation had given him an idea that should carry his plans to fruition.

"N-no, but they would hardly be rude to their betters."

"Class has nothing to do with it. They are accustomed to you, seeing only your character, not your foot. Just as society saw Byron."

She stared.

"Murch tells me the hill near Painswick offers a spectacular view. Have you seen it?"

"No."

"Then let us spend the day there. It promises to be warm, unseasonably so, possibly the last warm day until spring. We can picnic in the sunshine."

Her eyes gleamed, then faded. "Mr. Linden is not recovered enough for an outing, and you would surely prefer to work on this last warm day of autumn."

"An outing would be just the thing," claimed Jon, understanding Tony's purpose.

"And I cannot work in Miss Merideth's absence. She would be disappointed if I found anything interesting. Shall we leave in an hour?"

Her eyes moved from him to Jon. As she nodded, her face filled with joy and awe. And hope.

Tony swallowed renewed fury, wishing Sir Winton were at hand. The man deserved a thrashing.

Sarah paused on the carriage step to survey the hilltop, hardly noticing that it was Torwell who steadied her hand rather than the expected Linden. She'd never seen anything so lovely.

Her heart had been hammering ever since Linden's outburst at breakfast. Was it true that well-born people might not consider her an object of pity to be scorned or avoided? His shock had been real. As had Torwell's, but one expected tolerance from vicars.

She had accepted Linden's compliments as the pretense they so obviously were. He had no choice but to pursue the lady he thought controlled his birthright. Ambivalence about actually wedding her had caused so many blunders that first night, that Torwell had stepped in to bolster his courtship, dumping the butter boat over her head in an effort to soften Linden's reputation. But he was no more sincere than Linden. Once Alex confessed—she again cursed her cousin's vacillation—both men would ignore her. So their genuine shock over her lifelong incarceration was all the more exciting.

She had not traveled farther than the village since arriving at Vale House eight years ago. Her uncle had reluctantly taken her in after her father died, but he had made his conditions clear. She was to remain out of sight whenever he was at home, and she was never to flaunt her deformity before callers, particularly those of breeding. She had expected that reaction, for her father had demanded the same discretion. Her one trip into the world had been from Somerset to Vale House immediately after his burial, but she had been too grief-stricken to notice the scenery.

Now she trembled with excitement. For the first time in her life, she had allowed temptation to supersede duty. Hopefully her moment of selfishness would not lead to trouble. She owed Alex so much. Sir Winton would have ignored her existence without his daughter's pleas. And Alex had paid a steep price for her insistence. Sir Winton had yet to forgive her for overcoming his objections.

Now she stared in awe at the valley spread below.

"Leave the cane," said Torwell, tucking her arm firmly through his own. His long legs slowed to match her limping gait across the uneven ground. It was a courtesy even Alex sometimes forgot.

"Behold the Severn Vale," he said, sweeping his free hand toward the west.

"It is beautiful." He must be accustomed to such views, but she made no effort to hide her pleasure. She might never see it again. "I did not realize how much color there is this time of year."

"It is difficult to appreciate the variety from the valley floor. But from here, we see the fields and forests as the birds do. Strips of yellow where grain was harvested. Patches of green marking pastures. The glorious trees of autumn. Oaks turn to rust, others to gold. And look at that estate." He pointed to their left.

"Beautiful!" The word was inadequate to describe the rich tapestry laid out below.

"Like many landowners, he has scattered specimen trees across his park. The flaming orange is probably a maple from North America. Nothing else produces quite that color. And see that pale yellow? It exactly matches your hair. The blood red is equally spectacular. I wonder what it is."

"You could ask Mr. Hodges," suggested Linden. "The

groundskeeper at Linden Park," he explained when she frowned at the unfamiliar name. "Quite knowledgeable."

A breeze rustled through the grass. Though it was the gentle zephyr of summer rather than the nipping chill of the fast-approaching winter, she shivered.

Linden stepped closer to her side. This time the shiver was trepidation. For the first time since his arrival, Bessie was not with her. She had assumed that Torwell's presence would protect her, only now remembering that he might have as much at stake as Linden.

"This is a perfect day for an outing," she told him before turning back to Torwell. She must divide her attention between them, keeping the conversation light and impersonal. And they must keep the outing short. Linden was not as recovered as he claimed.

Why had Alex bolted this morning instead of confessing as she'd promised? It wasn't like her to run from duty, especially when it left a friend in the awkward position of staving off Linden's proposal for yet another day.

"Everything looks so tiny from this height," she said, smiling at Torwell. "And so clean. Look at that barge. I've never seen one ride so high."

"Because it is empty," said Linden. "That particular river is very shallow. It will doubtless stop in a mile or two to take on cargo. The Severn is another story. See the barge approaching Gloucester?" He turned her toward the north, then leaned over her shoulder to point into the distance.

"Goodness! Is that Gloucester? I hadn't even noticed it."

"You can see the cathedral tower quite clearly, with its four spires—beautiful example of perpendicular construction, and the east window is superb. We explored it while in town. Edward II is buried there. If you look past it, you'll see the barge I mentioned."

She followed his finger, hardly aware that she had released Torwell's arm. "Yes. Quite heavily laden."

"The one headed upstream is lighter. I wonder what it carries."

"At a guess, laces, silks, and French brandy, now that the war is over."

"Perhaps. Or Cornish tin."

"That would surely weigh it down. What is in the downstream barge? Grain?"

"Or shoes. Or maybe cheeses—Gloucestershire cheeses occasionally turn up in Lincoln," he said, smiling. "And very good ones, too."

She laughed. "Perhaps it is loaded with pins, so ladies' dresses don't fall off. There is a manufactory of pins somewhere near here."

"In that case, let us sink that barge without further ado."

The moment the words were out, he gasped, reddening as if embarrassed. Only then did she realize that he had suppressed his banter in recent days, managing a relaxed friendliness unlike any of his early manifestations. She liked him better that way, and despite Alex's warnings, she remained unconvinced that it was all an act. His core was good.

Torwell had slipped away.

Changing the subject to something less suggestive, she cursed herself for inattention. Linden's charm was catching her in a snare she must avoid. Just as she must avoid giving him an opportunity to propose.

"Do you suppose Cook included lemonade in that basket?" she asked when enough time had passed in innocuous conversation that she would not seem to be fleeing. "Your coachman has finished unpacking. And I suspect you need to sit for a few minutes."

He flushed again—definitely embarrassment this time. She should not have reminded him of yesterday. Gentlemen rarely accepted illness gracefully.

Tony smiled at Miss Vale's enjoyment—like a child celebrating Christmas for the first time.

Unfortunately, he reacted to her as if she really were a child. She could not be more than five feet tall. He had to stoop even to offer his arm. It didn't help that she was also delicate. Would he crush her trying to make love?

He stifled the image of the glorious Miss Merideth, who fit his arms as if made for them, and who had been as wild as he during yesterday's encounter. Why hadn't fate given Miss Vale even a little of her cousin's feisty wit or explosive passion? Instead, she was colorless.

A raven screeched, distracting him. He studied the bird and the rise upon which it sat, then circled slowly as he fought down excitement. It was more mound than rise. And not natural. In fact, it showed all the characteristics of buried stonework. Was this another Roman site, or an ancient tomb? The earliest tombs had been covered with earth.

Perhaps it was a Druid shrine, like the one beneath Miss Merideth's temple, or an ancient hill fort. This promontory would have offered security and the sort of view that could warn of approaching danger. What would Miss Merideth think? She knew more about the earliest people of this region than he did.

"Are you joining us?" called Jon, breaking into his thoughts. He blinked, startled to realize that at least an hour had passed. He'd completely forgotten Miss Vale.

"I beg your pardon," he said when he joined them. "I allowed my mind to wander. That mound is intriguing, but ignoring you was quite rude."

He concentrated on making conversation during their meal, trying to regain lost ground. And she responded, directing most of her comments toward him. But despite his best efforts, he could see no sign that she truly cared. As she had from the beginning, she turned to him from politeness. The perfect hostess, determined to entertain all her guests.

Cursing himself for digging his hole even deeper by demonstrating that a mound of earth was more interesting than she, he gave up. His father was right. He was a selfish fool, allowing his passions to divert him from duty. He might as well confess and get it over with. Nothing would improve his situation at this point.

He deliberately called up the image of his mother, wretched as she sobbed out her fears against his shoulder. Even her jointure was gone. His father's will provided for her, of course, but since her quarterly stipend was supposed to come from estate revenues, the provision was worthless.

So it was up to him.

"Shall we see what Painswick has to offer?" he asked, helping her to her feet as the coachman packed away the remains of their meal.

Interest battled uncertainty on her face. "Is Mr. Linden up to extending the day?"

"Quite," said Jon curtly. He glanced across the top of her head with a look that clearly ordered him to get on with business.

Tony grimaced. Jon was right. He'd procrastinated through breakfast. He'd eagerly trailed after a diversion just now. He was out of time.

Helping her into the carriage, he stared out the window, searching for inspiration. He needed to get rid of Jon for a few minutes.

You need a backbone.

Taking a deep breath, he opened his mouth, then sighed in relief when Painswick appeared. "What a remarkable church. Let's stop." It was as good a place as any.

Jon must have agreed. "I will remain here."

"You are tired," said Miss Vale. "I knew we should have returned."

"Nonsense. God might suffer an apoplexy if I turned up in two of His houses in one week." His eyes warned Tony that it was the last lie.

"Come, Miss Vale," he said, helping her down before she could turn stubborn. "We will leave him to his rest."

"Very well." But the worried glance she cast back at the coach had him gritting his teeth.

Like most of the nearby buildings, the church was constructed of local stone, but it appeared quite large for so small a village. Instead of entering, he led her toward the churchyard, which bristled with elaborate gravestones and chest tombs, some exhibiting superb carving.

"I should not be surprised that you are more interested in graves than architecture," she said.

"Actually—" His voice froze. He had done it again. *Tell her you're a fraud!* He opened his mouth, but he could not force the words past his lips. Deciding to work up to the confession, he seized on her assumption. "I am interested in both. But I usually start a church tour with the yard."

"Why?" She glanced along the row of yews leading back to the road.

"I enjoy looking at gravestones," he admitted in a moment of candor. "Many of the sentiments are moving. *Devoted wife and mother*," he read from a brass plate. "Not unusual, though I must wonder how true it might be. In my experience, a woman may be good at one duty, like my own mother, but rarely at both. And many abjure either role."

"In the upper classes that may be true," she agreed. "But you must know that churchyards rarely serve the great families. In the working classes, such devotion is common."

"An astute comment," he said, wandering among the stones. "Particularly from one who has spent her life in seclusion."

"Not entirely. I often visit tenants and villagers."

"When Sir Winton is away?"

She nodded, then paled.

"I would never criticize you for speaking the truth. Nor do I consider it undutiful to your family." He smiled into her eyes, struck again by how small and fragile she appeared. "You are a lovely girl, who should visit people more often. Of all classes. Perhaps—"

Again his voice froze as his gaze shifted beyond her to the village stocks, unexpectedly mounted just outside the church wall. Shackles. Bonds that tied a man down. That cut him off from his desires. That could turn him bitter if he accepted the wrong ones . . .

Some of his father's lectures had stuck, despite his youthful rebellion against everything Linden advocated. One was a deep-seated hatred of infidelity. Choosing a marriage of convenience would not negate that. So marrying Miss Vale would restrict him to bedding only her—forever.

Dropping her arm, he ran his hand over a marvelous chest

tomb, the weeping cherub on its end panel so lifelike he expected tears to flow from its stone eyes.

"Do not believe that I never get out," she replied, wandering to the far side of the tomb to face him across its width. At least she showed no sign that she recognized his turmoil. "Several neighbors call regularly, though I have hesitated to encourage visits in the last fortnight. You will surely understand, since you cited propriety when you went to Gloucester the other day. I've ignored the strictest interpretation of proper manners because Al—Merideth is so pleased to have your company."

Not anymore. The realization sent a sharp pain stabbing through his heart.

Enough! His conscience sounded exactly like Jon. *Stop thinking and do it!*

Drawing himself erect, which only made her seem smaller, he focused on the shrub behind her head. "Miss Vale, I must correct the mis—"

"Heavens!" she exclaimed, her eyes looking past him.

He turned, seeing only another chest tomb.

"Look at that carving." She giggled as she limped over for a closer look.

"Heavens, indeed." He laughed. The side panel was carved in lurid relief, depicting a man—identified as Farmer Parrot—being struck down by a flail. "*God's reward for working on Sunday*," he quoted the inscription. "I wonder who paid to produce so expensive an object lesson."

"Undoubtedly the local squire—who was probably a devout Puritan," she added after squinting to make out the date. "1645. I suspect he was one of Cromwell's fanatics. I doubt you'll find a more interesting inscription than that."

"True. I've never seen anything so blatantly moralistic."

"This side holds more details," she said, moving around the end. "He plowed, sowed, and harvested on Sundays, as well as threshed, *forsaking obeisance to his heavenly Father.*"

"Appalling." He was grinning.

"Given such insupportable disdain, the church itself might have commissioned this tomb." She giggled.

"Perhaps. How could they condone such heresy?" He drew in a breath. "Miss Vale, please allow me to—"

Again she interrupted. "Here is a newer monument." She ran one hand over an unadorned pyramid.

"John Bryan, stonemason," he read, even as he cursed his cowardice. The man's father, Joseph, was buried under an exquisitely sculptured headstone. Other examples by the same hand stood nearby, including an ornate stone honoring fellow mason Thomas Hamlett. "Beautiful. I'll wager these were John's work. What an artist. How sad that his successor lacked his talent."

"I suppose he considered it unlucky to carve his own stone in advance. Death is too final, so contemplating it casts a pall over life that can diminish even our greatest triumphs. Who will care once we are gone?" She shook her head over the pyramid, then headed toward the street. "We should start back. Those clouds will bring rain before much longer. And despite his protestations, you know that Mr. Linden needs his rest."

The sun had indeed moved behind storm clouds. He toyed for one brief moment with the idea of dragging her inside and forcing her to listen.

Yet his hand remained at his side. The words that might have stopped her froze in his throat.

Again he had failed.

He was a fool. Many times a fool. He deserved every curse his father had ever uttered.

But as he silently handed her into the carriage, a bolt of lightning rent the sky, illuminating the darkest reaches of his heart. His hand trembled, for he was more stupid than he'd thought, dooming them all. Contemplating death was not the only way to tarnish life.

He did not join Miss Vale's banter with Jon. Instead, he cursed long and hard. And futilely.

Chapter Twelve

Tony turned his tired horse toward Vale House, plodding along the lane at only a fraction of the speed at which he'd left four hours earlier.

His head had been swirling since he'd admitted defeat yesterday. Even before that bolt of lightning cleared the cobwebs from his mind, he'd known he could never wed Miss Vale. He didn't love her. He could rarely tolerate her company for more than a few minutes before shifting his attention elsewhere. When she'd left the churchyard, relief had buckled his knees.

The ride back to Vale House had been interminable, adding a layer of guilt to his other woes. Jon had clearly overexerted himself, falling into a doze before they'd covered a mile. Miss Vale had given up after failing in her third attempt to draw him into conversation. But his attention was focused inward. The excursion had been a disaster all around.

Jon had stumbled off to bed, with orders to remain there until morning. Miss Merideth had not returned by dinner. Though Miss Vale shrugged, making light of it, she was clearly anxious.

So was he, fearing an accident, an encounter with a highwayman, or some other calamity. Not until she arrived home at nearly midnight had he relaxed. But he'd not spoken to her. First he had to decide what to do.

His first reaction, while returning from Painswick, had been to leave, to abandon his shameful conduct, to abandon Linden Park and everything that went with it. The advantage was that Miss Vale would never know of his deceit. But such a course was cowardly—even more cowardly than hiding his identity to begin with.

His reputation had never seriously bothered him because he knew it was a lie. At heart he was an honorable man who had never harmed anyone but himself.

But turning tail to avoid embarrassment was inexcusable. No gentleman would consider it. So he must face the mess he had created. The question was how.

"Start at the beginning," he urged himself for at least the hundredth time.

What is the point? You've been over every fact.

"True."

The first rays of dawn illuminated an oak, its burnished leaves blazing like Miss Merideth's hair. Yesterday's lightning had awakened him to a truth he'd been trying to ignore since their embrace: She had become the most important person in his life—more vital than Jon, more precious than his mother, more deserving than himself.

He stopped at a crossroads, peering at the faded signpost as he tried to remember which lane led to Vale House. His life was at a similar crossroads. It was time to change directions.

He turned right.

If he hadn't been so stubbornly arrogant, he would have recognized the truth sooner. *I always keep my word.* He'd said that only two days ago. Well, this was one vow he must break.

Stupidity didn't begin to explain his blindness. He should have realized the truth the day they'd climbed the cliff. Or during those evenings they'd spent in exhilarating debate. Or any of the thousand times lust had distracted him from digging.

Or the last time she had pulled Jon aside, leaving him free to court Miss Vale. He'd paid little attention to his own conversation as his eyes strayed to her corner, his ears straining to hear every word. Keeping Jon under control, he'd told himself, but it had been a lie. He rarely fretted when Jon was entertaining Miss Vale. It was Miss Merideth who drew his eye. He'd begrudged his cousin every smile, every laugh, every twinkle of her warm brown eyes. Her delight had sliced a knife into his heart.

It still did.

He wanted her with an intensity he had not known was possible. He needed her to ease the ache she had ignited with that fevered kiss. And that need surpassed the physical. She stimulated his mind as well as his body, fulfilling dreams he had never put into words. He could be himself with her.

Be himself...

He shifted in the saddle. Was she really that different? Perhaps she was only responding to his own unusual openness.

He knew only three people well enough that he could relax in their presence. Yet he was not fully honest with any of them. His mother knew nothing of Torwell, and he hesitated discussing his frustration, his reputation, or his father with her, knowing that it would add to the burden she already carried. Jon was so innocent that he often censored tales to keep from shocking him. Simms listened to any complaint, but he never forgot his place, so friendship was impossible.

Now he had found a fourth in Miss Merideth. Despite his masquerade, he felt free with her. And he had not played a role in days, for they discussed only antiquity while on the site. Torwell was his natural role. When he was digging, he forgot that he was anyone else. For the first time, he'd been able to discuss his excavations. Of course he would revel in it.

It is more than that, countered his conscience, even as pain stabbed his heart.

True. She was more than a colleague willing to debate theories. He could never forget that mouthwatering figure, or the way her eyes sparkled with excitement, or the eagerness with which she had returned his kisses, or . . .

Go ahead and say it.

"All right! I love her."

It was the first time he had put it into words, though his conscience had known it since yesterday. But he could no longer deny the truth. He loved her. That was why he had failed with

Miss Vale. He could never offer for her, knowing that he loved another.

Maybe Jon would be willing to take her. She might even prefer Jon. Her solicitude over his illness went beyond the duty of even the most conscientious hostess. But he would not suggest such a match. And he would never count on Jon to care for his parents.

He could not in good conscience walk away from them. They were family. Since fate had left them in worse circumstances than him, they were his responsibility, so he must offer them a home. This disaster might even shame Linden into keeping his mouth shut. Not that it mattered. Somehow they would work out an amicable arrangement. But it would strain his budget to the limit.

Which meant he might not be able to offer for Miss Merideth. Providing for her would be tricky at best. He hated nipfarthings, but he would have little choice but to become one. Buying an estate would use up his investments and encumber him with a mortgage. The estate income must cover living expenses, mortgage payments, and the cost of whatever excavations he found time to pursue—once the world learned his identity, he had no guarantee that anyone would support his digs. Another disastrous harvest like the one just concluded could cost him everything.

Turning through the Vale House gates, he examined the problem from all sides. Buying his own estate was the only sane path. Renting a house that would accommodate his parents, his wife, and any children they produced, would require more than his current income, forcing him to dip into the principal. That would soon exhaust his resources, so he had to have a property that produced income. The one he had been considering in Somerset would provide digging sites for at least the first year, but then he would have to spend months in other locations if he wished to pursue the one activity he truly loved. And that would cost money.

So he would become a nipfarthing. To win Miss Merideth's hand, he would do whatever was necessary and pray that she

could accept it. She was the woman he had dreamed of, someone who complemented every part of his life.

The next problem was finding her. Leaving Orpheus with a
footman—he didn't want to explain to the groom why he'd
taken a horse out in the middle of the night—he headed for
breakfast.

She was avoiding him. That sudden trip to Stroud had been a
clear case of running away. It hadn't been planned, and Miss
Vale had made no mention of an emergency. So it must be his
fault.

He hoped their embrace had awakened similar feelings, but
he could not be sure. Perhaps their passion had frightened her.
Or maybe she thought he was trying to seduce her. Companions
were often targets of lecherous guests. And considering the sort
of men Sir Winton befriended, she had undoubtedly been approached before.

The problem couldn't be his identity. She had no way of
knowing he'd considered her ineligible until now. Vicars often
chose companions as wives.

Whatever her reasons, he had to see her. He would explain
everything—including his identity—then hope she would accept his proposal. Pray that she would accept it. She'd decried
deceit more than once.

He didn't miss the irony of having planned the same approach with Miss Vale only yesterday. But the stakes were
much higher today. He was putting everything on the table, including his heart and his soul. He didn't know what he would
do if she refused. The very thought froze something inside.

Taking a deep breath, he opened the door of the dining room.
She was seated in her usual chair. But the eyes she raised
flashed with fury. Crumpling the letter she'd been reading, she
rose.

Jon awoke before dawn, as he often did. Pulling on his
clothes, he headed for the library, where he could read until the
others were up. But this time he didn't escape unnoticed. He
nearly ran down Miss Vale when he turned a corner.

"You are up early." He felt his face flush. Though he had all but abandoned the role of rake, he still managed to embarrass himself. Why had he mentioned her sleep habits? Or uttered yesterday's horrid remark about sinking a barge of pins.

"As are you," she said in that sweet, calm voice he was enjoying far too much. "Are you recovered today?"

He nodded. "Thanks to your excellent care. Are you going down for breakfast?"

"In a few minutes. I need to check the music room first. We've a new maid in training."

"No housekeeper?" Another stupid remark, he realized, kicking himself. He'd seen no sign of one in a fortnight of living under this roof.

"Sir—Father sees no reason to employ one when A— Merideth and I can both work."

Jon let the observation pass, but he had a sudden urge to adjust Sir Winton's attitude—by force. "If you don't mind, I will accompany you."

"Not at all." She smiled warmly, reminding him of her pleasure at yesterday's outing.

"Did you enjoy our excursion to Painswick?" he asked, offering his arm. She limped less with help.

"Very much. I had not realized how beautiful this area is. My only regret is that we did not postpone it a day, so you could have enjoyed it more. I feared you would suffer a relapse."

"Not at all. Sitting in the drawing room would have left me just as weary. Besides, today is colder. But tell me about the church." Since she treated him exactly the same, Tony must have postponed his confession yet again. Avoiding unpleasant duties was so unlike his cousin, he was beginning to think that some other force was at work. Had Tony realized that Miss Vale deserved better than a marriage of convenience?

He was entertaining a strong desire to wring the Honorable Anthony Linden's neck. Every new delay made the situation worse. By now, truth was so entangled with lies that he doubted they could straighten out the mess without hurting both ladies.

Miss Vale laughed. "We never got inside. Mr. Torwell wished

to see the churchyard. That is another reason I wish we had
waited until today, for you would have loved it. One tomb had
an elaborate carving that showed God smiting down the sinner
who dared to work on Sunday."

"Was he struck by lightning?"

"No, he was hit in the head by a flail." After running a hand
over the top of the harpsichord, she inspected the edges of the
carpet for hidden dirt.

"A flail?"

"If the carving is accurate, he smote his own temple while
threshing grain."

He chuckled. "Possible, but quite odd. Did you see the
church?"

"No." She turned away to straighten several piles of music
that didn't need straightening. "I was concerned about your illness, so once we'd explored the churchyard, I demanded that
we return." The back of her neck turned red. "I owe him an
apology, for it was quite bad of me, particularly after he expressed an interest in the church. I do hope he doesn't think me
rude. I really did enjoy the outing. It was kind of him to suggest
it."

"But typical, for he knew you would welcome it. He has always reached out to help others." Making the praise sound sincere was difficult, for he remained irritated with the man.

But you owe him so much.

Memory drove his anger away. He had arrived at Linden
Park at age ten, alone, still in shock from his parents' deaths,
hardly able to string two words together without blubbering
like a girl. Many boys would have resented having a cousin
thrust into their home, especially a cousin who monopolized
everyone's attention for months. Yet Tony had welcomed him,
willingly sharing his possessions and his heart. That selfless-
ness had done even more than Aunt Mary's love to pull him out
of his grief.

It was a gift he could never truly repay, though he had tried.
He'd often pleaded Tony's case with Lord Linden, and he'd
made sure the tenants and villagers knew Tony's true character.

He'd even ignored Tony's wishes by revealing who had paid to repair the church roof, to provide pensions for three old servants, to send a village boy to school so he could win a post in the solicitor's office . . .

"I suppose that is why he chose to enter the church," said Miss Vale, jerking him from his memories.

"Chur—" He recalled himself in time to change the words to, "Yes, it was an ideal career." She did not seem to notice the strain in his voice.

"I wish all vicars were so kind. Our local one ignores the parishioners, and the one who replaced Father was cruel, tossing me out on the street without even asking if I had a place to stay."

"What an awful—" He stopped as her words registered. "*Father?*"

"Dear me, I must be babbling again." Her face had flushed crimson.

"Who are you?" His heart pounded.

"Miss Vale."

"The truth."

Her shoulders slumped. Limping closer, she faced him, though the terror in her blue eyes revealed the courage it took to do so. "Miss Sarah Vale. Please don't hate Alex, sir. It was only supposed to last a day or two, but she has been so excited about working with Mr. Torwell, that she keeps putting off ending it."

"What do you mean by *it?*" He couldn't be hearing right. But his head was already cataloguing the evidence that should have told him the truth days ago—the stumbles whenever she mentioned her supposed father, Sir Winton's disdain for her foot, the portrait that must be Miss Merideth herself. He cursed himself for not realizing that the clothes in that picture were barely ten years out of date.

Her face grew even redder, though he had not thought it possible. "You must know your r-reputation, sir. Alex was appalled at what Sir Winton had done to your family. She never wanted to wed anyone, but when she discovered that there was no way to return your property, she knew that marriage was the only way out. But she feared your reputation. When you turned up so unexpectedly, she thought you meant to force her, so she asked me to exchange identities with her until she discovered if she could tolerate you—even a man of your reputation would think twice before seducing a cripple."

"Stop this!" he ordered, furious that she would demean herself so badly.

"I know you are angry, sir, but I beg you. Don't blame Alex. I could have talked her out of it, but it did seem to make sense. And she never expected it to last past a day. But she was so thrilled to meet Mr. Torwell that she lost her head, postponing her confession for another day, then another. She's learned so much from him—not that it excuses her deceit. I've begged and begged her to end it, but she's as stubborn as a mule at times. Now I've let her down. How can I face her?"

"That is not what I meant," he said, fighting to sound calm. He set his hands on her shoulders. "I understand her reasoning completely. What angers me is hearing you slight yourself."

She snorted. "You, of all people, should know how society views anyone who fails to meet their standards."

The enormity of the farce suddenly shattered the shock that had held him in thrall. Miss Merideth had not diverted his attention to protect Miss Vale. And all her quizzing hadn't been helping her employer learn more about him. She'd been trying to figure out if she could put up with him.

He laughed.

Tony's indecision . . . He laughed harder.

This girl's ambivalence . . . He collapsed onto the floor, shouting and snorting and choking with laughter. Tears rolled down his cheeks, leaving him helpless, barely able to gulp air between debilitating peals of laughter. Tony was about to find his head on a pike. It served him right.

Miss Vale stared. "Of all the possible reactions we considered, laughter didn't even make the list."

Jon tried to catch his breath. "You d-don't know the h-half of it," he managed before another fit convulsed him.

"Are you all right, sir?"

He couldn't breathe. She knelt beside him, looking anxious. He grinned up at her. "Miss Va—May I call you Sarah. This is too much."

"Of course." She helped him sit up.

"Sarah. My dear Sarah. I know absolutely nothing about society, for I've never entered it." Tony had had his chance. Now he could live with the consequences. "You are not the only one put off by Tony's reputation—which is totally false, by the way. He knew Miss Vale would never look twice at him—"

"*He?*" She recoiled. "Who are you?"

He laughed. "Mr. L-Linden. Mr. J-Jonathan Linden, vicar to Linden P-Park." Flopping back to the floor, he gave up any hope of control.

Sarah stared, her eyes like saucers. "Then Mr. Tor—"

"Is T-Tony Linden, heir to Lord Linden, who p-precipitated this entire mess."

She shook her head. "But why would he pretend to be an antiquarian?"

Pulling himself together, Jon softened his tone. "That was not pretense, Sarah. His full name is Anthony Torwell Linden. The history of his reputation is a very long story, much of which I cannot reveal without his permission, but the rumors are totally false. Yet society is unwilling to admit the truth. To pursue his interest in antiquity, he was forced to use another name." He saw the same understanding burst through her eyes.

"Heavens! No wonder he looked so green in the churchyard yesterday. I thought he was ill, but he must have been trying to confess." She laughed. "For t-two weeks we have all been w-walking around in the wr-wrong roles." She collapsed.

"P-pretending—"

"You were a r-rake."

"T-Tony shuns churches."

Laugher convulsed both of them, blinding them, choking them with hilarity. By the time Jon recovered enough to think, Sarah was in his arms. It seemed natural to kiss her.

She froze, and for a moment he feared he had pushed her too far. Then she returned the kiss—fervently.

His arms tightened, sending sensations knifing through his body that he had never known. Rolling her beneath him, he trailed kisses over her face, groaning when her hands lifted to his head, pulling him back to her mouth.

"Sarah . . ." One hand fumbled upward, colliding with her breast. She moaned.

He recoiled. "Forgive me, Sarah. I'm forgetting myself."

"You are Jonathan Linden, vicar to Linden Park." She laughed as her hand traced the line of his cheek. "Maybe I should pin a tag to your jacket so you can remember."

His breath whooshed out with that touch. It was a miracle. "Thank God you are you, Sarah." He stared into her eyes. "I love you. I've been denying it for days, ignoring it, cursing it, berating myself for letting it happen when I knew you would have to accept Tony. Now we are free. Marry me, my love. Make me the happiest man in the world."

"Jonathan—"

"Tony calls me Jon. It's a name only very special people use."

"Jon." She smiled. "Am I dreaming?"

"Never. I love you."

"Yes." She grinned. "Yes, I love you. Yes, I will marry you." The grin faltered. "But are you sure you won't mind—"

"Your foot? Never. The body is but a shell that houses us during our sojourn through life. It is easily marred, but that does not affect the person inside. I love *you*, Sarah—mind, spirit, soul, however you wish to define it. And I will always love you."

"And I, you." She kissed him again, held him close for another minute, then sighed. "Much as I would love to stay here, we've already strained propriety to its limits. Shall we find breakfast?"

"Calm and practical, as always. I do love you. You bring comfort to everyone around you, and peace." He helped himself to one last kiss, then scrambled up, pulling her to her feet.

She smiled. "I want to shout our betrothal from the rooftops, but springing it on the others without warning is not a good idea. Alex has an explosive temper."

"I am tempted, though. This entire imbroglio was their idea, but you are right. I will tell Tony in private."

"And I will tell Alex that you know my identity. I want you at my side when they learn the rest. So we have one more imposture to carry off. They will undoubtedly be at breakfast. This seems to be their usual time."

He nodded. "Excellent. Once we've eaten, I will inform Tony that the imposture is over. I will give him one hour to inform Miss Merideth—heavens, she pulled the same ruse he did with the names. Why didn't I notice earlier?"

"Why would you?"

"Because I looked up her full name." He bit off mention of the special license, but couldn't help grinning. It might be used yet. "We can retire to the drawing room after delivering our ultimatum. Once they confess their own sins, we can announce our betrothal."

"I wonder how they will get on."

"That is out of our hands, though I have rarely met two people so well suited."

Chapter Thirteen

A lex pulled her hair into her companion style, then shook her head. She was through hiding. From now on, she would wear her own style, assume her own identity, and confess to whichever man she saw first.

Murch had treated her to a rare scold last night. And he was right. Leaving without warning had been inconsiderate, placing Sarah in the questionable position of entertaining two gentlemen alone. And it was unconscionable to remain away so late that Murch had been forming a search party when she'd finally returned. But his complaints hadn't stopped there. He'd laid all her sins before her—her behavior for weeks had been arrogantly selfish; Sarah deserved better, as did her guests; it was unfair to expect the staff to perpetuate this fraud a moment longer.

She agreed, having reached the same conclusion during a day of hard thought. She might not enjoy being a woman, but that did not excuse poor manners. So she would confess. No more procrastinating as she devised dubious schemes to catch Linden alone, or sought one more day of working with Torwell. That was finished anyway.

Poking the last pin into Alex Vale's hair, she headed for the dining room.

It was empty.

She nearly screamed in frustration. After bracing for an unpleasant encounter with Torwell, it was a shock to find it postponed yet again. Might he be avoiding her?

It was far too likely, she concluded. Murch had mentioned

that he'd taken Sarah out yesterday. He'd probably decided to press his courtship. Or Linden may have suggested the excursion, though Murch had described him as half-dead from his illness.

But no matter. She would speak to both gentlemen as soon as possible.

She jumped as the door opened. But it was only Murch.

"This just arrived."

As he proffered his tray, she recognized her father's hand on the letter. Her hand trembled, but she quickly stifled any fear. Even if Bushnell had gone straight to his bedside the moment he arrived in London, his response could not arrive before tomorrow.

"Did he write to anyone else?"

"Only you."

Not a demand that they raise rents, then. Perhaps he had further orders about her Season. Or Richard might be in trouble at school. Or he could be announcing the imminent arrival of yet another friend.

Waving Murch away, she pushed her plate aside and broke the seal.

I cannot believe my eyes, he wrote. *Had the letter come from anyone but Bushnell, I would question whether even you could be so criminally stupid. Speaking to Linden was bad enough, but inviting his bird of paradise into my home is beyond— Words fail me.*

"Damn," she muttered. Bushnell had not waited to reach London. Either he hadn't believed that Linden would travel with a vicar, or he'd sent a letter immediately after their initial conversation.

"Does he think I have no intelligence at all?" she muttered. "He should know Bushnell always exaggerates."

Obviously not.

You need not bother considering fortune hunters, he continued. *I would never place the burden of screening suitors on your shoulders. Sir Alfred Mabury called yesterday, seeking permission to pay his addresses. He is a kind and gentle man*

*who would cause you no grief. Or you might prefer Mr. Patrick,
who has visited daily since my fall, anxious to ease my suffering. He, too, has expressed his fervent desire to make your acquaintance.*

She cursed. Regret was already eating at him. Did he think
her too stupid to recognize his ploy? She nearly tossed the missive aside in disgust, but stopped herself. Neither of his supposed paragons was remotely interesting, but he might already
have dispatched them to Vale House. She must be prepared.

He urged her to carefully consider these suits, and warned
against the stratagems men like Linden might employ, then finished by describing Linden's reputation in greater detail than
she had ever heard.

Phrases jumped from the page—*seducer of innocents, like
the Pauley girl, whom he refused to wed . . . will wager on anything . . . prankster decried by every decent man . . . carried
home most nights too drunk to walk . . .*

"They must be exaggerations," she murmured, though that
last was an uncomfortable reminder of the night he'd arrived.
But the rest did not fit the oddly soft-spoken man occupying the
best guest chamber.

—*disappears for long periods of time, indulging in the most
scandalous orgies . . .*

"And how would you know, unless you accompanied him?"
she scoffed.

*His vicious attacks on women have earned him the moniker
the Green-eyed Monster. Items of value disappear whenever he
visits a respectable house.*

"The pot calling—"

She gasped, staring at the recrossed page. Surely she had
misread it.

But the damning words remained. *Green-eyed Monster.*

Mr. Linden was tall, with dark curly hair that framed his
brown eyes. Not a trace of green shimmered in their depths. But
she had seen green eyes often. Her own closed, remembering
the way Torwell's had laughed as he spun her around the mosaic.

"The bastard!"

Why had no rumor mentioned his penchant for pranks? If she'd known, she would have suspected deceit. Instead, she'd trusted him, shown him her most precious treasures, shared her site. And all the time, he'd been plotting against her, even using her awe of another man to seduce her. How could he warn her against looters and thieves, when he was one himself?

Nausea doubled her over. Dear God! Had he already hacked out that mosaic? Selling something that fine might negate the need to take on an unwanted wife.

The door opened again, revealing the man himself.

"Bastard!" she hissed, rising to lean on the table. "Impostor! How dare you make a mockery of everything decent?"

"Wha—" He paled. "You know."

"Of course I know. Did you think you could gull us forever?"

"Let me explain."

"Explain what? How you plotted against us? How you schemed to win back the fortune that supports your revolting debauchery? I care nothing for excuses."

"You care nothing for truth, either." His eyes flashed.

"Hah!" Her hands fisted, crumpling the letter. "You lied from the moment you arrived. Pretending to be a man I respected, so I would welcome you. My God! How could even you stoop so low?"

"What did your welcome have to do with anything?" he demanded harshly. "I didn't even know you existed before arriving. Yes, I hid my identity—for this very reason. That reputation is false from beginning to end, but I've been saddled with it for most of my life. Can you blame me for avoiding that handicap when I came to meet the woman who was throwing my parents out on the road? Not that it matters anymore. I had already abandoned—"

"No, it doesn't matter." Her fury rose as he twisted even his own dishonor to avoid blame. "I'm not the one who turned them off—in fact, I tried to allow them to stay. But I won't allow a hypocritical Judas to betray everything I've worked for. I despise deceit."

Those betraying eyes narrowed. "I'm not fond of it myself, but there are times—"

"Never! I should have known you were too good to be true. You are no different than any other man—and worse than most. An arrogant, posturing liar who will say anything to gain an advantage. I can't believe you took me in."

"I didn't," he protested, turning those faithless eyes to the window. "I've told only one falsehood—"

She hardened her heart against the pain in his voice, cutting him off lest he talk her round. What an actor he was! "Enough, Linden. Get out of my house! Get out of my life! And if I find even one trinket missing, I'll have every magistrate in the country on your trail. Your father may be a lord, but you are only a treacherous commoner. I'll see you hang!"

"You?" He blanched, whipping his head around to stare at her. "My God! How dare you criticize me when you are just as devious, Miss Vale."

"As if you didn't know. Why else would you impersonate Torwell?"

"I *am* Torwell," he shouted, lunging around the table to shake her shoulders. "Will you listen to me?"

"Never!" She slapped him. "I'm through being cozened by a liar."

"The pot calling the kettle black. You can't have it both ways."

"I had to protect myself!" she protested, then cursed him for putting her on the defensive.

"How? By tossing your innocent companion into a situation you dared not face yourself? Coward! Your father must have meant your character when he called you a deformed freak. I wish I'd known that earlier. It would have saved me some trouble." He dropped his hands as if touching her contaminated him, his scornful stare raking her from head to toe.

"You insult Sarah by calling her deformed."

"Don't twist my words. She's the sweetest girl I've met in years. And she has more integrity in a single finger than you've demonstrated in weeks. I could forgive you for fearing the rumors. I expected that. But I'll never forgive you for hiding behind her skirts. That is worse than the blackest deeds a disapproving world has imputed to me. You are unworthy to wash her feet." He turned to leave.

"That's not what—" The contemptuous glance over his shoulder froze her tongue.

"Feels different when you're on the other end, doesn't it, Miss Hypocritical Vale? You are just like your father, and no better than any other scheming jade. Despite your demands for respect and equality, you moan and groan when people judge you by the same standards you use on them. Well, I've got news for you. What's sauce for the gander is sauce for the goose. You might think about that the next time you feel like throwing stones. I can't believe I thought you might be different. I must be the world's greatest fool."

"How dare you criticize me! Even hell hasn't a pit deep enough for you."

"Close-minded, as well. Enjoy fending off the fortune hunters, Miss Vale. The most desperate will need your dowry badly enough to overlook that sharp tongue. Of course, the winner will lock you in an attic so he needn't live with you. But what do you care? By admitting his avarice, he will meet your exacting standards."

"I hope you rot!"

"Sorry to disappoint you." He flashed a cheeky grin. "I always land on my feet. The only reason I approached you was to save my mother from dying in a hovel. But I shouldn't have bothered. I've known your estimable father for years. The fruit rarely falls far from the tree."

"Get out," she ordered through clenched teeth.

"I'll always thank God that I learned your true character before it was too late, Miss Dishonorable Vale. My mother would prefer that hovel to welcoming you into the family." Another of those crooked grins lit up his face. "Hold that image close and think on it. Maybe you'll get lucky, and it will eat a hole big enough that the gods can insert a heart into that barren chest."

"Get out! Get out! Get out!"

Sweeping her a flamboyant bow, he complied.

His eyes are devastated.

"Hardly." She stifled the voice. "He enjoyed watching me squirm." How could she have been so stupid? His dishonesty had been obvious from the beginning. She should have turned him away the moment he'd faked that accident, but curiosity and guilt had weighed her down.

Shock had numbed her since the moment she'd realized his identity, but that immunity was now gone. As the full pain of his deceit sank in, nausea returned in choking, bitter waves. She bolted for her room.

Tony retained his control long enough to fling an order to Murch, but pain overwhelmed him long before he reached his room. Damn her! And damn him for falling in love with her. Her words had sliced him to ribbons, flaying him until he doubted it was possible to register more pain. Someone could stab him in the back and he would not notice.

He'd known that revealing the truth would cause trouble. In fact, he'd racked his brains all the way to the house, searching for a way to broach the subject. But never had he pictured this.

He had postponed confessing once too often, he admitted as grief penetrated the shock, lashing his heart in its turn.

He'd been wrong. The pain was already worse.

Someone must have written to her, for she'd been clutching a letter through much of her diatribe. Though how anyone could have known—

The how didn't matter. Only the result. She was so incensed that she refused to listen, refused to think, refused even to recognize the facts staring her in the face.

Recalling her disbelief sent his temper soaring. It had been wishful thinking to hope she might care. Even a mild *tendre* would have prompted her to listen. But she hadn't. Miss Holier-than-thou Vale wanted everything her way. She could do whatever she wanted, but everyone else must be a saint.

Damn her to hell! And damn himself for forgetting how scheming and cunning women were. One couldn't trust them a moment. She might well have conceived this farce so she could wrest control of her dowry while he was reeling from shock. It was the sort of ploy her father often used.

Ringing for Simms, he stuffed clothes into valises, letting the anger build. She was as arbitrary as his father—blind, deaf, unwilling to accept anything that didn't fit her neat little image of the world. Damn her for acting so confounded superior when her own sins were as bad as his. He should have known that Sir Winton would never have produced an honest daughter.

Idiot!

"Tony—" Jon was pushing the door open.

"Pack. We're leaving," he ordered. "I want to be out of here in five minutes."

"But—"

"Move! If you aren't ready, you can find your own way home." He flung one valise toward the door while dumping cravats into the other.

Jon gasped.

"Well?"

"Immediately." He ran for his room.

The coachman was slow, but they pulled away only ten minutes later. Murch's frown followed them down the drive.

Alex retched until the pain in her stomach matched that in her heart, then cried until she was dry. Then she repeated the cycle. She finally shoved the sodden pillow aside, disgusted with herself for caring. He wasn't worth this much upset. He certainly wasn't worth tears.

How could she have been so stupid? The signs had been there from the beginning. He was a schemer and liar of the first order, who hadn't had time to get comfortable in his role before arriving—which explained his nervousness when she'd questioned him that first night. At the very least, she should have suspected manipulation when she realized that he knew Bushnell. Torwell supposedly knew no one.

Damn the man! How dare he sneak into her house and steal her heart? How dare he feed her dreams—and even incite new ones—then dash them to pieces, grin, and walk away? That bow had mocked her even more than his scorn.

Deformed freak . . . meant your character . . .

The words sliced deep, hurting more than everything her father had said in six-and-twenty years. New tears coursed down her cheeks, sending her back to the chamber pot.

Thought you might be different . . . scheming jade . . . hiding behind her skirts . . . coward . . . coward . . . coward . . .

She moaned, stifling the sound in a pillow. "What have I done?"

No more than you had to.

It was true, she insisted, whipping up her fury. How dare he hide from what all the world knew, then blame her for protecting herself? He could protest until his face turned blue about his innocence, but people did not make up tales. No one woke up one morning with the bright idea of ruining Tony Linden's life.

He was the villain. *He* was the schemer. Dear God, why had she been born a woman? It left her vulnerable to wretches like Linden. Even his respect had been a lie. He'd manipulated her from the start so he could get what he wanted. He cared nothing for her, even using her most cherished dreams against her. Life was unfair.

A soft rap penetrated her fuming.

"Who is it?"

"Sarah. I need to talk to you."

"Not today."

"Are you ill?"

She exhaled slowly, forcing control over her voice. "I am fine, Sarah. But I do not wish to be disturbed today."

The door rattled, but the lock held. "Alex! We have to talk."

"No!" she shouted, desperate to be alone. "Get out."

"What is wrong, Alex?"

She gave up responding, unwilling to explain. The burst of fury had died, leaving excruciating pain and desolation behind. Clasping pillows over her head to deaden Sarah's voice, she sank into misery.

Chapter Fourteen

"For the last time, no! I will not return. I will not wed that scheming witch. And I will not listen to another word!" Tony twisted sideways to stare out the window.

"The tiff cannot be that serious," protested Jon. "I have never seen two people so perfectly suited."

"Enough, Jon." Anger faded into weariness. "I am pleased that you are betrothed, and I understand that you want us to share your joy, but neither of us is interested. If you continue harassing me, I will have to ride on the box."

The carriage fell blessedly silent.

Hard travel had exhausted him, numbing his wounds, though the agonizing pain still lurked, ready to pounce the moment he relaxed. Yesterday, he had stopped only long enough to change horses until Jon's concern for the coachman had prompted a brief midnight halt at an inn. But despite a sleepless night and long day, he'd found no rest, plagued by nightmares whenever he dozed off, each harsher than the last. Now the sun was again setting, its last rays turning a passing tree red.

The same red as her hair.

No!

Remembering was pointless, he reminded himself. Forgiveness was an alien concept to Miss Lying-Through-Her-Teeth Merideth-Vale. She wanted absolutes in her life—absolute honesty, absolute purity, absolute respect for her talents. Well, she could have her absolutes. He was absolutely gone and he would stay that way.

He recognized the church spire in the distance. They would

push on for another three hours before stopping. A dawn start would bring them to Linden Park by three. Speaking with his father was a meeting neither would enjoy, but he could not postpone it. Only days remained before they must be gone.

She would never forgive him. She might have eventually done so if his only crime had been that insane deception. But he'd lost his temper, deliberately hurting her in childish retaliation for his own pain, tossing out words he knew would slice deep into her heart. He'd watched each one hit, taking satisfaction at every cringe, every blink, every tightening of her fists. It had been a stupid revenge. He shouldn't have done it. Every one of her flinches had scraped a new strip from his soul. And he had stepped outside the bounds of civilized conduct.

Maybe she was right. His character was fatally flawed. He might protest that he was innocent, but his reputation was a product of his own behavior. New anger had prompted a tirade consistent with that reputation, despite being alien to Torwell's usual conduct and his own self-image. The hole he'd dug himself into was now six feet deep, and the coffin lid was sealed. He was the last person on earth she would consider forgiving.

So he must move on. Once he confessed this latest failure and made what peace he could with his father, he would look to the future. Yesterday's plans were even sounder without the added expense of a wife and family. He could not allow his mother to suffer. Sharing a roof with his father would be a well-deserved punishment for throwing his reputation to the dogs.

When Tony entered the study, Linden ignored him. He'd drawn his favorite wing chair close to the fire, but not a muscle moved as he stared at the flames. In the weeks since their last meeting, he had aged at least ten years.

"Father?" Though nervous, he sat in the other chair. This was a time for confession and compromise, not confrontation. Pacing or looming above Linden's head would create the wrong impression.

"I am surprised that you returned." His voice lacked its usual harshness. "There is little point. Sir Winton's trustee will take charge in two days."

This was not the reception he had expected. He scrambled to revise his planned opening as his father continued.

"But at least this gives me an opportunity to beg your forgiveness."

"It is done. Nothing can be changed. As you pointed out at our last meeting, the estate was yours to dispose of as you pleased."

"That is not what I meant." Linden shifted, revealing the tension his pose had hidden, a tension growing from pain rather than the anger and arrogance he usually radiated. "The estate was a family treasure, to be guarded and nourished by each custodian until it passed to the next generation. When we last spoke, I was still trying to deflect responsibility for my poor stewardship."

"I understand. We all find ways to excuse ourselves, but it is done." He was more uncomfortable than if the man had ranted in his usual way. At least he knew how to deal with that.

"Yes, it is done, but I must apologize. Losing everything is my well-deserved punishment for a lifetime of poor decisions and inexcusable arrogance. I can live with that. What I find hard to accept is that others must also pay for my crimes—you, your mother, the servants, the tenants . . ."

"This is not necessary, Father." Had the man been drinking again? Never before had he been maudlin. But a quick glance found no sign of wine.

Linden bit his lip. "I do not expect forgiveness, but at least hear me out."

Tony nodded. Listening hurt, but he'd been on the other end of that request only three days ago. Refusing made him no better than Miss Vale. If he ever hoped to build rapport with his father, he must let him explain.

"I have ruined your life, for you would never have followed this course had I not railed so loudly against it."

"Perhaps, though I have made plenty of mistakes on my own."

"I wanted to protect you from repeating my errors." He seemed not to have heard the interruption. "You were such a bright child, Tony. Happy and healthy, with charm to spare. I prayed that you would always remain happy, but I feared what would happen when you grew older. You were so like my brother Daniel—and me."

Tony stared, unable to recognize this blue-deviled man as the disapproving autocrat he usually faced. Something was happening that he couldn't explain. Had Linden spent the entire month in maudlin contemplation? "What do you mean?"

"I was wild as a youth," Linden admitted, briefly raising his eyes before returning his gaze to the fire. "As was Daniel, though he quieted once he married. Thank God Jonathan inherited that calm while avoiding Daniel's instability."

"What tale is this?"

Linden shrugged. "I should have told you years ago. Daniel ran berserk one day, killing his wife and then himself. Explosive tempers are the family curse."

"My God." He'd always thought Jon's parents had died in a carriage accident. Did Jon know the truth?

"In my case, temper combined with the arrogance of knowing I was heir to a title. My father's discourses on the exalted deeds of our ancestors made that arrogance worse. I never allowed anyone to question my actions—which cost me dearly enough. If someone challenged my courage or my expertise, I had to prove them wrong. Winton Vale took advantage of that failing. I lost a good portion of my allowance to him nearly every quarter. Though I knew I was a terrible card player, I would invariably respond to his taunts and dares by accepting a game. He always won."

Biting his lip to remain quiet, Tony sifted the words. He had never met anyone whose luck was consistently out, so it was more likely that Sir Winton had already mastered the art of sharping cards. Even if prudence prevented him from cheating others, Linden had been an unsuspecting victim.

He knew other men who needed to prove themselves superior. They jumped at any challenge, never considering the consequences. Some complained loudly and bitterly when they lost—and fought frequent duels when their complaints included charges of cheating. Others crawled away to lick their wounds in private, feeling ill-used. But none learned anything from the experience. So why had he never detected such a fault in his father?

"When I reached London, I tried to avoid him," Linden continued. "But he had a knack for finding me when I was in my cups, then talking me into just one game. But my luck was always out with him."

He leaned forward to dangle his hands between his legs, turning toward the fire so he could only see Tony by looking over his shoulder. "My skill had improved with time and study, so I played often with others, amassing a fortune to protect me from Winton. But even skill does not guarantee success. The culmination of my folly occurred two years after you were born. Winton was not in London, so I feared nothing. I was well into the second bottle when Lady Luck deserted me. Hand after hand fell to my opponent. By evening's end, he held vowels for nearly everything I owned. In desperation, I offered one last wager—Linden Park against that mound of vowels, the winner to be decided on a single cut of the cards."

"My God."

He glanced back. "Insanity, I agree. I turned up a four and was calculating how long it would take to stagger home and put an end to my life—"

Another gasp escaped his throat.

"—when he drew a three. I'd escaped by the narrowest of margins. Even drunk, I swore I would never wager again. By morning, I'd renewed that vow. I left London immediately and never returned, fearful that a taunt would draw me into another game. And I swore that somehow I would keep you from making the same mistake. Yet in the end, I broke both vows. Sir Winton found me, enticing me into a game of dice. And I drove you into the very trouble I had hoped to avoid."

"No, you didn't."

"Don't be kind, Tony. I know you would never have pursued the course you've taken without my constant nagging."

"True. Tossing my reputation away in response to your pressure was stupid—though even that first year, my behavior was never as sordid as gossip suggested. And it has been many years since it matched at all."

Linden again glanced over his shoulder, then sighed. "Then I have more to repent than I thought, for my continued laments over your excesses must have contributed to public perception."

"Undoubtedly." This was one point that he would not concede. He had done nothing for at least eight years that would support that reputation, yet it continued to grow.

"Our last meeting was the first time I suspected I might have been wrong," he said wearily. "You reminded me that you have never overspent your allowance. It was not a point I had considered, but I cannot think of a single friend whose children can make that claim. How can you support yourself? You receive no more from the estate than I did forty years ago, but surely prices have risen. If you won significant amounts at the table, rumor would have reported it."

"Actually, I have done little gaming of any kind since leaving school," he admitted. "And even in school, I usually won as much as I lost—not that you would have heard; one large loss is noteworthy while ten minor wins pass unnoticed."

"And I suppose you will claim that those very sordid house parties you attend are merely a way to reduce expenses?" This time his voice contained a hint of his usual displeasure.

"Gossip." Tony shook his head. "Once one acquires a lurid reputation, people will believe any tale. While I am sure that such parties exist—though not as many as rumor would have us believe—I have never attended one. But that has become the accepted explanation for any absence from town. I'm sure most of society believes I am engaged in yet another orgy right now."

"Then where do you go?"

He paced the room, though he had decided even before arriving home that he would have to reveal everything. "I realized long ago that nothing would overturn the reputation my temper had created. Yet it barred me from pursuing any of my interests. I could have become yet another useless fribble content to prance about London until the title fell into my hands, but society bores me, and I have never aspired to leisure. So my only choice was to become someone else. Because he cannot risk meeting anyone who knows Tony Linden, Mr. Torwell is a recluse. Yet his excavations have drawn considerable interest in antiquarian circles."

"You dig up remains?" demanded Linden.

"Roman sites in remote areas, for most of each summer. I've been fascinated by the past since finding a Roman denarius in the stream twenty years ago. Torwell is now considered an authority on the period." He spotted several copies of *The Edinburgh Review* on a shelf. Opening a six-months-old volume, he dropped it in his father's lap.

"*Regional Differences in Roman Mosaic Design, a comparative study of themes and ornamentation found in decorative flooring from Lincolnshire and Gloucestershire,*" Linden read, each word sounding more incredulous than the last. "You wrote this?"

He nodded.

"Yet you've never shown the least interest in that site Frosham is so proud of."

"Who do you think discovered it?"

"B-but that was fourteen years ago."

"I didn't consider how that coin might have washed into the stream until several years after finding it. Its condition was too good to have tumbled for long, so I poked about upstream, finally stumbling across Frosham's villa. I had to return to school, so I could not do the actual excavation, but I had dug out enough to know what he had."

"I've never known you at all, have I?"

"That is as much my fault as yours, Father. I was too stubborn to admit that your antagonism grew from concern, and even after I realized that my rebellion was childish—and was hurting me far more than you—I made no attempt to reveal the truth. But we can discuss that later. Now we need to consider the future. I tried to regain the estate by offering for Miss Vale, but I handled it very badly." He explained his sojourn at Vale House, though deleting any mention of her villa. "She will never forgive me, so the estate is truly lost."

"I know."

"Torwell received grants from several patrons, so I've been able to invest most of my allowance in recent years. The income is not quite large enough to support me, but my secretary is arranging purchase of a small estate in Somerset. Once people recover from the shock of learning that Torwell is the notorious Tony Linden, I may receive funding for new excavations. In the meantime, the estate income will do. You are welcome to join me."

"I am delighted that you will have a roof over your head, Tony, and more relieved than I can say that you have prospered despite me," he said, then shook his head. "But living together would never work. The habits of a lifetime will not change overnight. And it seems we are more alike than I'd ever thought. I, too, need to remain occupied, or I will become even more annoying."

"Have you anything in mind?" The refusal was a relief, though not in the way he would have expected even an hour ago. They were both revising a lifetime of beliefs, but their new rapport was too fragile to tolerate strain.

"Possibly. I will know more soon. In the meantime, I've accepted an invitation to visit an old friend. We will leave as soon as the estate transfer is concluded. Will you be staying?"

"Only until morning. I must meet with the bankers and pray they will allow me to explain why Tony Linden expects a loan."

"Why not Torwell?"

"I am done with deceit and done with skulking about the shadows. For good or ill, I will play myself from now on. Let me know your new direction. I will be in London for at least a month."

Excusing himself, he went in search of his mother.

Three days of soul-searching had led to this decision. Living dual identities had influenced every aspect of his life, always negatively. The fiasco with Miss Vale was merely the latest example. He had to plan every move, every word, even his gestures, to keep the two lives separate and to prevent misunderstandings. Linden was flamboyant and frequently irreverent, inserting suggestive innuendo into even innocuous conversation. Torwell was staid, methodical, and emotionless about everything but the Romans. Neither character was natural.

Now it was over. Though it was too late for happiness, at least he could achieve a modicum of comfort.

Sarah sighed. A third reading of Jon's letter confirmed that she had missed nothing.

He had written it shortly after leaving, providing the first explanation she'd received for the events of three mornings past. All he'd managed in that last mad scramble was a murmur to Murch to *tell Sarah I'll be in touch*. She hadn't even known he was gone until Murch found her beating on Alex's door.

Alex had remained in her room until early this morning, but even after emerging, she refused to reveal what had happened or why. In fact, she ignored any reference to the gentlemen's visit, aside from offering belated congratulations on her betrothal.

When she'd pressed for answers, Alex had ordered her to be quiet or leave Vale House.

So she had welcomed Jon's letter.

Unfortunately, he knew little more than she did. Apparently Alex had discovered the deception on her own and attacked Tony. He'd retaliated. The ensuing argument ended with Alex throwing both men out of the house—or with Tony fleeing. It wasn't clear which.

Alex's temper had often led to trouble, and her stubbornness usually made that trouble worse. If her curt refusal to speak was any indication, she was already regretting her reaction. And it sounded as if Tony was just as unhappy. But Jon described Tony as the stubborn sort, which didn't sound very promising.

She sighed.

The least thought proved that Alex and Tony were perfectly suited, not that either would admit it at the moment. So it was up to her and Jon to bring them together. The first step was to make sure that each understood the reasons behind the other's charade. And perhaps Murch would know more about that disastrous argument. Only after learning the facts could she plan a way around Alex's stubborn pride.

Her own future looked rosier. Smiling, she slipped the letter into her writing box, hardly believing that Jon really loved her. They would be married in two months.

In the meantime, she would tell him everything she knew about Alex, and hope he would respond with similar information about Tony.

She sharpened a pen.

Chapter Fifteen

Alex scraped another layer of soil from above the temple, keeping her back firmly turned to the villa.

A week had passed since she had emerged from her room, but this was the first day she had come to the site. Though her enthusiasm for excavating was gone, he would not have the satisfaction of destroying her interest in antiquity. She had already put off resuming her work far too long. She was lucky that no one had stumbled across the mosaic.

The weather had helped. Cold rain had moved in the day after he left, keeping most people indoors and adding to the protection already provided by the haunted wood. But it wasn't enough.

So security was her first concern. In spite of his faults, she could not ignore his warnings. How he chose to use his own knowledge was out of her hands, but at least she could hide the mosaic from others.

Rain had washed a thin coat of mud over the tiles. She'd spent the morning filling the trench and tamping it solid. Then she'd dragged dead grass, leaves, and debris across the area until it was indistinguishable from the rest of the clearing. But despite frequent reminders that she was protecting the treasure from vandals, her heart knew that her real purpose was to erase the scene of that torrid kiss.

No wonder it had melted her bones. Tony Linden was a rake of the first water. He probably had more experience than all the men in the village combined. And their encounter had meant no more to him than any of his others.

Cursing, she hacked at a mat of grass and roots that had transformed into his treacherous face.

"Damn you!"

Squeezing her eyes closed helped no more than keeping her back to the villa or burying the mosaic. Awake or asleep, all else faded, overlaid by images of the wretch—wading along the stream, oblivious to his ruined boots; scrambling up the cliff, his shoulder brushing hers as he pointed out hints of Roman foundations; heaving stones aside, muscles rippling under a thin cambric shirt; debating where to lay out exploration trenches . . .

The mat disintegrated under her assault.

She had won as many debates as he had, some leading to success, others to frustration. But neither of them had expected to find that mosaic. Her hand shook, rekindling every image of that celebration . . .

Stop this, Alex!

Pain crashed back. And desolation.

He could hardly have reached the village before the first regret set in. Despite her charges, she knew he really was Torwell. He could not have discovered her interest before arriving, for no one knew outside the household. The staff would never have revealed it to a stranger, not even one as beguiling as him. And no man could have learned enough about Torwell and Roman remains to fool her. Not in the time he'd had available. He'd turned up on her doorstep only a few days after his father had lost Linden Park.

In retrospect, it was obvious how he'd managed to live two separate lives. Torwell was reclusive. His response to her dilemma over Mitchell's suggestion spoke from experience. His assistant presented his papers to the Antiquarian Society, so he'd probably never met the men who held his scholarship in esteem. And he worked in remote areas from necessity, hiding his notoriety beneath a facade of shyness.

"It doesn't matter," she said aloud, hoping to convince her stubborn conscience.

It had been plaguing her for days. She hadn't lost her temper so badly in years, lashing out in a pointless attempt to assuage her pain, saying anything that might hurt, and denying even obvious facts. His deceit still hurt. She'd respected him, trusted him, loved him . . . Yet all the time he had been living a lie.

So were you.

But that was different. She'd been protecting herself from harm, not hiding her character. *Tossing your innocent companion into a situation you dared not face yourself . . .*

But she'd been right that Sarah would be safe. *She has more integrity in one finger . . .*

Yes, Sarah had been safe. He respected her too much to cause her any grief. And he had rarely been alone with her. He wasn't all bad.

He isn't bad at all, insisted the voice.

Well, maybe . . .

You know he's not. And so does Sarah.

Sarah had been driving her crazy with *Jon this* and *Jon that.* He wrote nearly every day—*so considerate, Alex; he even gets his uncle to frank his letters so I needn't pay for delivery*—always including long descriptions of his cousin. Sarah insisted on reading the letters aloud over breakfast, which she was unaccountably sharing these days, and referring to them in every conversation. It was one reason she'd come to the villa today.

Why couldn't Sarah accept reality? It was over. Nothing could put their partnership back together. It was irretrievably broken. The only way to survive was to put him behind her and get on with life.

Yet Sarah persisted, painting word pictures that merely added to her pain.

Tony was far from the care-for-naught rumor described. He often helped servants, tenants, villagers, and even area residents with no claim on Linden Park. But he never took credit, using Jon to administer the anonymous funds.

Only two people mattered to him—Jon and his mother. He would do anything to protect them, particularly his mother. Most of the pranks he had perpetrated in his youth had been deliberate attempts to distract his father from castigating her. At other times, Tony had shouldered the blame for acts he had not committed, or had deliberately broken his father's rules, again to deflect the man's attention.

Lord Linden was a harsh man who forbade everything enjoyable. He was even harsher with Tony than with his wife, setting spies to watch his every move and waging a war of wills. Instead of submitting tamely, Tony had fought back, finally exploding in a display of every vice his father abhorred. Thus was born his reputation. Despite repenting—and avoiding any repetition of that spree—rumors followed him to this day. Ten years ago, he'd given up, inventing Mr. Torwell so he could pursue his love of antiquity.

She could understand. Embracing masculine mannerisms and flaunting her education had been a futile attempt to show the world that her own father's criticisms didn't hurt. And hadn't she also adopted an alter ego with Lord Mitchell? Having a father like Lord Linden would be enough to make anyone rebel.

Not that it mattered. It was too late for truth. After that exchange of insults, deceit was irrelevant. No man would forgive her taunts and stabs. She had meant to hurt him, and she had. Even if she could stretch her own love far enough to put that argument behind her, he could not. Sarah's report confirmed his own words upon arrival, words he had repeated before she threw him out: He had come here solely to protect his mother. He cared nothing for Miss Alex Vale. He might have accepted Sarah as the price of restoring his mother's home, but he couldn't accept her.

"Pay attention," she admonished herself, scraping at the next layer of soil. The temple was the one area where he had never worked. Thus it was the only place she had any hope of maintaining her composure.

The trowel struck another rock.

Sighing, she concentrated on removing it. It would be the third today, each surrounded by shattered roof tiles. She'd carefully extracted fragments, hoping to find intact floor beneath, yet so far, nothing else had turned up. Maybe the temple had held no decoration.

Interest stirred as she exposed a curved edge. It was neither stone nor tile. The color was wrong.

Excitement mounted, driving everything else from her mind. Slowly, an amphora emerged from the ground. Intact. Even its delicate handles remained.

She had never seen one before, though one of her books contained an illustration. Ancient peoples had used them as storage jars for wines, oils, grains, and possibly other things. To find one here, undamaged, was almost miraculous.

Tony was right. The site must have flooded, cushioning corners with mud that had protected them from the slide.

He would love to see this, wouldn't he, Alex?

How true. He would be so excited. He might even kiss her again . . .

Heat instantly seared her body.

"Damn you!" she shouted as tears coursed down her cheeks. "How am I supposed to work with you looking over my shoulder?"

Scrubbing her face dry with her skirt—she had locked the pantaloons in her workroom, determined to set the past firmly behind her—she put away the tools. "I won't let him ruin this excavation. I won't let him invade my dreams. And I will *not* shed another tear for that man."

She pulled out a sketch pad.

Her life was her own, just as she had always planned. His intrusion had been too brief to matter. Her disappointment would fade. So would her pain. In the meantime, she must stay busy.

Once she finished the sketch, she gently lifted the amphora from its bed of mud. Cradling it in her arms, she headed for her workroom.

Jon ignored Tony's glare. He'd expected it, though understanding the cause did not negate the pain.

Tony had left Linden Park the day after they'd arrived, without even bidding him farewell. Nor had he responded to letters in the two weeks since. So he'd come to London.

"Don't let that stubborn temper build a new barrier between you and the world," he said now. "You are behaving just as stupidly over this as you did about wrecking your reputation."

Tony slammed a fist onto the desktop that separated them. "I cannot believe you came all the way to London to meddle in my affairs. Are you sure Sir Winton's agent did not throw you out?"

"Positive. He has kept the staff intact and approved the plans for next year's planting. That is as far as his concern extends, for his tenure will end next summer. Sir Winton has already told Alex that she will be unwelcome at Vale House after the Season. Either she weds or she starves."

"It's her choice," he said.

"It is also yours. Alex is miserable."

"Because she has to find a new companion—if she bothers doing so. She's odd enough to flout even that convention. Now change the subject. I am not interested in her activities, her looks, or her feelings."

"But Sarah says—"

"Enough, Jon." He strode to the window, keeping his back to the room. "It's over. I misplayed the hand and lost. End of discussion. It's time to move on."

"I don't believe that. Nor do you, if you would only look beyond your grief and pain."

"Much of it caused by your persistence, Jon. Why must you torment me?" His fists clenched.

Jon flinched. "I owe you too much to let pride destroy your best hope of finding the happiness you so richly deserve."

"You owe me no—"

"You welcomed me, Tony," he said, hoping a reminder of those days might soften Tony's antagonism. "You supported me through the worst period of my life, accepting my intrusion into your world, giving me more affection than most boys accord a brother, and not once criticizing my tears or demanding to know why it took me more than a year to recover. Many children lose their parents, but they manage to move on."

"You needn't refine on it. I was lonely and needed a playmate." But he'd stiffened.

"Uncle Thomas told me he'd let the sordid details out of the bag. But even he doesn't know everything." He had to inhale deeply to keep his voice steady. "I found them that day, sprawled in pools of blood. I held my father's hand while he begged my forgiveness, tears streaming down his face. I watched him draw his last breath. So don't talk to me of finality and impossibilities. As long as you can breathe, you can repair any breach."

"A lovely thought," said Tony, walking to the door. His averted head hid his own tears. "But not in this case. You don't know the facts, Jon. Nor does Sarah, or she would not keep pressing. It's over."

Jon gave up, allowing Tony to push him out—for now.

Tony grimaced as he returned to his desk. It was bad enough that Jon had shown up in person to berate him. But why had he trotted out his parents' deaths? Dear Lord, it had been worse than he'd thought. No wonder Jon had been so distraught.

But he had done nothing to help Jon recover, so bringing up such ancient history was merely another way of applying pressure. And this was only the beginning. They had agreed to dine together.

He should have stopped at the vicarage before leaving Linden Park, but he hadn't felt up to facing those judgmental eyes. Not when he was already reeling from emotion. Leaving the Park for the last time had been harder than he'd anticipated. Despite years of conflict, the Park was home. He'd expected to live out his life there and be buried with his ancestors.

As if that wasn't enough, a host of other feelings had swirled through his head—hope that the fragile truce with his father would continue, guilt for failing his mother, pain . . . He couldn't have faced another of Jon's sermons.

The Vale House fiasco had strained their relationship badly.

He had never expected Jon to become a dedicated matchmaker. This latest confession merely made it worse.

"It's over," he repeated, focusing on piles of paper atop his desk. "Everything's over."

He'd finished the article for *The Edinburgh Review*, working late into the night so he'd be tired enough to sleep without dreaming.

Surprisingly, Simms had found a banker willing to loan Tony Linden money, though the letter of recommendation from his father might have helped. An agent had settled the purchase of the Somerset property, so at least part of his life was proceeding smoothly. He could take possession within a fortnight. Not that he would personally do so. It was too close to Gloucestershire. Before heading west, he had to put the Vale House visit behind him. So he would go north.

Despite the season, he had requested permission to excavate a Roman encampment near Hadrian's wall. It was a site that had intrigued him for fifteen years, ever since he'd visited a schoolmate whose father owned the land. He'd signed his request *Torwell*, though Lord Pembroke would recognize him the moment he arrived. But explanations were better made in person.

Northumberland in November matched his mood. It would be cold, windy, and gray. Very gray. Very cold. Perhaps freezing the pain would lessen its impact.

And the project would serve other purposes. It would begin the difficult process of redeeming his reputation, for this was the last time he would hide behind the Torwell name. It would keep him busy, exhausted, and fed without having to sell the first editions that had been a parting gift from his father. And it would take him a long way from Gloucestershire.

He could not afford to go within a hundred miles of Vale House. If she were near, nothing would stop him from calling, on his knees if necessary, to beg. And she would laugh in his face, witch that she was. He could not survive another encounter.

Look to the future, he reminded himself for the thousandth time as he banished her face from his mind. His hopes were as dead as the Romans he studied. Nothing but pain would come of dwelling on them.

Focusing once more on the job at hand, he resumed sorting notes and papers. Those to be kept went into trunks that Simms would move to Somerset.

A week later, Simms escorted Lord Linden into Tony's denuded study.

"Did you change your mind about joining me?" he asked, pouring wine.

"No. I accepted an appointment as governor of Elboa."

He nearly choked. "What and where is Elboa?"

"An island in the Caribbean. The previous governor died last month, so the government is pleased that I can sail immediately."

"How does Mother feel about leaving the country?" His head was spinning at the unexpectedness. His father had never hinted at an interest in government service, nor had he mentioned the sort of connections that could obtain a post so quickly.

"Pleased. The winters have bothered her in recent years. She looks forward to the warmth." He hesitated before pulling out a letter. "Jonathan asked me to deliver this. He is concerned about you."

"He needn't be." He set the missive aside, fighting temper at Jon's continued meddling. "He has fallen into the euphoria that too many newly betrothed men experience. Having settled his own future, he wants his friends to join him. But he does not realize that some alliances are impossible."

"Don't—" Linden started to speak, but changed his mind. "I am not qualified to question your decisions, Tony. Or even to offer advice. But I hope that you are not suffering the same blindness that afflicted me for so many years. The Linden temper takes many forms, but it will destroy your life only if you allow it to." He set his glass on the desk. "We sail tomorrow. Will you dine with us this evening?"

"I would be delighted. And I am equally delighted that you arrived today. I signed the purchase papers for Nolton Grange yesterday. Tomorrow, I will be leaving London."

"Excellent. We will expect you at the Pulteny at seven."

Tony passed a pleasant evening with his parents. Bidding them farewell was surprisingly difficult. He was only beginning to know his father, but that process would now be postponed for several years. Yet it could not be helped. The appointment offered Linden a new life, restoring his self-respect. If he remained there long enough, he might even rebuild his fortune.

Once they sailed, Tony directed his carriage north, hoping that frost and snow might freeze his heart enough that he could survive. Simms would move his belongings to Nolton, then await further instructions. Jon's unopened letter went with him.

Chapter Sixteen

Cold November winds whipped across the clearing. Alex shuddered, despite her heavy cloak. Digging in this weather was incredibly stupid, but she couldn't help herself. The last month had been the longest she'd ever known. Only constant activity kept the tears at bay.

She had expected time to ease the pain, but it hadn't. Bluedevils escorted her everywhere. She no longer cared that her father had found three more men eager to wed her dowry—she'd refused admittance to the first two—nor that he was selling centuries-old silver to cover another disaster at the gaming tables. Even the plight of a tenant whose roof leaked raised only passing sympathy. Perhaps it really was possible to die of a broken heart.

Ironically, the most comforting spot on the estate was this clearing. His ghost might permeate the very soil, but at least those memories were good. She hadn't entered the family dining room since ordering him away. And the drawing and music rooms echoed with evidence that he'd been courting the fortune. But the villa had been real. They'd become friends and partners here as they pursued the one interest they had in common.

So she spent ever shorter days here. It reminded her that at least one man had respected her intelligence. It kept her too busy to fall into a decline. And it avoided Sarah.

Thank God, Sarah would be gone in another month. As uncharitable as that thought was, she was heartily sick of her constant chatter. Too much of it concerned Tony. Recalling the good times was one thing. Remembering his lies was quite another.

She was tired of hearing about the rift with his father, his love for his mother, or even the improbable claim that he was miserable.

Many of Jon's explanations were biased—like Tony's courtship of Sarah. He may have stepped aside once he learned that Sarah did not control his fortune, but he'd assiduously pursued her until the moment she accepted Jon. In all that time, his expression had rarely varied from Jon's, so she could only interpret it the same way. Jon loved Sarah. So how could he claim that Tony didn't?

Jon saw only what he wanted to see, as did Sarah. In their own happiness, they ignored the most obvious fact of all. Tony hated to lose, fighting for anything he truly wanted. Why else had he created Torwell? Why had he come to Vale House in the first place?

But he was not fighting now. He'd made no attempt to return. He'd ignored Jon's pressure, refusing to respond to letters since leaving Linden Park. Jon only knew where he was because Lord Linden had posted one last note before sailing. Either he loved Sarah, or he hated Alex. Perhaps both.

If he regretted this break, he would have forgiven her diatribe by now, just as she had forgiven him—mostly. He would have tried to change her mind—battering the door down, kissing her senseless, scrambling her brains until she believed anything he said. She had no doubt he could do it.

And he knew it. With his experience, he could hardly have missed her reaction that day. It was an unwelcome reminder of how he'd stiffened when he realized who he'd been kissing.

She had to accept reality. He hadn't made even a token effort to change her mind. Instead, he'd arranged a new excavation in Northumberland, moving on with his life. He'd probably forgotten all about her—unless he was entertaining his friends with bawdy jokes about the ungainly redhead who'd thrown herself at him.

"Damn the man," she swore, whipping up her fury. He must have welcomed an excuse to leave. And now that his mother was provided for, he was probably thanking fate for his lucky escape.

Sarah was all about in the head to think that he cared. The man was an actor so at home with deception that he no longer recognized truth.

Swiping her foot across the ground to clear it of dead leaves, she drove in her spade.

She was a fool to wear the willow for him. The temple would be finished soon. Once her notes were complete, she would decide what to do with it. Aside from the amphora, it had contained nothing her father would value. She'd found no sign of an altar, which might have been swept away, so perhaps she would follow the debris trail for a short way.

She had covered the other trenches, obliterating anything that might encourage a search of the clearing. All she'd left were half a dozen sterile pits strategically scattered around the temple. But perhaps she should bury everything. Come spring, she must leave Vale House. She might never return.

Plummeting temperatures finally drove her back to the house. Her teeth chattered so badly that she actually welcomed Sarah's company, for it included tea.

"You are making yourself ill, Alex," Sarah chided.

"I am never ill."

"Alex!" Sarah's temper exploded for the first time in years. "Look at yourself. You've lost more than a stone because you won't eat. You haunt the villa regardless of the weather, returning drenched with rain and stiff with cold. If this keeps up, you will die of lung fever before the winter is out. Admit it. No matter how impossible Tony is, you love him. Isn't it time to abandon your stubborn pride and do something about it?"

"You cannot remake the world just because you want everyone to be happy," she said wearily. "If he cared, I would know."

"How? You are blind, Alex. Can't you accept that his reputation is a charade?"

"You convinced me of that weeks ago."

Sarah paced the drawing room. "But you refuse to consider what that means. Think about it, Alex. How must he feel to be reviled for things he didn't do, to be shunned as if he had some horrid disease, and to have his name bandied about the country as a representative of the devil? He is intelligent and sensitive. Despite knowing the tales are false and that most were a product of his own invention, part of him must believe he is a pariah. And things like this can't help." She tossed the latest *Morning Post* onto her lap.

A small paragraph in the society column was circled. *Drawing rooms are agog at Mr. T— L—'s latest prank. Impersonating a respected scholar adds a new twist to a reputation already beyond repair. A— T—must be appalled!*

Alex set her cup carefully aside. She had soothed her own pain by finding excuses for his words—he didn't truly know her; her attack had shocked him into responding without thought; he'd been justifiably appalled at her treatment of Sarah; words spouted in anger didn't count, so he hadn't really meant them. When he stayed away, she had cursed him for toying with her affections and stealing a heart he didn't want. But not once had she considered how her insults had affected him, expecting him to know that she had only been in a temper, so the words meant nothing.

She had flung charges at him without remorse, tossing out anything that might hurt. Just as society had done for most of his life. Just as his own father did. So he'd reacted as he always did when people turned on him, picking up the pieces and moving on, seeking out an isolated ruin where he could lose himself in work. Why would he think about her again? She'd demonstrated that she was just like everyone else, refusing to even listen to an explanation. He would do nothing to reopen old wounds. *I always land on my feet.* Why hadn't she recognized the agonizing loneliness underlying that cocky grin? He'd even told her—*I thought you were different . . . what a fool I was.*

Sarah must have realized that her words had finally made an impression. "You are so much alike," she said, resuming her seat. "Unfortunately, two of the things you share are stubbornness and temper. Yes, your last meeting was painful. But forgiveness is possible—provided one of you sets pride aside long enough to make the first move. He loves you. Why else would he flee as far from here as possible? No one of sense would excavate in Northumberland this time of year. He's killing himself trying to forget you. Jon described him on that trip to Linden Park. He was devastated, so brittle that Jon feared he would shatter. Believe me, Alex. His emotions are firmly engaged. You can sit here and pray that someday he might return—though I would not count on it; his confidence is even more fragile than yours—or you can apologize for being a quick-tempered fool. I know what I would do. But then, I love Jon. I would do anything to make him happy."

Without another word, she left.

Alex shivered.

Pride. Was that what she was suffering? It didn't seem possible, for she had often regretted her words. Tony must know that. Jon would have told him.

Assuming he'd read any of those letters he refused to answer. It would be just like him to toss them away unopened. He was the most stubborn, irritating man she had ever met.

Or was he?

Sarah's words gnawed at her mind as she soaked in the warm water Murch always had waiting. She had also been ridiculed most of her life, though nothing like what he had faced. But even Torwell's reclusive facade would not have protected him from society's disdain, merely emphasizing his predicament. Torwell could only be respected from a distance. He could not enter the world to which he had been born as anyone but Tony Linden. The moment he met someone face-to-face, his reputation would determine his status—as she had proved.

She shivered, recalling some of the charges she'd flung at his head. Despite knowing him first as Torwell, despite her reverence for Torwell's knowledge and accomplishments, she had judged him solely by rumor, innuendo, and spite.

Was that why he'd abandoned his last sanctuary by saddling Torwell with Tony Linden's reputation? Had he quit trying? But all he'd accomplished was to draw censure for a new crime.

She had hurt him badly. Worse even than she'd thought. Perhaps enough that he could never forgive her.

Coward!

He had spoken truly, for she really was a coward. She'd hidden from the world by pushing the world away. It was time for truth. She would never know if forgiveness was possible unless she tried.

Heart pounding, she threw on a wrapper and headed for her workroom. A letter of apology would do no good. He would toss it aside with Jon's. So she had to approach him in a way he would understand . . .

Tony plodded back to the manor from the most frustrating dig he had ever conducted. He tried to blame the weather—though snow had not yet made an appearance, the frigid wind penetrated even the heaviest clothing, and the ground grew harder every day—but weather had little to do with his blue-devils. Nor did the site, which was fascinating. Only a few coins and scraps of metal were turning up, but the foundations were nearly intact, providing an excellent picture of the encampment's design.

A picture that meant nothing.

The real problem was himself. Only two weeks of working with Alex had ruined him for working alone. He missed their debates. Each new find excited her, prompting speculation about its nature. She was a knowledgeable partner who could fill hours of unproductive digging with stimulating conversation. But most of all, he missed celebrating successes, like finding that mosaic.

He tightened his jaw.

Excavation was a lonely business. Not that he was entirely alone this time. Pembroke had assigned several gardeners to help him, but they had no interest in the work or understanding of what they found.

"Get used to it," he grumbled, climbing the stairs to his room. The butler would have warm water and a fire waiting.

Pembroke had been shocked to see him—and wary. If the man had not recently married off his last daughter, he might well have barred the door.

It was no more than he'd expected.

They had talked quite late that first night. Tony had set out the basic facts of Torwell's creation, then described his exploration of the fort during his brief visit fifteen years ago.

"But I thought you spent that week at the Spotted Dog," Pembroke had exclaimed, naming the local inn.

"Youthful foolishness." Tony had shaken his head. "I wanted to punish my father. It took a few years to realize that I was only hurting myself."

Pembroke had quizzed him on the Romans, but by the end of the evening, he accepted the truth. The rest of society would be harder to convince, though, if recent gossip columns were any indication.

But that was a problem for later. Pushing his bedchamber door open, he froze.

"What the—"

A crate sat on the hearth rug, his name on its label. But that label offered no clue to either its contents or its sender. The direction was not written in Jon's hand, or any other he'd seen.

Cold forgotten, he pried open the top and gingerly removed packing material until he reached an amphora. A letter lay on top. His heart pounded. This hand he recognized.

Mr. Linden,

When I found this, I knew you would wish to examine it. Its survival is astonishing, for it was surrounded by broken stone and shattered roof tile. Judging by the quantity of shards I found, there must have originally been a dozen or more, though only this one remains intact. Perhaps they held ritual wine. I would appreciate your thoughts.

I have reburied the villa, particularly the mosaic. Father has lost consistently since rising from his sickbed, so I dare not reveal its existence. What further security measures would you recommend? If I can deflect Father's plans for the Season, I hope to search for the temple's missing altar.

Alexandra Merideth Vale

Pain nearly blinded him. He read the note again, then a third time. Each reading increased his agony. Imagining her burying the mosaic recalled their embrace, doubling him over. Would the memories never subside? Damn her for bringing it all back.

But even pain could not stifle his excitement. He picked up the amphora, running his hands over the surface as she must have done. She'd cleaned it beautifully, but it was too small to have held wine. Perhaps it had contained ritual oil.

But he would speculate later. Holding it nearer the lamp, he turned it between his hands, reveling in its survival, a jewel plucked from a sea of mud.

Survival.

A landslide had buried the villa, crushing the walls, shattering the roof, battering the debris into unrecognizable chips. Yet this remained intact. The violence that had desecrated hearth and home, sacred and profane, had left this untouched.

Like his love. It burned as bright as ever. Escape had not lessened the pain. The cruelest words had dimmed nothing.

That was her message, he realized on a surge of hope. No matter how vehemently others rejected him, she would not. Though angry words had buried their love, it remained undamaged, waiting to emerge into the light of day once they scraped away that obscuring veil of doubt and distrust. She was offering him a second chance.

What a stubborn fool he had been. He should not have quitted the field without a fight. Pride was an empty thing, especially when clinging to it consigned him to misery. How long would he have wallowed in grief before he admitted that he couldn't live without her? Thank God she'd been forgiving enough to reach out.

By the time he finished packing, he was certain. Why would she have mentioned her father's plans if she did not hope for rescue? And why search for an altar if not to wed . . .

Tony reached Vale House five days later, hardly believing he'd shaved three full days from the journey. Of course, his carriage was still somewhere in the Midlands, and he'd managed very little sleep.

Murch's greeting was curt. Only the fact that Jon was due within the hour kept the butler from turning him away.

Cursing himself for burning Jon's letters unread, he checked his impatience. "When is the wedding?"

"Tomorrow."

Murch made no attempt to mask his scorn, so Tony Linden's standing must be even lower than he'd feared. Not knowing the date of his cousin's wedding was yet another sin to hang on his conscience. Yet she'd sent him the amphora.

"Is Miss Alex at home?"

Murch glared, then jerked his head toward the wood before slamming the door in his face.

Why had he approached the house? He should have known she would be at the temple. If she hurt even half as much as he did, only constant work would keep her sane.

Shivers of excitement tickled his spine as his horse entered the wood, but trepidation grew stronger with each step. Had he misunderstood?

It was a question that had bedeviled him for days. He had flung the most hurtful words he could think of at her. Even if she knew he hadn't meant them, the pain would remain. Forgiveness might be possible, but could she ever forget?

He stopped at the edge of the clearing and slowly dismounted, drinking in the sight of her, his hands shaking so badly, he could barely tether his horse.

She was kneeling near the temple, facing away from him, patiently scraping soil from a shard. Longing shuddered through him, freezing his tongue. He forced his feet closer.

Was he about to make an ass of himself? She looked calm, as if nothing mattered but the work at hand. Maybe she had put him firmly in the past. She must have sent that crate weeks ago. Did she still care?

Questions surged through his head, feeding his uncertainty until he wanted to flee. Perhaps it would be better to meet in the drawing room, where convention would cover any awkwardness. Or in church tomorrow at Jon's wedding. Or in London next spring.

His foot stepped on a branch, cracking it. She jerked her head around and froze.

He cursed. She was too far away to read her expression. Thirty feet separated them, to say nothing of the gulf of harsh words . . .

A smile split her face as she sprang to her feet.

Unaware of moving, he caught her up in his arms, managing only, "I've missed you," before his lips crushed hers.

Alex threw her arms around his neck, hardly believing he was here. When she'd spotted him, it had seemed like yet another ghostly image of days long past. But he was real, in her arms, pressing her close to his hard body as his mouth devoured hers.

Their moans mingled.

"Alex . . . Alex . . ."

He trailed kisses across her face, murmuring her name again and again, distracting her from the knees that could no longer support her. She had yet to say a word.

Threading her fingers into his hair, she pulled his head up until she could see those incredible green eyes. "Tor— Lin—"

"Try Tony," he suggested, the undercurrent of laughter back in his voice.

"Welcome home, Tony."

His arms tightened. "This is hardly the proper time or place, but I must finish the business I meant to start at breakfast that day. I love you, Alex. I've tried living without you, and it doesn't work. Will you marry me?"

She cupped his cheek. "I cannot think of a better place," she murmured, then stiffened as his words sank in. "Dear Lord! What have I done?" He'd planned to offer for a companion? Abandon his inheritance and ignore his mother's need so he could be with her?

He froze. "Is an offer so shocking?" His voice had turned brittle.

"No— Oh, God, I'm doing it again. Forgive me, please? I love you."

His eyes warmed as he relaxed. "Then what was that all about?" He released her, stepping back as he ran his hands through his hair—and treading on his hat. She'd knocked it off.

"I just realized I was more in need of forgiveness than I'd thought. I never considered the possibility that you might offer for a companion, particularly one with so many faults." She'd hurt him worse than she'd known. No wonder he'd fled.

"What faults?" he demanded, grasping her shoulders so she had to meet his gaze.

"Too tall, too—"

He snorted. "And Jon claims *I'm* blind. Alex, my love, you are perfect. Surely you noticed me drooling over you from the moment I saw you. Rigging you out in my clothes was the stupidest thing I've ever done. Having to look at you every day nearly drove me insane with desire. I tried to pass it off as lust, but that horse wouldn't run. So no more talk of faults. I would change nothing, for you are beautiful, desirable, intelligent, loving, caring, a true original—"

"I also have a temper," she said dryly, as heat poured into her face.

"I love it, for I will never be able to ride roughshod over you the way my father always did to my mother. Now, let's return to business—in proper order this time. Please accept my heartfelt apologies for my cruel words at our last meeting. I meant none of them, but struck out to hide my own pain."

"As did I," she admitted. "Let's put the incident behind us and try to stick to truth in the future."

"Gladly. So on to more important business. I love you, Alex. Two months without you make hell look benign. Will you marry me?"

"I love you, Tony. I never want to go through such misery again. Yes."

This kiss was even headier than the others. His hands roamed her back, inciting waves of heat that melted her legs until she was hanging onto his shoulders to keep from falling.

"You've lost weight," he said a long time later, scooping her into his lap as he settled onto a pile of stones.

"So have you, and your eyes look so tired." She ran a finger over the circles that spoke of sleepless nights.

He grinned, looking every inch the rakehell she'd once thought him. "Not as tired as they'll be by morning."

"What *do* you mean?" But her shocked tone carried little weight, for her hands were buried in his hair.

He pulled out a special license.

"Is that still good?"

"Barely. It expires in two weeks, so we cannot take a chance on another argument postponing the ceremony. What do you say to an immediate wedding?"

"I would be delighted, but I doubt you can convince the vicar."

"The last time I checked, Jon was a duly ordained representative of the Church of England, authorized by the archbishop himself to administer sacraments. According to your estimable butler—whose eyes tried to cast me into eternal perdition when I showed up on your doorstep unannounced—Jon is due any minute. Considering the number of missives he's sent me in the past two months, I doubt he would object to marrying us."

"Nor do I."

"Once Jon and Sarah are wed, we will tell your father to cancel your Season, then head for an estate I recently bought in Somerset. It includes a most intriguing mound."

She glanced at the villa. "What about—"

He sighed. "It isn't ours, Alex. We should fill every remaining hole and allow winter to hide evidence that anything has been disturbed. Sir Winton would not appreciate it."

"I agree. But the estate is entailed, so Richard will eventually inherit it. Perhaps he will let us excav—" She lost track of her words as his hand teased one breast, raising so much heat she wanted to tear off her cloak. There were definite advantages to being a lady—especially Tony Linden's lady. "We'll cover the site tomorrow. But I'm keeping Minerva—she brought us together."

"And the amphora, which will keep us that way. Love can

survive the harshest challenges, and it endures even beyond time."

"I knew you would understand."

Setting an arm around her waist, he led her to the horses. "We have many years of excavating ahead of us, love. And we'll do it in the open. I've already begun redeeming my reputation."

"And you've made peace with your father." When he raised his brows, she laughed. "You aren't the only one Jon has been plaguing. I cannot think of a more fitting parson to spring this mousetrap. He has fought tooth and nail to bring us together."

"Thank God."

Exchanging one last kiss, they headed for home.

SIGNET REGENCY ROMANCE

Lord Dragoner's Wife by Lynn Kerstan

Six years ago, Delia wed Lord Dragoner, the man she'd loved from afar. But after only one night, the handsome lord mysteriously fled the country...only to return amid scandalous rumors.

Can love bloom again in the shadows of the past—and the danger of the present?

0-451-19861-1/$4.99

The Holly and the Ivy by Elisabeth Fairchild

Mary Rivers's Gran has predicted a wonderful Christmas in London. And when their usually prickly neighbor, Lord Balfour, is increasingly attentive, Gran's prediction may come true—if the merry Mary and the thorny lord can weather a scandalous misunderstanding and a chaotic Christmas Eve ball!

0-451-19841-7/$4.99

A Regency Christmas Present

Five exciting new stories by Elisabeth Fairchild, Carla Kelly, Allison Lane, Edith Layton, and Barbara Metzger.

0-451-19877-8/$6.99

To order call: 1-800-788-6262